MY TYP

G

1

Copyright © 2024 Garry Kay

The moral right of the author has been asserted

All characters and events in this publication are fictitious (other than those mentioned in the acknowledgements) and any resemblance to real persons, living or dead, is purely coincidental

All rights reserved

No part of this publication may be reproduced, stored in a retrieval system, or transmitted, in any form or by any means, without the prior permission in writing of the author

Cover design **Sam Kay**

Also by Garry Kay
Break Free
The Door
Don't Fear The Reaper
Jagger Black

For the rest of the team
Twinkle and Oscar

Tender

Chapter 1

2015, June 18, Thursday
Hotel Petra, Southside, 10 years before the trial

'My type on paper,' Tasha announced to the other girls around the table. She looked over at him again, alone at a large table with his laptop open. He didn't notice her. She looked back at the girls.

The bride-to-be pointed back at him. 'Really? With the computer? Don't be silly. Looks like a knob. And what the fuck does my type on paper mean anyway?'

This time the man across the room looked over briefly as the laughter intruded on his work. He was a long way from home, in town for an interview for a new job as a GP that would force a relocation from one end of the country to the other, far away from his failed marriage. The joy of a hen party wasn't helping his mood, although there was one young lady that he reluctantly admitted to himself was rather easy on the eye, with a smile that said confident but not too serious. He concentrated harder on his preparation notes. He had to be well prepared.

'Doesn't mean anything,' Tasha had to raise her voice. 'It's just Love Island bollocks.' She took a sip of her Martini. 'But you know what I mean don't you?'

'S'pose, but he looks a bit nothing. Thought you liked lively. Jokes and stuff.' The hen took another look. 'Not bad looking actually, but nah. Not your type. Certainly not mine.'

They both looked again along with the other hen party guests. Mixed opinions.

'Hot.'

'Gay.'

'Burglar.'

'Murderer.'

'Paedo.' More laughter.

'Married.' That killed the mood.

Tasha didn't think so. 'He's not married. He's focussed. Looks quietly determined. Any money says he's divorced. That's why he's focussed. Fighting back.'

'You don't half talk shite sometimes Tash.'

'Won't argue with that, but I bet I'm not far out.'

'Go on then. Divorced, I get the next round. Anything else, you're buying.'

They shook. Then paused for a moment all looking at each other.

'Well. Someone has to ask him.'

'Best you do it. The paedo won't get the wrong idea if the hen asks.'

'He might. You go over.'

'No. Tash should.'

'No. Safety in numbers. Two should go.'

The hen took the lead. 'Defo. Safety in numbers. C'mon. Let's all go.'

They grabbed their drinks and bags, headed across the room slowly and sat themselves down at the stranger's table. He stopped typing and slowly looked up at the seven members of the hen party.

'Evening girls. And congratulations,' he nodded towards the hen. 'Can I help?'

They all looked expectantly at their leader.

'Could you settle a bet for us?'

He waited briefly before replying. 'Maybe. I can try.'

'Tasha here,' she waved her hand in her direction, 'thinks she knows a bit about body language and reckons you were married but got divorced.'

They all stared at him and waited.

He half smiled, looked again at Tasha, surprisingly enjoying the drama, despite feeling just a little intimidated by the attention.

'How much did you bet Tasha?'

She was surprised at how much she enjoyed hearing him say her name and was disappointed with how uninspiring her answer was.

'Round of drinks.'

'Wow. For seven?'

She nodded, suddenly not her usual confident self.

'Well?' Impatient hen. 'Were you?'

'Let me think,' he replied, hand on chin.

'What about? Either you were or weren't. Not something you'd forget in a hurry. What's to think about?'

Again he paused.

'I'm thinking about whether to be honest or not?'

Collective groan.

He made them wait. His eyes on Tasha. She was even more attractive close up and her smile was full of kindness and warmth. She had read him spot on. He had to admit that raised his heart beat a little. His divorce came through six months ago. He had always got on well with his ex-wife. Still did. There had been no children, no anger and no fights. But, looking back now, if he were totally honest, there had been no love either. He thought he had loved her, but what he actually loved was probably the whole package; respected job, beautiful wife, nice house. Not what every young man craves, but certainly what they instinctively gravitate towards, the comfort blanket of conformity. He had no idea if there were any easier routes to happiness, but he knew he had to get away from his whole life in Manchester, which he had built around his marriage and successful career as a blood specialist at the hospital.

He wasn't sure why he had chosen Southside or why he had gone for a more mundane role as a GP, but it was a place he knew well. A large town outside London where he studied medicine, met and married his wife, had great friends, played football, enjoyed parties, but ultimately ran away from ten years ago when his wife slept with his best friend. He forgave her at the time because she had suggested the new start. He accepted it was a never-to-be-repeated mistake. He wanted it to be. It wasn't. But they both tried for almost a decade before the inevitable divorce. She had probably been with him for the same comfort blanket of conformity, but she had always craved excitement and someone less predictable than him. That's what she had seen in his best friend and, unfortunately, others that followed. He couldn't give her what she wanted and he didn't love her enough to keep trying. The divorce was best for both of them. But he had to start again and rewinding to a point where he had been happy seemed wise.

He returned Tasha's warm smile. He liked her. A lot. Dangerous. Then he addressed them all. 'Okay.'

They nodded encouragement.

'It's delicate.' He raised his eyebrows. 'I'd prefer not to share.'

The bride-to-be threw her hands in the air and rolled her eyes 'like a slot machine,' as her husband-to-be often told her, a stolen line.

He closed his laptop and stood up. 'But I'll get the drinks.'

The girls cheered and shouted out their orders all at once.

He held out his arms like the shrugging emoji. 'Might be pot luck if I forget anything.'

Tasha stood up. 'I'll help you. I know what everyone wants.'

They headed to the bar. It was a busy night at Hotel Petra and the only gap had two empty bar stools. They took them and Tasha placed the orders for the girls' drinks, a Martini for herself and turned to him, 'And you?'

He fancied a beer, but he'd been on diet coke all evening. To stay sharp for the interview. One beer? No. Bad idea. 'Diet coke please.'

'Really?'

'Yes. Big day tomorrow.'

Before she could react, the drinks started appearing on the bar. She added the coke order and carried some drinks to the table, came back for more, then returned for her Martini. She sat back on the bar stool and took a sip when it arrived along with his coke. He paid before raising his glass to hers.

They clinked glasses, then sat and looked at each other enjoying the effortless flirting that was nudging them together, even in the brief moment of quiet.

'So what's the big day?'

He took a sip of coke and faced her, struggling to hide a smile. He instinctively scanned for a wedding ring. Or engagement. Any clues.

'Interview tomorrow.'

She acknowledged his answer with the slightest tilt of her head.

'Job?'

'GP. All Saints' Surgery.'

'Oh wow. I went there once. You could be my doctor.'

'Maybe.' He smiled warmly. 'But not for ages. I'm on three months notice up in Manchester, so, like I said, could take ages.'

She nodded again. 'Manchester eh?'

'Born and bred, but I actually studied here in Southside and worked down here for a few years.'

Before she could ask why he went back to Manchester, he dived in with his own question.

'How about you? Always been in Southside?'

'Born and bred.'

'And the other girls.' He waved his arm in their direction. 'Work colleagues?'

Tasha looked over at them briefly as she worked out how to answer. She settled on honest but vague.

'We're all on the same netball team. And all in the middle of a mad week at Vicar Insurance.'

Vicar was one of the biggest employers in town.

She took another sip of Martini before looking up at him with a mischievous smile.

'So Doctor. Are you gonna tell me?'

'Yes,' he knew what she was asking. 'Divorced six months ago.'

'Woohoo,' she smiled triumphantly before remembering her manners and forcing a frown. 'I'm sorry to hear that.' She looked down at the bar for a second. 'Hope it wasn't too painful.'

He took another sip of his coke, looking up at the glasses stacked on a shelf above the bar before turning back to her. 'Yes. Painful, but worse things happen and, truth be told, it was over years ago.'

She nodded.

'I'm totally focussed on the future now.'

They clinked glasses again. The future.

His grin widened. 'My turn.'

She was allowed to smile again. Due reverence completed. The chatter around the bar and the soft music wasn't overpowering, but they edged ever so slightly closer so they could hear better.

'How? From 20 feet away, were you able to tell I was divorced. And? How did you notice such detail while in the middle of a hen party?'

She thought about it. 'Do you watch much telly?'

'More than I used to.' Ironic smile.

'Love Island?'

'Funnily enough, yes.'

Now she raised her eyebrows in surprise. 'Really?'

'Yes. I listen to Radio 2. Steve Wright was talking about it. Said it was gonna be good. So, yes, I had a look.'

'Okay. They've got their own language. You know, stuff like my type on paper, where's your head at and everything is a hundred per cent.'

He nodded.

'We'd been talking about it and to show what my type on paper meant...'

'Go on.'

She hesitated. Looked down at the bar. 'Bit embarrassing.'

He saw what was coming, could have made it easier, but took playful pleasure from her discomfort.

She looked back at him. 'You know what I'm going to say and I can see you're enjoying it.' She slapped his arm gently. 'Okay. I pointed you out.' She placed both hands on the table and looked firmly at them and went on. 'Just to make a point. Don't get too big for your boots. You're not James Bond.'

Now he helped her out a little. 'Well Tasha. I'd certainly noticed you. The pick of the hen party.'

Now he was a little unsure. The chemistry was like nothing he'd ever experienced. When she touched his arm it was like an electric shock. A jolt of pure pleasure. She was definitely dangerous. He was down for an interview and, even if he got the job, he had a long wait before he made the permanent switch back to Southside. Just one thing had given him a slight sense of unease. He didn't know why, but he had a deja vu when she said don't get too big for your boots.

'So after I pointed you out, I looked over now and then. Curiosity. You were concentrating on your laptop. Determined.'

'Yeah. Okay.' He edged a little closer.

'Nothing distracted you until that Blur song came on.'

His head moved just a fraction urging her to carry on.

'*Tender.*'

He smiled again, but a sad smile. A defeated smile.

'You stopped focussing on your work and stared aimlessly into the distance until the line about moving on from a split.'

He paused for a moment before replying, '*I need to find someone who can heal my mind.*'

'That's the one. Then as the chorus started, your eyes dropped back to your laptop and refocussed.'

They sat quietly for a moment.

He was miles away. Again. As he had been during the song earlier, but he inwardly slapped himself around the face. Look forward.

'Well. Very astute. Impressive Tasha. Although it could have been a girlfriend... or a boyfriend.'

She smiled and reached for his forearm, giving it a gentle squeeze.

Blur were back in his head. 'Beautiful. Possibly my favourite song at the moment.' He nodded gently upwards to underline the sentiment.

They smiled at each other. Thoroughly engrossed. Both had forgotten why they were there. The hen party. The interview.

They looked into each others eyes, both filled with anticipation. The sexual tension was building.

He watched without moving as she reached a hand up to his face and gently squeezed his left earlobe. He fought the urge to pull her towards him. Didn't move at all. Eyes locked. She slowly pulled her hand away.

She broke the silence.

'Wow... never done that before.'

'Clubbin' Tash?' the bride-to-be asked from a couple of steps away.

The Doctor and Tasha heard nothing. Stuck in a moment.

'Tash, we're off to the club.'

Nothing.

'Tash.' Louder.

Her shouted name broke the trance. She looked round, a little flustered.

'Yeah. Sorry. Clubbing.'

She was thinking fast. It was her friend's big night. She had to go. But she wanted to stay. She badly wanted to stay.

The hen noticed the hesitation.

'You could always bring My Type On Paper.' She looked at him. 'We owe him a drink.'

Tasha looked back at him with raised eyebrows asking the question.

He raised his hands in submission.

'Love to,' he said, hoping it sounded genuine, because he had never liked nightclubs, but he didn't want Tasha to go without him. He was hooked and even the ordeal of a nightclub couldn't stop him.

'Lovely. Let's go then.' The bride-to-be also hoped she sounded genuine, but was not as convincing as My Type On Paper.

'Actually,' he hesitated. 'Can I catch you up? I'll need to change and take the laptop back to my room.'

'Sure,' the hen replied quickly reaching for Tasha's hand.

Tasha stood to leave, thinking fast.

'Do you know where it is?' she asked looking back at him.

He did. There was only one nightclub in Southside, but he saw an opportunity.

'No.'

Tasha stopped. The bride-to-be reluctantly waited as Tasha struggled with directions. After much confusion and with her friend showing a touch of impatience, Tasha took a chance.

'Why don't I wait. Then I'll walk with you.'

The hen rolled her eyes. Again. Accepted the idea and spoke softly to Tasha before she caught up the others by the door.

'Don't forget Denzil.'

The Doctor and Tasha sat back on their bar stools and watched as the noisy hen party headed for the door.

The spark returned instantly, although he couldn't help asking.

'Denzil?'

Tasha was quick with her reply, but faced the bar as she answered.

'My dog.'

He nodded.

'He'll need letting out.'

Facing him again and smiling. 'Let me get you a drink before we go. There'll be a queue at the nightclub now.'

She caught the barman's attention, ordered Martini and suggested another coke. His commitment to good interview preparation melted.

'Jack Daniel's please. Neat. Ice.'

Tasha smiled and quietly hummed approval.

Again they clinked glasses. The future. Unsaid. The conversation flowed. They were tripping over themselves wanting to share more ideas, stories, opinions, hopes, dreams. More drinks.

'How about you Tasha? Favourite song?'

She rubbed her chin gently and looked up at the glasses above the bar as she thought. 'Ooo. Tough one. I'm gonna say Pogues, *Dirty Old Town*.'

'Great tune.' He nodded approval. 'Ironic though.'

'Yeah?'

'Well. You live here. In the London commuter belt. Miles away from Manchester.'

'And?'

'The dirty old town is Manchester.'

'Ah yea. Ha.'

'*My* dirty old town.'

She nodded.

'*I dreamed a dream by the old canal*.'

She smiled. Reached again for his forearm. The line was on repeat in her head.

'Always wanted to *kiss my girl by the factory wall*.'

They both had the song on repeat as they edged slightly closer together.

He wanted to kiss her.

She wanted him to kiss her.

They edged closer.

He noticed the light dancing on her shiny lips.

'Last orders mate,' said the barman firmly, crushing the moment.

'I'll get these,' he said. 'Jack Daniel's please. Straight. Ice. And a Martini.'

She took a swig. 'So Doctor, if you studied here, you'd know there's only one night club and you'd know where it is,' she said with a challenging smile.

'The Skin Shop in John's Passage off Talk Drive.'

They both laughed.

'We goin' then?'

'Sure...' He hesitated.

'Go on.'

'But first...'

'Go on Doctor.'

'A few hundred yards from here down Horngrove Lane, there's a walk by the river opposite the industrial estate, there's something down there I'd like to show you.'

She thought briefly. 'Okay. Let's go.' She grabbed his hand and led him towards the door.

He grabbed his laptop and dropped it at reception as they left the hotel, her arm through his, crossed the road and turned down towards the river and the tree-lined walk along it's bank.

It was a beautiful warm summer night with moonlight dancing across the ripples from a gentle breeze. They walked hand in hand along the bank. An orange glow from the street mixed with the moonlight in the rustling leaves above their heads. Soft sounds in the distance. Traffic, some shouting, a dog barking. He stopped under a large oak tree.

She looked around expectantly but there was nothing obvious. She raised her eyebrows.

'Up there,' he replied, pointing at the tree.

She looked a little closer. There was a large M carved in the bark. A long time ago. The bark had almost grown back into the grooves.

'Took me and a friend half an hour to do that. We were gonna do my whole name, but it took too long.'

'Nice,' she nodded. 'That's not why you bought me here though is it?'

He nodded, put one arm around her waist and pointed towards the river with his free arm. 'This is the closest I could think of for a canal.'

She smiled appreciation at the sentiment.

'And those industrial units across the river are the closest I could think of to a factory wall.'

They kissed, slowly, not greedy, not impatient, but warm, almost loving. Neither of them wanted to stop. The moment was special. The kiss was enough. She reached up to his face, held his cheeks. He had one hand still around her waist, the other in her hair.

A duck swimming past flapped it's wings and the sound stalled the magic. They pulled slightly back from each other, their eyes locked. They had been together little over two hours, knew so little about each other, but it had seemed so natural. A match that some people search years for and never find.

Moments later they walked slowly back towards the hotel arm in arm. They'd only covered about ten yards before they faced each other and kissed again. The same fire, the same warmth and excitement.

The same duck followed them, determined to intrude on their connection, this time noisily taking off.

'We should get to the nightclub. The girls will be wondering where I am.'

'Yes,' he replied reluctantly. 'Yes we should.'

Getting back to the hotel was slow with so many stops. They were struggling to keep their hands off each other.

He collected his laptop from the reception. 'Wanna wait here or come up and pick my outfit.'

She took his hand and headed for the stairs. 'Let's go Doctor M.'

They were both patient after closing the hotel room door, savouring the moment, enjoying the anticipation. She pulled the wardrobe doors open, then turned smartly round to face him with a mock scowl. 'This it? Two shirts, one pair of trousers and a suit?'

He shrugged his shoulders. 'I travel light.'

She reached for the furthest hanger, pulled out a plain blue polo shirt and faced him again. 'Okay Doctor. Shirt off.'

He pulled it over his head and took a couple of steps towards her. 'Wanna pass a hanger?'

She took the shirt off him and threw it on the bedside chair, her eyes taking in his toned smooth chest.

'Okay,' he laughed softly, took the polo shirt and pulled it on. He held a strong pose waiting for her opinion.

'Not your colour.'

He slipped it off and held it out. 'Oh okay. Matches your eyes. Maybe you should try it.'

She unbuttoned her blouse slipped it off and threw it over the same bedside chair.

He now took in her curves, smooth skin, black lace bra. His heart was racing. He could see hers was too, her chest rising and falling rapidly.

They grabbed each other and kissed again, more passionately now. A little impatient. Wanting more. His fingers found the clasp and her bra was quickly off. She reached for his buckle, then zip and hurriedly pulled downwards. They fell on the bed. The sexual tension had been growing all evening and was now racing to a crescendo.

They never made it to the club.

Two hours later he sat up in bed, a single bedside lamp catching the glistening sweat on their bodies, Tasha resting her head on his chest with her hands round his waist.

She listened to the steady beat of his heart. Comforting. Secure. This was new. It was a feeling she had never had before. The holy grail. Like she had found her soulmate, but that didn't seem possible. How could it be? They had only just met. But surely, when you meet 'the one', you know. It's instant. Maybe even love at first sight, but she was too pragmatic, too real to believe in something as Utopian as that. But whatever it was, without question it was the happiest most real connection she had ever made. She snuggled closer and caressed his warm flesh.

He kissed the top of her head. He'd travelled halfway across the country hoping for a job that would give him a fresh start and help him move on. Instead, he'd met the sort of partner that was too good to be true. Too perfect. Tasha knew what he was thinking, she liked what he was thinking and it went both ways. The little things they valued were the same. The big things they valued were the same. They frowned at the same things. He savoured every second as she rested her head on his chest, all the time waiting for the bubble to burst and reality to come crashing back into his life. If they had been on Love Island, the producers would have interviewed him as he raved about her ticking all the boxes. But Love Island isn't about the love, it's about drama. He knew the programme makers needed drama, and if there was none, they'd find a way of making it. There must be a catch.

Then it happened.

Two seconds after her phone started vibrating, there was the sound of a car horn in the road outside the hotel.

Tasha sat bolt upright in a flash, reached for her phone and read a text. Then the panic started as the horn sounded a second time.

She grabbed his forearms and looked pleadingly at him. 'I'm so sorry Doctor. I have to go. I'm supposed to be staying with one of the girls from the hen party tonight.'

'Okay. So what's happened? The text? The car horn?'

He could see she was thinking fast. Planning.

'She just got a text from Denzil. He's on his way over to hers. To pick me up.'

'What? The dog?' He was lost now.

'No.' Then she remembered she'd said Denzil was the dog. 'Yes.'

She dressed fast and raced for the door. Stopped. Turned again. 'I'm so sorry Doctor. You are literally the most beautiful person I've ever met. I will sort this. Wait for me.' A pause. 'I *will* sort this.'

The door shut and she was gone.

Ten minutes later, he still hadn't moved. All he could think about was Alton Towers. Oblivion. Billed as the world's first vertical drop roller-coaster falling 180 feet straight down to a hole in the ground at almost 70mph. How was it possible to follow the most special moment of his life with the worst? He reflected on what had happened. Yes Ronan Keating. Life *is* a roller-coaster. But Oblivion is a bit of a stretch. Wow.

He didn't know her full name. Just Tasha. Worked at Vicar Insurance. No help. So did most people in Southside. She didn't know his name at all, just one of his initials and his planned occupation. After his interview, in little over seven hours, he'd be on a train to Manchester over 200 miles away.

He jumped out of bed and hurried around the room hoping for a Cinderella moment. A glass slipper. Any clue. Nothing. She'd left in a hurry and taken everything.

His interview preparation had been trashed, but he was determined to get the job and be back in Southside in three months.

Then he would find her.

Chapter 2
2025, August 1, Friday
Southside Crown Court, trial day 1

A large middle-aged man wearing football shorts and a white sleeveless T-shirt two sizes too small struggled with the early-morning heat. It's going to be much hotter later, but he was already agitated in anticipation. He put down his toast to finish later. His stomach spilled out from below his food-stained shirt as he opened a chilled can of beer, drinking half of it before sitting at the kitchen table scowling in the direction of his wife, sat on the far side of the room watching catch-up TV uncomfortably loud to drown out the unusually noisy square below their third floor one-bedroom flat. Windows wide open.

Having been voted as the couple least likely to work on the outside, Sasha and Melik received a text informing them that their Love Island journey had come to an unexpected end.

'That's a shame. She was sweet,' his wife said. Not to him. More to the telly.

The man took another swig of beer. Shaking his head. There were few things more annoying than Love Island, and his wife's obsession with the show was a constant source of friction.

'Well. That's it then. The final five.' Talking to the telly again. 'Should have been Sasha. Nicest by far. It was Melik. Nobody liked Melik. Cost her.'

She was shaking her head.

Now she looked over at her husband. 'Gonna have to be Trudy and Carlos now, but if Goran wins, I'll be livid.'

'*You'll* be livid!' he replied with unhidden venom. He finished his beer and crushed the can with his fist. It wasn't enough to satisfy his anger and his eyes danced around the table looking for another target to vent his frustration on. Love Island had been belting out of their telly every day for eight weeks with the Aftersun spin-off show compounding his trauma.

He noticed a fly struggling on the sheet of fly paper he had taped to the corner of the table, now part covered with last night's takeaway wrappers and foil trays. He pushed aside the crushed beer can and raised his fist before crashing down on the table making his wife jump.

'What the fuck?' she shouted, now matching his aggression.

He looked over. Still scowling, unapologetic, stood and left the room brushing past the table, dragging the foil cartons to the floor and looking at his fist. No squashed insect. He'd missed.

The fly, which had been stuck to the sticky paper by just its left front leg for three and a half hours after entering through the open windows in search of a nice meal, found in the takeaway remains, had seen the man's fist approaching. With an ability to process visual information seven times faster than the man, the approaching fist advanced as if in slow motion. Something distracted the man and the line of trajectory changed ever so slightly. As it did, the fly flapped its wings to avoid the impact, although it could not move far with one leg stuck to the paper. It was enough and the edge of the man's flesh brushed against the fly pushing it free, whilst at the same time detaching its front left leg.

With five legs remaining, the fly buzzed over to the counter and settled on the man's toast. It walked around slowly, the receptors on its legs taking in the tastes as it moved. A fine feast and having been stuck on the paper for so long, the fly now took the opportunity to eat before laying 150 eggs in the toast, rubbed it's remaining legs together for five minutes and headed for the window.

It flew over the packed square outside Southside Crown Court. Normally mid morning on a Friday the large open space surrounding the bandstand would be almost empty. The busy shopping streets were one block further west, but today there was standing room only.

A murder trial was about to start and the circumstances were so unusual that there had been, and continued to be, since the story first broke, a nationwide media frenzy with crowds sucked in by the whole circus as much as the detail surrounding the accused.

One man charged with murdering his best friend's brother. The same man had been hailed a hero in the Press for saving his best friend's life, but within days, the surviving best friend had triggered a chain of events that now saw him squared up in crown court with his friend of nearly 30 years.

The fly headed towards the court house over the line of television vans with satellite dishes on their roofs and wires heading in all directions. The reporters with microphones in hand looking for anyone related to the trial in the crowd for interview. A comment. A prediction. Anything that nobody else had. Something to give them the edge. A scuffle broke out on the steps leading up to the court entrance. A dispute over holding space for a friend still parking their car. A police constable stepped in.

The fly went through an open first floor window at the side of the building, circled above the jury box, over the witness stand, along the bench and settled on the ceiling above the dock, where the accused had been eating a jam sandwich. There were a few crumbs and a dollop of spilled jam in front of the defendant. The fly rubbed her legs together to consider her next move.

After eating his jam sandwiches, Doctor Flick Mendy looked blankly around the courtroom in disbelief. How did he get in this mess? The short answer was his inability to multi-task. When doing something difficult, it required his total attention. When focussed on a challenging task he gave it absolutely everything as if he were in a cocoon. It was like an imaginary forcefield developed around him to prevent distraction.

He knew, from painful experience many years ago, that his forcefield, although it guaranteed a higher standard of care, had drawbacks. He had once been told important information during a procedure, but it failed to penetrate his forcefield and he continued to stitch up a patient with swabs still in place. The beautiful job he had done on the wound looked very messy after the stitches had been removed to get the swabs out and restitched. Action against him and the hospital Trust had been narrowly avoided following a delicate exchange between the patient's lawyers and the Trust.

He didn't consider himself a spiritual person, although mainly because his knowledge was limited, but after 'swabgate', as his colleagues described it, he found himself reading about a popular belief among certain Japanese communities, who thought some personality types were caused by physical characteristics such as blood type.

Doctor Flick Mendy was blood type B negative, very rare, only two per cent of the population, and the Japanese associated this blood type with a person who would put all their focus into one activity, with the possibility of neglecting other less vital actions. He felt comforted to think that his mistake could have been something unavoidable and not the result of his incompetence or poor judgement.

Part of the reason he was in court was because he had been told vital information before another extremely difficult medical procedure and his forcefield had stopped that vital information getting through. Swabgate and the Japanese spiritualists were chasing each other around his head. He could not be absolutely certain what he had and hadn't heard or why he pressed on with a procedure that cost a man his life. He told himself he was a good man. He knew he was a good man. But he couldn't be certain. He followed the Hippocratic Oath religiously. The preservation of life was his driving force. He was a good man. If he told himself enough times, it must be true.

And yet, here he was charged with the murder of Juan Prost, older brother of his best friend of nearly 30 years Venga Prost. And the younger brother Venga was the one who triggered the police action against him.

Doctor Flick Mendy continued to stare at nothing in the courtroom. The forcefield was up and he was questioning himself with the same intensity he expected from the prosecution counsel.

A small movement distracted him and broke his trance. A fly landed on the dollop of jam from his sandwich. Flick watched, captivated by the fly's struggle. It appeared to be caught, its back right leg stuck to the jam. The doctor raised his fist and bought it down on the desperate insect.

The fly saw the fist approaching. Its ability to process visual information seven times faster than humans had already saved it earlier that day and, again, it flapped its wings to avoid the impact. It was enough and Flick's fist brushed against the fly, pushing it free, whilst at the same time detaching its back right leg.

With four legs remaining, the fly returned to the ceiling.

Red tape

Chapter 3

2024, October 7, Monday
Southside to Scotland, ten months before the trial

Doctor Flick Mendy zipped up his overnight bag, put it next to his medical bag by the front door and headed to the kitchen for more food.

The doorbell rang.

Beaming and holding up both arms in greeting, Juan Prost stepped into the open door to shake Flick's hand and squeeze his shoulder. 'Taxi for the dream team.'

He smiled back warmly and shook his hand firmly. It was always good to see Juan, such a nice bloke, and the mood was upbeat. Juan was collecting Flick and they were both joining the rest of the gang at Juan's younger brother's house on the other side of town to head off on an adventure team-building trip.

'Nearly ready. Just eating. Come in.'

There was a tiny delay before Juan stepped inside, looking around, the smile briefly replaced with a more cautious expression.

The hesitation was understandable and Flick said nothing, despite knowing that his house was full of triggers for his friend. It had been Flick's house for nearly three years now. He bought it from Juan at the back end of the Coronavirus pandemic. Juan had lived there for almost two decades with his wife, loved the place, many happy memories, but she had been one of the early victims of Covid. Her work at a nursing home coupled with her asthma had made her vulnerable. Juan spent most of lockdown on his own in the place missing the love of his life, all the time wanting to move away for a fresh start but unable to because nothing was happening in the market. Flick had the opposite problem, keen to buy but very hard to do viewings with Covid shutting down the housing market.

It was a private deal that helped them both. Juan moved to a smaller property that needed work. The work distracted him. The ‘project’ property was cheaper so he was able to help Flick, who was £100,000 short of his price, by accepting what was basically an IOU. Flick agreed to pay interest until his ex-wife moved out of their house releasing more than enough to make the final payment.

It was an unwritten agreement. No need to waste any money formalising it. They’d been good friends for years. Juan’s brother Venga was Flick’s best friend and all three played together, back in the day, for Southside YMCA Football Club, along with Jack String, now chairman of the club, who was the fourth member of the gang heading off on the team-building trip. All four now well past their playing days, Flick and Venga both 46, Juan 51 and Jack 60.

‘Coffee?’

‘No. I’m good thanks.’

Flick nodded as he opened a bag of crisps.

‘Would love a coffee, but I’m guessing Venga will have us driving somewhere as soon as we all meet.’

They had a rough idea of the plan, but Venga was organising it all. He was meticulous and thorough in his preparation and expected total commitment from all involved. They knew this when they signed up.

‘And it’s so uncomfortable needing a wee when my super-efficient brother is unwilling to throw in an unscheduled stop.’

Flick smiled, knowing Juan was right.

'Actually. Mind if I visit now? To be sure.'

'Go ahead.' Flick waved his hand in the direction of the hallway.

Juan headed upstairs to the bathroom. Finished. Flushed. Washed his hands and stared at his tired old face in the mirror. It felt like his wife was there with him, looking over his shoulder at the same reflection. He savoured the moment. It was such a vivid memory. Felt so real. He didn't want to let go. He had no problem picturing her, always with a warm smile. Her voice was clear as a bell in his head. Her laugh never faded. That was the strongest, but how he felt in the simplest of moments was hard to recreate in his mind. Nothing moments. They were the best. They were fading, so he stood, looking in the mirror. A couple of minutes passed before he dried his hands and headed for the top of the stairs.

Another hesitation. Then he turned left, along the landing and into the small room at the end. He expected to see silver stars painted on the ceiling, soft pink walls and an unused cot. It was all gone. Now all white, although he could just about see some of the stars, their shape given away as the light falling on them picked out the edges of the thicker paint. He sat on the single bed that now filled the space once occupied by an empty cot.

Flick had crept upstairs and gone straight to the former nursery. He now stood in the doorway feeling his friend's pain.

Juan looked up with a wry smile.

'All those years of IVF after the miscarriage. Nothing.'

Flick nodded. Understanding.

'All we ever wanted was a child. The missing piece of the jigsaw.'

'I know.'

'At the same time, Venga, who's never married, never had a girlfriend for more than two years and has no interest in being a father, still manages to have a daughter. A reluctant single parent.'

Flick put a hand on Juan's shoulder.

'Venga has a wonderful daughter. He's been lucky.'

Juan nodded gently.

'You had a wonderful wife. *You've* been lucky.'

Juan sighed, acknowledging his half full glass.

'Come on.'

They headed downstairs.

'All set?' asks Juan.

'Let me just grab a treat.' He heads for the fridge. 'Want anything?'

'What you got?'

'Cornettos.'

'Wow. Posh.'

'Well, not proper ones. Tesco equivalent. No. Think they may be Co-op.'

He thought about it, but not for long. He had a sweet tooth. 'Okay. Yes please.'

'What flavour?'

'Vanilla please.' Juan followed him into the kitchen. 'You know I'm a vanilla man.'

They both laughed at the Fifty Shades reference.

'Unlike your brother.' Flick smiled.

Juan laughed as he thought about Venga's creative sexual appetite. 'He'd be raspberry ripple and tooty fruity with sprinkles and a flake.'

They both laughed together as they binned their wrappers and headed for the door.

Jack String dropped his overnight bag by the front door and turned to hug his wife, kiss her on the cheek and playfully slap her bottom.

'No parties Mrs String, and make sure you miss me.'

She slapped *his* bum playfully. 'The whole football club will be round later drinking cocktails, fighting over me, playing poker and watching porn.'

'Fair enough. Don't let them drink my best whisky.'

'Okay Mr String.' She hugged him again. Now more serious. 'You will be careful won't you? You know what Venga's like. Adrenalin junky and they're all younger than you.'

'I *know* my limits,' he said with some reassurance. 'I'll keep you posted.'

Jack walked across the marble hall, out through the double oak doors, threw his bag on the passenger seat of his convertible BMW Z4 and headed along the sweeping driveway lined with granite mushrooms, past the ornamental lake and out on to Wheel Road through the large wooden gates. He admired the nameplate Ring Of Fire in his wing mirror as he pulled away towards Venga's house.

Venga Prost opened the boot of his large black SUV on the drive in front of his tidy detached house in the leafy upmarket suburbs of Southside and ran his eyes over his carefully packed supplies; food and drink for a long overnight journey and emergency supplies in case they broke down. What the gang of four needed specifically for the team-building exercise would be packed while they were all together, so it could be shared evenly and every member of the group would know what they had with them and who was carrying it. The detail was important to Venga and he wanted to make sure the whole team was completely up to speed. He looked up as Jack's convertible pulled up alongside, immediately followed by his brother Juan's pokey, economic, sensible Korean car parked with two wheels on the grass. He thought about asking him to stick to the Tarmac, but didn't want the bickering to start straight away. He thought about suggesting that Juan bought a decent car with a full-size engine instead of trying to single-handedly save the planet, but, same, avoid the bickering.

It was a team of four, trialing what Venga hoped would be a popular team building exercise for about ten. Not his bread and butter trips that had helped him build his corporate-supporting company TV Rush (team Venga), but a newer more niche market aimed at wealthy monied young men who were already successful businessmen but craved adrenalin-charged opportunities to show off their dynamism, strength and leadership qualities. Good trips to bring in the money but far away from the team ethic that motivated him to start the company in the first place. He had worked for similar companies after leaving college, but had always wanted to be the boss, running the show.

His first adventure trip had been with his best friend Flick Mendy during their days at Southside University in the 90s, when they had both gone down to the river on bikes aiming to carve their names on a tree by the river and return to the halls of residence without either of them touching the ground with their feet. Leaning on each other and the tree while they carved a large M had been as far as they got. Two attractive girls walking past had been too much distraction. Now 26 years later, the same Flick Mendy was helping him trial a new venture that promised thrills for the wealthiest upwardly mobile leaders of the business world.

He ran his fingers over the TV Rush logo across the back of his car before turning to greet his volunteer team. He hugged his brother warmly, careful not to give away his irritation at his poor parking.

'Thanks for coming Juan.'

'Wouldn't miss it for the world Ven.' Juan patted him on the back as they hugged. 'Surprised you haven't complained about my parking tbh.'

Venga avoided eye contact as he turned to Flick, grabbed him around the waist with both arms and lifted him off the ground with almost shouted greetings. 'Dream team baby.'

Flick struggled and smiled at the same time. 'Put me down Vee.'

Venga growled as he planted him back on his feet.

Venga then grabbed Jack and shook his hand vigorously with both hands. 'No team is complete without The Wise Old Man.'

'Thanks Ven.'

'We haven't got one so you'll have to do Jack.'

They all laughed as they grabbed their bags and headed for the house.

Once they were all seated around the kitchen table, Venga checked his watch before clearing his throat to silence his team.

'You want to know what we're doing and where we're going. And you're probably wondering if Storm Vicky is going to be a problem.'

They all nodded and waited. Juan was prepared to pull out if the fast-approaching storm was standing in their way, but was happy to wait for details and reserve judgement.

'We leave at 7pm and drive just over 500 miles to Oban in Scotland.'

'Wtf?' Juan. 'Scotland overnight?'

'Yes Juan.' Venga was now very calm and had expected resistance from all of them, especially his brother.

'I appreciate you are volunteers helping me test this new adventure package, but the distance covered in a short space of time can only be done if we work as a team, which is what this is all about.'

'Fuck.' Juan.

'Wow.' Jack.

Flick's eyes were wide open in surprise. 'Okay boss. Keep talking.'

'We're catching the 6.45 ferry tomorrow morning to the Isle of Mull. We land at dawn. Around 7.30. Then we travel another half hour to Tobermory. Anyone ever been there?'

Juan and Flick looked at each other blankly. Jack smiled approvingly.

'Beautiful place.'

Juan was anxious now. 'In a storm? Boats?'

Venga had been expecting the question. 'Storm Vicky is just about to hit Land's End a glancing blow as it passes up the English Channel. Most of the damage is expected in northern France. Some on our south coast but then it'll be over mainland Europe and we're 500 miles away. No danger. If there were any danger I would have pulled the plug.'

No audible complaints, but Venga could see they were worried, but hit them with the rest before a protest could build. 'I have rented a rigid inflatable boat with a large engine near Tobermory and we will take it eight miles around the headland to the small island of Skerryn.'

'As long as the seas are calm enough and Storm Vicky is no threat?' Jack, acting wise.

'Absolutely.'

Murmurs of reluctant agreement.

'Skerryn is a small island about two miles long. It lies between Mull and Coll. Used to have a population of about 50, but there's nobody there now, hasn't been for about 40 years. There's a big sandy beach at the southern end and a small hill of about 200 feet towards the northern end. The only other point of interest is a wrecked lifeboat, went aground on rocks at the end of the beach back in the 90s. Was never recovered. Salvage value less than the cost of recovery. Apart from that, just a few derelict crofting houses and grass. No trees. Too exposed.'

'With the right weather,' Flick rubbed his chin in thought, 'this doesn't sound that much of a team test. I am, well *we*, I suppose, are waiting for a catch.'

Venga let the pause drag a bit for dramatic effect. Then screwing his face up a little, went on. 'Well… I wouldn't exactly call it a catch, but there is always some meat in the sandwich to keep things interesting.'

Juan rolled his eyes.

Flick nodded knowingly.

Jack smiled with relish. He enjoyed a challenge as much as Venga.

'I've also ordered a 35 foot class 6 wooden telegraph pole. Second-hand mind. I'm not made of money.

It weighs just over 600 pounds, so, not far short of the four of us added together.'

Now they were lost and just waited for more.

'We collect the pole at the same place as the boat and we take it to Skerryn, land on the beach and carry it up the hill at the far end of the island. Then, using four ropes, we pull it upright with a flag on top, which reads TV Rush.' He stopped and waited for reaction. It was quiet for a while as they digested the plan.

Flick was very practical and asked the first question. 'Most RIBs are smaller than 35 feet. How will we carry the pole on the boat.'

'Excellent question Flick,' Venga said, pointing at him. 'We tow it with one of the ropes. It will slow us down but, like I said, we have a big engine.'

Juan chipped in. 'Wouldn't that be a danger to other boats and what if the tow rope got tangled in our propeller?'

'Fair shout Juan.' Venga nodded. 'I have two signal flags, which we fly from our boat. B for bravo and D for delta. B means we are carrying a dangerous cargo and D means we are manoeuvring with difficulty. Combined they should keep others at a safe distance.'

'And the tow rope?'

'I have an 8 foot length of guttering downpipe. The section of tow rope closest to the RIB passes through the pipe so it can't sag and foul the propeller.'

Flick was working it all out. 'So the team thing is that the pole weighs the same as us and the goal can only be achieved if we work together?'

'That's right.'

'And we can't even get there unless we all work together in the car taking turns driving.' Flick considered his thoughts a little more, before adding, 'About three hours driving each and everyone gets more than eight hours sleep?'

'Not quite. We need to have two pairs of drivers. One drives while his "buddy" navigates and keeps him awake. Then they swap after three hours.'

'What? Like talking and stuff?'

'Yeah. Changing the music, directions whatever it takes to keep the driver alert.'

Nods.

'Okay. So who's with who? Draw straws?' asked Juan.

Venga smiled, knowing he was about to wind his brother up. 'Already sorted. I'm with Flick.'

Juan wasn't happy. Would have preferred some choice. Might have chosen Jack anyway, or maybe Flick, certainly not his brother, but didn't like not being consulted. 'Why? If you don't mind me asking.'

'Because he laughs the most at my jokes.' Venga laughed loudly at his own wit and, much to his embarrassment, Flick laughed the most out of the others.

Venga moved on quickly. 'To be fair though, me and Flick are the youngest so we'll both do the late shift so Juan and Jack can start as it'll be tough to sleep early on.'

Jack could see Juan was put out and tried to lighten the mood. 'I thought your grandson might have been driving us Venga.'

That caught him off guard.

'What? Eight-year-old Zac?'

'You never know Ven. Story came up on my screen at work last week about an eight-year-old girl in Ohio. Took her parents' car, drove 13 miles to the shops, parked it and the police eventually found her walking around a shop.'

Juan looked bewildered. 'You making that up?'

'Nope. True story. All she hit on the way was a post box.'

'Wow.'

Venga carried on, his glance briefly resting on Juan's thick jeans, which weren't the best choice, but best not say anything. 'Thanks Jack. Okay. Next I have to make sure we're all carrying the same weight. One backpack each and nothing we don't need. Maximum mobility. And no, my grandson won't be helping.' He shook his head and pointed towards the row of bags against the wall. 'Each bag has a share of the food and drink we need, along with the equipment. Ropes, flares and the like. They all have space for you to add one change of clothes and a waterproof coat.' He held out a hand. 'You did bring them?'

They all nodded.

'The black bag on the left has less in it. That's yours Flick. I'm hoping you remembered your medical bag.'

'Yes. Battle bag packed.'

'Mobile reception on Skerryn is limited and space is limited, so unless you use the Vodafone network or EE, you may as well leave your phone in the SUV when we collect the RIB.'

Juan held up his arms in despair. 'O2.'

'Giff Gaff.' Flick. 'They use O2, so mine's useless.

'Vodafone.' Jack smiled.

'And I'm EE, so we should have enough emergency cover.' Venga looked down at Juan's jeans again and couldn't stop himself. 'It could rain and we may get wet landing the boat. Jeans may feel heavy if that happens and could drain your energy or limit your movement. Do you want to borrow something more suitable Juan?'

Juan felt belittled by his brother and quickly checked what everyone else was wearing. Mostly loose-fit light-weight tracksuit bottoms. Venga's even looked silky and probably waterproof. It would have been prudent to accept Venga's offer, but he felt slighted and wanted to save face. 'Thanks for the offer Ven, but I'm good.' Silent pause. 'Unless it's a deal breaker.'

The team was everything to Venga and he knew Juan's cooperation was vital, so he chose not to push it. 'Your shout Juan. Just thought I'd offer.'

Jack had no stories up his sleeve about eight-year-olds in Ohio wearing wet jeans so the quiet moment felt a shade awkward before Venga moved on.

'Last thing before we set off is introductions.' They laughed a little. Flick a shade more than the others. 'Yes. I know. We all go back years, but I'm trying to duplicate what would happen if I were taking paying customers, so if you don't mind, I want each of us to take a turn. Say who you are... Flick.'

'Ah right. Yes.' He thought quickly. 'Hello bunch of total strangers. I'm Flick Mendy from Manchester, now 46 years old, first came down to Southside in the 90s to study medicine, married and started work at the hospital. Moved back to Manchester and worked as a haematologist, divorced and moved back to Southside as a GP.'

'Cool.' Venga.

'Oh and I also work as a consultant for the army in Aldershot developing equipment for battlefield conditions. So my medical bag for this trip is a state of the art army battle bag. And I support Manchester City.'

'Thanks Flick. Juan.'

He cleared his throat. 'Juan Prost. 51. Care home manager. Better Monopoly player than anyone I know. Widower. Labour voter. Remainer. Passionate about the planet and every living creature that shares it with us. Arsenal fan.'

'Thanks Juan. Jack.'

'I'm apparently The Wise Old Man of the team at 60. Started work four decades ago as a trainee reporter for the Southside Gazette. Now the editor, although the paper is a shadow of what it used to be. Not my fault. Just the way things have gone for papers since the internet changed all our lives forever. Sensationally beautiful wife. I'm also chairman of Southside YMCA Football Club and I spend far too much of my time with my former team mates, who my sensationally beautiful wife believes are a bad influence on me. I'm passionate about anything competitive. I'm rubbish at Monopoly but am pretty confident that I was, and probably still am, a better football player than anyone I know.'

That sparked laughter.

'Bollocks. You're a donkey with no left foot.'

'Oh and yes, Man U fan, but always prepared to tolerate the *noisy neighbours*.' He patted Flick patronisingly on the back. 'Also, as a Man U fan I can sit smugly watching the *noisy neighbours*' number one fans from Oasis bicker and fight endlessly, but delighted to see them finally build bridges. And yes. I do have tickets.'

Groans.

'Just saying.' Jack nodded towards Juan and Venga. 'If the Gallagher brothers can stop bickering, I'm sure the Prost brothers could give it a go.'

'Thank-you Jack. You always were a dreamer. Okay. For completeness, I am Venga Prost, 46, owner of TV Rush team builders, the accommodating half of the Prost brothers.' Venga smiled. Juan shook his head. 'Single parent, very single in fact, never married, no woman has ever been able to tolerate me for more than two years and the only one that did, cut and ran leaving me with a child that didn't fit her social profile. I am incapable of making a relationship work. However, despite what you may have heard, I am a *very* gifted Monopoly and football player and support the only north London team with true pedigree, Spurs.'

With that he grabbed the bags. 'Game on.'

Juan drove as they headed towards the M25. His driving buddy Jack turned on the radio. 'Storm Vicky hit Torbay this afternoon with a beach bar swept into the sea in Torquay and major damage to beach huts in Paignton and Teignmouth, where a seaside skatepark was flooded.'

'Shit Venga. Thought you said it was just gonna tickle the south of England on its way past.' Juan was worried.

'Depends how you define *tickle*. Don't think I'm over-worried about a flooded skatepark. Besides, we don't know how hard France has been hit.'

Jack helped Venga. 'Fair point. This is English radio. They're not going to tell us much French news, so we're not going to have a clear picture of what Storm Vicky is doing.'

Flick wasn't worried. 'So Venga, what plans do you have for food? We stopping at all?'

This was much easier. 'Nope. Only stops will be to change driver. And when we do, it's a toilet break and petrol. I have food in the back. Hungry now?'

'Yes please.'

Venga handed out sandwiches.

They all ate while listening to Different Corner by George Michael.

'Beautiful song.' Juan.

Flick swallowed a mouthful before adding, 'Used to be "our" song.'

'Our?'

'Mandy.' Ex-wife.

Jack joined in. 'Flick. You do know what it's about don't you? It's not really a love song. It's about a lack of love. And one man wanting to walk away, but unable to do it.'

Flick looked surprised. 'Ah right. A surprisingly good choice then as it turns out.'

'Actually there's loads of songs that have a darker meaning than most people think.' Jack was full of trivia.

'Go on.'

'Foster The People. *Pumped Up Kicks.*'

Flick knew that one. 'Ah yeah. Something about school shootings in America. *Outrun my gun.*'

'Yes. How about *Every Breath You Take* by The Police?'

'Beautiful song.' Juan.

'Love song isn't it?' Flick.

'Not really.' Jack frowned. 'A bit of trivia by the way. Sting started writing the song at Ian Fleming's desk in Jamaica. The James Bond writer. And it's more of a stalker song. Every breath you take, every move you make and it's full of Big Brother references. So, as Sting said himself, it's surprisingly sinister.'

'What this tells us.' Venga joined in. 'Is that Jack is probably better at quizzes than either Monopoly or football.'

'Maybe. And I love winning. Wanna quiz now?'

'Sure.' Venga.

'I'm in.' Flick.

'How we doing it Jack?' Juan.

'Take it in turns to ask a question. Clockwise. I'll start. Buzz in.'

'Game on.' Venga.

Jack thought for a moment. 'Okay. How many moons has the earth got?'

'Buzz.' All three at once.

'Wow. Three-way tie. I'll count to three and you all give me your answer at the same time.' He counted and they all said one in unison. 'Sorry. All wrong. At the moment, and for about two months, an asteroid has been caught in the earth's gravitational pull so we temporarily have two moons. You can't see the new one without a very powerful telescope, but, sorry, all wrong. Juan's turn.'

Groans all round.

'Right. Here we go. Name a country beginning with O.'

'Buzz.' Jack. 'Oman. One, nil, nil, nil. Your turn Flick.'

'Most southerly point in Africa.'

'Buzz.' Juan. 'Cape Of Good Hope.'

'No.'

'It fucking is Flick,' Juan laughed. It was banter with Flick. It would have been tension if he'd said the same to Venga.

'No. Sorry Juan.'

'Buzz. Cape Horn.'

'No. Sorry Venga. That's South America.'

They all looked at Jack, albeit very briefly by Juan, as he was watching the road.

'Just giving you all a chance. Buzz, Cape Agulhas. Two,0,0,0.'

Venga couldn't think of anything sensible. 'In what sport does Fanny Chmelar compete?'

'Buzz.' Juan. 'Skiing. Two,1,0,0.'

Laughter.

'Back to you Jack.'

'Topical one for you. What is the most westerly point of mainland Britain?'

'Buzz.' Venga. 'Land's End. And I'm guessing topical because that's where Storm Vicky first hit.'

'No.'

'Buzz again.' Venga. 'Okay clever dick. Cape Cornwall.'

'No.'

'Fuck.'

'Buzz.' Flick. 'Gotta be somewhere in Northern Ireland. I dunno. County Fermanagh.'

'No. Northern Ireland isn't Britain. It's UK. Come on. Topical.'

Juan slapped the steering wheel. 'Buzz. I know this.' He paused for dramatic effect. 'Ardnemichael Point. Somewhere in Scotland. Two,2,0,0.'

Jack smiled. 'Not quite Juan. Not sure I can give you that.'

'Jack. Don't be an arse. *What?* Did I pronounce it wrong?'

'Well. I'm prepared to take your guess as Ardnamurchan Point, so pronunciation isn't the issue.'

'What's the issue then?'

'Well. Ardnamurchan Point is commonly described as the most westerly point of mainland Britain. But it isn't. Corrachadh Mor, half a mile further south, is actually a few metres further west. And we'll probably be able to see both points from our RIB when we get close to Skerryn.'

'*Commonly*. Sounds like my point.'

'Fair enough Juan. I'll give you it. Two,2,0,0.'

Jack's lead grew.

'I've got one.' Venga. 'Why do mermaids wear sea shells?'

'Not sure we can accept that Venga.' Jack.

'I'll allow it.' Flick knew the answer. 'Buzz. Tits too big for B cups.'

Cheers from all but Jack. 'Go Flick.'

'Here's one.' Flick. 'Why should you avoid a Brazilian wax?'

Jack, smiling, knew he was back in the game. 'It's a total rip off.'

Juan saw an opportunity. 'Buzz. It's a total rip off.'

'Wanker Juan.' They all laughed.

Venga stared out the window at the passing traffic on the M25, lost in thought during a quiet moment, before turning back to the others. 'I had a girlfriend once…'

Groans and smiles all round. That line was like grandpa from *Only Fools And Horses* saying *during the war*. They all knew it was the start of one of Venga's tales of sexual excess.

'Go on.'

Venga took a sip from his water bottle. 'Well… this was years ago. I only saw her for a couple of months. Lithuanian masseur. Don't ask me how we met. Anyway. She was staying over one weekend and I heard a high-pitched squeal in the bathroom.'

They nodded encouragement.

'Couldn't be sure if it was good or bad. Went up. Door was open and she was waxing her legs…'

Venga stopped.

They waited. They knew there was more.

'She pulled another strip. Eyes locked on mine. The squeal turned out to be good. She was enjoying it. Then she passed me a fresh strip.'

'What? She wanted you to wax her legs?'

'Yup. And not just her legs. She loved it. Lead to great sex.'

Again they waited. There was always more.

'Okay. So this happened a few more times. Odd foreplay, but, not gonna lie, loved it. You know when my birthday is don't you?'

'April 23.'

'Yup. St George's Day. She had a surprise for me on my birthday. Went round to her place and she had a dressing gown on. Nothing else. I sat down on the sofa. She stood facing me and dropped the dressing gown.'

They waited again.

'She had dressed herself as the flag of St George with two inch wide red gaffer tape.'

'What? On her body?'

'Yes. Top to bottom. Literally. Through her legs. And side to side over her tits.'

'And she wanted you to pull it off?'

'She did. And it was a step up from waxing strips.'

All three were wincing and laughing at the same time.

'And she liked that?'

'Fucking loved it mate.'

More howls.

Jack, always practical, had to ask, 'Gaffer tape. Strong stuff. Couldn't you have injured her? You know? The more sensitive bits?'

'Pretty sure she'd thought of that. Can't be sure as it wasn't my main priority at the time, but I think she used a bit of Vaseline here and there for protection.'

'Wow,' Flick laughing hard.

'So why did you stop seeing her? Was it the language barrier?' Jack. Practical again.

'Hmm. You probably won't believe me but I think she was a bit too adventurous for me.'

None of them believed that. Venga was insatiable.

'Two things. She wanted to pull tape off me. Never going to happen. I'm very hairy.'

'And?'

'She wanted to film it.'

'Ha. Sex tape.' Jack was quick.

'Yes Jack. Very good.' Sarcasm from Venga. 'Time for a driver swap.'

Almost 400 miles later, Venga was at the wheel with Juan and Jack both asleep in the back. Flick was finding songs on the radio to keep the driver awake. He settled on *Rubber Ball*, Bobby Vee.

Venga tapped his fingers on the steering wheel and quietly sang along. 'Have you finally ditched that crazy bitch from the hospital or is it back on? Yet again?'

'Yes. I have been the mother of all rubber balls.'

Flick found himself falling asleep as his mind went in never-ending circles with his girlfriend/ex girlfriend/girlfriend/ex. Fuck it. Stay awake. The driver needs me. 'Yes. The *crazy bitch*. I think it's definitely over this time. Couldn't really say for sure that it was ever on. I know I never loved her. She told me she loved me all the time, but it didn't stop her moving out four times.' He thought about it. 'No. Five times.' Thought about it some more. 'Six… I dunno. She's moved to Brighton. It's over. I hope it's over. It's too much stress. Maybe I'm better off alone. How about you? Any Lithuanians at the moment?'

Venga smiled. 'Not seeing anyone really. I am definitely better on my own.'

Flick dug his nails into the back of his neck to try and keep himself awake. 'Seriously though Vee, you've never really been on your own. Your daughter runs your whole life. She's a single parent of two... her own kid and you.'

They both concentrated on the road ahead. They were close to Oban and in good time for the early ferry.

Venga was about to speak, opened his mouth, but stopped.

'Go on. What?' Flick had noticed.

'Was gonna admit to a weakness, but it's not in my nature, so I changed my mind.'

They looked back at the road. Two miles to go.

'Didn't think we had any secrets bud. Spit it out.'

Venga liked to be seen as confident and strong willed, even to his closest friends, especially to Flick, his closest friend, but there were no secrets, so he should be comfortable sharing anything.

'Okay. It's nothing really. All I was gonna say is you're right. I lean on her more than she leans on me and that's probably been the case since her early teens.'

Flick nodded.

'I am a confident bloke… most of the time. And I blag it when I'm not.'

'I know.'

'But she's genuinely confident all the time. No idea why. Doesn't get it from me. She's never even met her own mum. So yes. I lean on her a lot.'

'There should be a left... Soon… Probably signposted *ferry*.' Flick checked the map on his phone again. 'Here.'

Venga made the turn. 'Don't remember much about her mum myself. But she was classy. So much swagger. I loved being seen with her.'

'Yes. I remember. She was sassy. To be honest, I found her quite intimidating. In a good way.'

They both focussed on the scenery lost in memories from so many years ago.

Then Flick remembered to ask, 'Also Vee, when I asked if you were seeing anyone, you said *not really*. That's not no is it. So let's have it.'

'Doctor Flea. Nothing gets past you.' Venga took a sip from his water bottle. 'This will surprise you.'

Flick laughed.

'I went online and met someone.'

'That's…' Flick struggled for the right word. 'Okay. Surprising. But nothing wrong with that. What's she like?'

'Witty. Educated. Sharp.'

'Cool.'

'And she's a single mum… with one daughter.'

'Perfect.'

'Best thing, she laughs at my jokes even more than you.'

Flicked laughed. 'How long has this been going on then?'

'Couple of months.'

'Wow. You kept that quiet. But wow again, some of your women don't make it to two months.'

Venga smiled.

'So when am I gonna meet her?'

'Hard to say Flick. Not met her myself yet.'

'What the fuck?'

'Slow and steady wins the race.'

'Yeah right. But the race hasn't started yet.'

'Now Flick. Don't be so shallow. We're building rapport. There's no hurry.'

Venga slowed the car, looking around, checking the signs.

Flick pointed ahead to the right. 'Think that's the queue.'

Venga joined them, pulled on the handbrake and stopped the engine. Jack and Juan stirred in the back.

The darkness fell away during a choppy crossing with a brisk breeze under heavy skies. There was no sun. The cloud cover was solid. Venga drove the final half hour from the ferry port at Craignure that followed the coast road up the top of the island along the beautiful Sound of Mull.

Flick turned up the radio for the weather report.

'Storm Vicky has left a trail of destruction along the north coast of France with less powerful, but still strong winds hitting towns along the south coast of England. However, Belgium and Holland may avoid the worst impact of the storm as it has now turned up the North sea heading towards Scandinavia.'

'Fuck.' Venga banged his fist on the steering wheel. 'Fuck. Fuck.'

The worry spread through the SUV as they crept along the narrow road towards Tobermory.

'What do you think?' said an alarmed Juan, leaning forward on the edge of his seat.

Venga thought fast. His mind racing as they closed in on Tobermory with well over 500 miles on the clock and a considerable amount already invested in a trip that provided no immediate returns.

'It's still not heading towards us, but even passing up the North Sea, we could feel it a bit. Could make things uncomfortable.'

'Was a bit choppy on the ferry.'

'About a three to four. Storm Vicky on its way to Finland would make it about a four.' Venga held his left arm up in a shrugging movement. 'Storm Vicky on its way to Norway would make it about a five.'

'How bad is that in our boat?'

'Like I said. Uncomfortable. A bit wet, possibly, but we'd be alright.'

'I'm okay with that.' Jack was still up for it. It took a lot to put him off.

His confidence encouraged Flick. 'I'm still in.'

Venga knew they couldn't do it unless they all agreed. 'Just you Juan. How about it?'

He wasn't worried about getting wet and didn't want to spoil his brother's trip. 'As long as you think we're okay, I trust your judgement Ven. Game on.'

The buoyant mood had faded a little as they pulled into the boatyard and Venga got out to find his contact.

Five minutes later, he returned to the SUV with more bad news. 'Mixed new boys. The boat is great. Ready to go. But the 35 foot class 6 wooden telegraph pole that has been procured for our trip isn't quite what I had in mind.'

'What's wrong with it?'

'It still has all the metalwork attached.'

'You mean like the steps near the top and the cross trees that the wires sit on? All that stuff?'

'Yes.'

Jack was always glass half full. 'Not that much heavier then?'

'I'm not worried about the extra weight. It's more the possible danger posed. It's a heavy pole and just a bit more dangerous with chunks of metal attached.'

'Can't they take them off?'

'I asked them to when I booked it but he said they were in such good condition, he thought I might want to keep them. And if we want them off now, he can do it, but it will take about two hours.'

'Can we wait?'

'We could, but we caught the dawn ferry to maximise daylight and we don't know what will happen with Storm Vicky, so if we're gonna do it, we go now and work around the metalwork.'

'I'm in.' Jack.

They all looked at each other.

'Sure.' Flick.

Now they all looked at Juan.

He kept them waiting.

'Fuck it. I'm not spoiling the party. Let's go.'

They cheered. Venga hugged his older brother and they all headed for the boat with one final thought from Venga. ‘We’ll be fine as long as Storm Vicky doesn’t change direction again and head for Scotland.’

Foreign accent

Chapter 4
2025, August 4, Monday
Southside Crown Court, trial day 2

Rebecca Pooley, juror number one, was a 48-year-old nurse with three children and a husband she adored and almost lost to a heart attack nearly 10 years ago. It was her first time as a juror. It was actually her first time in a court room and she was determined to consider all the evidence and give a well judged verdict. But she found herself fixed on Dr Flick Mendy. He didn't look like he would murder anyone. He was a good looking man about the same age as her and he had a warmth about him that said 'trust me, I'm a doctor' and, on first impressions, she did. She remembered the news stories hailing him as a hero for saving a life in appalling conditions. Then she remembered the stories that followed of his arrest for murder. Hero to zero. The stories were the same, but there were new twists and motives. The judge had told them to ignore what they had seen in the media and focus entirely on what they heard in court. She had so many questions. How was such a good looking doctor still single in his forties? How long would the trial keep her from her work at the hospital? When was she going to have time for food shopping during such a long trial? She had a large family to feed. And where did the name Flick come from?

Behind her, juror number seven Steven Robinson was listening studiously to court proceedings, but his attention was more on his fellow jurors. He was a 58-year-old retired police superintendent and his court experience was massive. He was ready to hear both sides in every detail and his default setting was focus on the courtroom and ignore the media distraction. His plan was to be elected foreman so he could enforce the same discipline across his fellow jurors. He noticed Flick's smart blue shirt with a subtle pattern of small darker blue stars with just the top button undone and thought the defence counsel would have worked hard on his appearance to give a casual but serious look, in the hope that some jurors, possibly the women, would see him as a warm trustworthy doctor.

Flick couldn't help studying the jury. It must be the same with every trial. He was as fascinated by them as they must be of him. He wondered if he had dressed right, but remembered he'd forgotten to do his laundry and wore the only clean shirt he had and hoped the star pattern wouldn't make him look flamboyant. He soaked in the whole jury desperate for a positive connection from fleeting moments of eye contact and speculative interpretations of body language. Juror number seven Steven, he was good with names, the big friendly giant, seems okay. Think he can be trusted. He talks a lot, but you can see he doesn't just speak over people. He's listening to everything that comes back. Juror number one Rebecca, seemed nice, probably early forties so nearly his age, that might help, nice looking actually, wonder if she's married, looks a bit like the receptionist from his surgery nearly a decade ago. She had moved on since.

He remembered his colleague from his first day as a GP in Southside. She had greeted him and shown him around. He could picture her and remember her voice as if it were yesterday. Lovely woman.

'Hello. How can I help you sir?'

'You're expecting me... I hope... Dr Flick Mendy, the new GP.'

'Ah. Great to meet you.' She came out from the front desk and shook his hand. 'Let me show you round and get you settled in your consultation room. The "boss" said he'd catch up with you early on, but I have appointments lined up for you from 11am, so a bit of time to settle and get your head round things.'

They were all mostly busy with patients, but he met two doctors, the physiotherapist and a nurse before the receptionist showed him into his room.

'I've set you up on the system.' She handed him a piece of paper. 'And here's all your login details. Obviously you can change the password once you're in.'

'Wonderful.' He hesitated briefly, looking around, taking it all in. 'All looks lovely. Great team.'

'Oh they are.' She was reassuring. 'And most of the patients are...' now she hesitated, 'good. I suppose. Mostly. Same as any surgery really. Little surprises around every corner,' she quoted Willy Wonka. 'But nothing dangerous. The last patient for the woman you replaced, she left a month ago, was an odd one.'

Flick nodded.

'I booked her in for a bad chesty cough. She wanted antibiotics. She saw the doctor. Turns out it wasn't even for her. Was her dog. The doctor told her she should have booked a vet and refused to help and then,' she paused, 'and you won't believe this, she put in a formal complaint.'

Flick laughed.

'Boss threw that out and she went to the ombudsman. Same result.' The receptionist threw both arms in the air in despair. 'Some people. I dunno.'

'Can't wait to get started. Sounds like fun.' Flick smiled. He put his bag on the desk and thanked her.

'The kitchen is behind the front desk and there's always coffee, tea and biscuits.'

As soon as he was alone he logged into the system and did a search for Tasha. She had been on his mind every day of his three months notice since he accepted the GP job in Southside.

No hits. He tried Natasha. Three hits, two older than him and another the same age. Not gonna be her. He then took a gamble and rang Vicar Insurance.

'Hello, Vicar Insurance. How may I help?'

'Ah hi. Morning. Err. Dr Flick Mendy here. I'm calling from All Saint's Surgery, Southside.'

'Do you know what extension you want?'

'No. Sorry. This is a little awkward.' Then he lied. 'We had a call at the surgery recently from a woman at Vicar Insurance on a personal matter. Gave her name as Tasha. I have the information she needed, but she didn't leave a surname. Can you help?'

The line was quiet for a minute, and he heard a muffled conversation.

'Hi. Doctor Mendy.' It was another voice. Smooth. Assured. 'We have over a thousand staff and countless visitors. There are five Natashas. Have you any other information that could help us narrow it down?'

Flick felt a surge of excitement. This was promising.

'Hard to say from just a voice.' More lies. 'Sounded mid twenties.' He wanted to say friends with someone who got married three months ago, but would give himself away.

Four of our Natashas, as far as I know, are well past 40, one's mid 30s. Maybe it's her? She's Nigerian, but speaks immaculate English. Did she sound African?'

Flick's optimism melted.

'Not that I remember.'

'I'll pass your number on to her if you like, and if it was her she'll have the opportunity to call you back.'

'Thanks very much.'

His disappointment must have been obvious as the woman clutched at straws. 'We had a work experience girl from the sixth form college a few months ago called Tasha, but beyond that. I'm out of ideas. Are you sure it was Natasha? We have a few Natalies.'

Flick sighed. 'Definitely Tasha. No worries. Many thanks for your help. Fingers crossed it was the Nigerian woman. Thanks again.' He hung up.

The boss then kept him talking for 45 minutes, before a message popped up on his screen letting him know that it was time for his first patient. The boss left his office as a young man with thick blond hair knocked apologetically on the open door and waited to be invited in.

Flick offered him a chair, introduced himself and asked how he could help.

'About a couple of years ago, I noticed a large spot, no, growth on the back of my head. I sometimes catch it when combing and was worried that it may be a problem.'

'Okay, let's take a look. Where abouts?'

The young man indicated an approximate area and Flick ran his fingers through the thick hair, parting it to get a better look at the scalp. He tried a few places in the area he had been shown but couldn't find anything.

'Can you show me again?'

'Shall I put my finger on it to guide you in?'

'Okay, let's try that.'

The young man routed around in his hair. Flick waited. He looked some more, but the young man couldn't find it either.

'Blimey. Ever so sorry doctor. I can't find it. Weird. It's so big as well.'

'Would you like me to take another look?'

The young man thought about it, clearly quite flustered.

'No. Thank you. Sorry. I'm wasting your time. I'll have to leave it.'

He picked up his jacket and left.

Flick saw on his screen that his next patient was ready, but quickly scanned his emails in case he had anything from Vicar. Nothing. There was a knock at the door. He opened it and a woman of about 40 with long black hair marched in and sat down in the seat by his desk.

Again he introduced himself and asked how he may help.

'I know what's wrong with me 'cause I saw it on the telly last year.'

'The telly?'

'Yes. A woman called Zoe had functional neurological disorder, FND, and nobody could help her.'

'Okay.'

'FAS they said it was. Foreign accent syndrome.'

'Right. I remember that.'

'She was from Lincoln. Woke up one morning with a German accent, which morphed into a Welsh accent after six weeks and never went away. Never been to Wales in her life. Or Germany.'

'I do remember that. So, has that happened to you?'

'I would have thought that was blatantly obvious. I'm a Southsider. Have been for my whole life, 43 years. Home Counties. But I woke up this morning with the strongest Liverpudlian accent you've probably ever heard. Pure Scouse. You've got to help me.'

Flick didn't know how to react. The woman with long black hair had the most standard Southside accent in town and there was nothing that remotely sounded Liverpudlian.

At that point there was an urgent knock at the door.

'Come in.'

The young man with the thick blond hair hurried through the door with a finger pressed against the back of his head. 'I'm so sorry to barge in doctor, but I've found it. I was walking towards my car feeling around my head and there it was. Big as ever. So I put my finger on it and ran back.'

'Ah. Right.'

Flick made his apologies to the woman. She stayed in the seat while Flick checked the young man's spot.

'It doesn't hurt doctor. It's just like a Sugar Puff has half buried itself in my scalp.'

'Oh, I've got a couple of those,' the woman volunteered. 'Had them for years. Showed my doctor when I first had them and he said nothing to worry about. They'll probably go on their own. And they did. I had others, but they all went away in the end.'

'Did they ever bleed when you caught them with a comb?' the young man asked.

'Couple of times, but scabbed over quick. Wouldn't worry about them if I were you. Don't want to waste the poor doctor's time do we now?'

'Quite agree. Thanks for your help.' He made to leave again.

'Hold on.' Flick felt like an intruder. It was his first day and his patients were consulting each other. 'It is, as she says, fairly harmless, and, as she says, it will probably go away on its own eventually. But if you are worried about it I could cut it off now.'

'Thanks doctor, but I really am squeamish, so if there's no real danger, I'll just wait for it to fall off.'

Again he made to leave.

'Hold on.'

He stopped in his tracks and turned back.

'I have one more question for you.'

The young man raised his eyebrows.

Flick looked at the woman, then back at the young man. 'Where do you think this woman comes from.'

'Southside.' Instant.

The woman looked put out.

Flick pressed his advantage. 'Not Liverpool?'

The young man actually laughed out loud. 'Okay. Thanks again doctor and thanks to your assistant.' He left.

Flick didn't correct him but faced the woman.

'So I can't detect any Liverpool tones in my "assistant" and nor can the man with the spot. I think you should see how you get on and come back and see me in a couple of weeks if you still feel your accent has been distorted.'

She thanked him and left.

Flick looked back at Rebecca, juror number one. He had been very fond of the receptionist so he attached his positive feelings for her to the first juror. Now he felt he was winning them over. Juror number seven was a good listener.

Very positive. Along the row, juror number four Joe Wareham caught his eye. Looked like a surfer, striking, late twenties, watching everything, switched on, but Flick couldn't think of anything positive because he was back in the surgery on his first day.

After lunch, a man, looking very like juror number four but much older, so possibly juror number four's dad, had sat himself down in the chair next to Flick's desk in his consulting room and proceeded to list all the symptoms associated with an enlarged prostate gland. The symptoms were so closely matched to those of an enlarged prostate gland that Flick thought he may have self diagnosed and memorised the common symptoms of the condition he thought he had to ensure the desired response from his doctor.

Flick talked his patient through the possible cause of his symptoms, the best action moving forward and booked him a blood test to check for evidence of cancer, so that, hopefully, the worst case scenario could be ruled out. Which left him needing to do a rectal examination on his very first day as a GP to see if the prostate gland was as it should be. He pulled the curtain around the bed and instructed the patient to pull down his pants and lie on his side with his top leg over the other and his knee pulled up to his waist. When ready, Flick opened the curtain, pulled on a pair of surgical gloves, lubricated the patient, warned him that he may feel some discomfort and inserted his finger up the man's anus.

At the point of maximum penetration as Flick was feeling for the prostate, the patient said, 'I was supposed to be playing five-a-side football this evening, but it's been cancelled.'

'Oh dear. That's a pity. How come?'

'Sports hall is double booked. Netball cup final apparently.'

Flick removed his finger with some excitement. He hadn't thought of that angle. He should be getting in touch with netball clubs. The girls on the hen night were all from the same netball team. They could lead him to Tasha.

The patient was delighted to hear that his prostate was normal and very surprised at how interested his doctor was in the venue of his five-a-side football and all the other clubs that shared the facilities.

Unfortunately a series of carefully worded emails to netball clubs in and around Southside over the next couple of weeks provided very few answers and no clues.

He looked back at juror number four unsure whether he could be trusted. He was trying to feel positive about the jury, but it was a mixed bag. All they had done was remind him of a bizarre first day as a GP when he had failed miserably to find Tasha.

Juror number three Imelda Morse, a 36-year-old sports therapist, had been watching the accused closely all day. She was surprised at how much he focussed on the jury instead of the prosecution counsel, who had been making their case. While those in the public gallery followed the questions and the witness's answers, the defendant had watched the jurors' reactions to the questions and the witness's answers. Mind you, she couldn't criticise him for that because she was watching him, watching them, watching the questions and the answers.

For a short while she stopped watching Flick, who she couldn't read at all, and watched a fly. It landed on her forearm. She didn't move at all as it walked erratically up her arm, frequently stopping, changing direction, stopping again, then rubbing its legs together. And that wasn't easy. It only had four. It flew away.

Chapter 5
2024, October 8, Tuesday
Mull to Skerryn, ten months before the trial

Venga's contact, Baxter, lead them to a small jetty in a sheltered bay and they loaded their gear on the rigid inflatable boat alongside.

'What you doing with the pole?' asked Baxter.

'Towing it round the headland and over to Skerryn.' Venga had already told him, but, like removing the metalwork, he hadn't taken it in. 'About eight miles I reckon. Shouldn't take more than a couple of hours.'

'If you're lucky. Wind's picking up and veering. That's never good news. Looks like about a force 4 at the moment. Gonna slow you down.'

'As long as Storm Vicky heads for Scandinavia, we should be fine. Forecast is only for a three.'

'Forecast will be wrong today.'

'What makes you think that?'

'Seen it before. Storms just miss England and that pisses them off, so they try and turn round for another shot with a handbrake turn in the North Sea, then the fuckers miss again and hit Scotland.'

Venga laughed.

'Not kidding mate. We always get your shit.'

'Maybe.'

Baxter pointed out to sea. 'Look at the waves. The long bigger swell has come across the Atlantic pushed by the outer edges of Vicky. But there are smaller waves whipped up in the opposite direction, pushed by today's wind from the mainland. They're breaking on the bigger waves. Look. The white choppy bits. That'll get worse. I *know*. I'm telling you. Fuck the forecast. It's wrong.'

The four of them looked at each other. Nobody reacted straight away but Venga's expression said, 'Don't listen to the witchdoctor.'

'I can see you don't believe me, but just in case I'm right, and the weather whips up bad, you shouldn't try coming back in anything over a force 5. Touch and go in a force 6. Best sit it out on the island and wait for the weather to pass.'

'We don't have tents.' Venga had no plans to stop over.

'No need. Skerryn used to be occupied, till about 40 years ago. There's a few empty houses. Mostly derelict, but one at the foot of the hill is still in good order and sometimes used as a shelter. Won't be locked.'

They all nodded appreciation for the gloomy advice.

Above the whistling wind they all heard a booming low sound in the distance.

Jack was fairly confident he knew what it was. 'Hey Baxter. Sounds like a humpback whale. You get many of them up here?'

'Very rare. Unlikely.'

'I had a story popped up on my screen at work last week.'

There was a collective groan from the others. While most of Venga's stories started with 'I had a girlfriend once', most of Jack's stories started with 'I had a story popped up on my screen'.

'Go on.'

‘There were pictures with it too. A humpback whale had opened its mouth to take in a load of fish and sea water and had accidentally scooped up a seal as well.’

‘Very rare. Unlikely.’ Baxter.

‘There was a picture of the seal in the whale’s mouth looking shocked and frightened. The whale closed its mouth, went under, then resurfaced and spat the seal out.’

‘Great story.’ sarcasm from Flick.

‘So Baxter, what d’you think? Was that a humpback?’

‘Unlikely.’ He seemed confident and pointed to the headland as a boat appeared in the distance. ‘I think it was the Kilchoan ferry sounding its horn.’

Jack’s face dropped as the others enjoyed a laugh at his expense.

Venga put up the bravo and delta flags on the boat and set about attaching the rope and guttering pipe to avoid the propeller being fouled.

Baxter had more words of wisdom. ‘Waste of time those flags.’

Venga was patient. ‘Why do you think that?’

‘Well… I know what they mean, being ex-Navy, but most of the idiots that play around the harbour wouldn’t have a clue so you’re not telling them anything. And anyone like me who knows what they mean would avoid you anyway ’cause you’re English.’ He almost smiled, but kept it very dry.

‘Thanks Baxter. Noted.’ Venga patted him on the shoulder.

The four members of the team spaced themselves evenly along the length of the pole and walked it along the jetty, Venga attached its rope to the back of the boat, then they all lifted it again and slowly lowered it into the water, climbed aboard, untied the rope, fired up the engine and headed for the open water.

As they pulled away, Baxter gave them a final vote of confidence. 'I'll let the lifeboat station know what you're up to just in case. Forewarned is forearmed.' He waved.

It was choppy, some spray, but no problem until they rounded the headland at the top end of the island and felt the full force of the large swell from the south. They turned south west and saw Skerryn a couple of miles beyond the headland in open water. The bow lifted over a wave and crashed down sending spray over them all. Loud cheers. The mood was again upbeat. Now committed to finish the job, it felt good. The decision was made. Crack on.

Flick felt the mood lift and launched into a football song from the club they had all played for, Southside YMCA. It was adapted from a Manchester City chant about the Toure brothers set to the tune of 2 Unlimited *No Limit*. But for YMCA it was brothers Micah and Zuri Kanye.

Flick belted it out, barely heard over the wind, waves and engine. 'Micah, Micah Micah, Micah Micah, Micah Micah Kanye.'

The others joined in like it was a football club night out and together the sound drowned out the elements. 'Micah, Micah Micah, Micah Micah Kanye. Zuri, Zuri Zuri, Zuri Zuri Kanye.'

Flick switched it to the Manchester City version with Kolo and Yaya Toure. The others immediately stopped and booed.

Venga reprimanded him. 'Nooo Flea. Don't get too big for your boots.'

Jack pointed north and shouted over the wind, 'Over there. Can you see the lighthouse?'

'Ah yes. I've got it.' Juan.

'That's Ardnamurchan Point.'

Nod of approval from Flick and Venga.

Sarcasm from Juan. 'It's hard to see for that massive headland below it sticking out 5cm further west Conrad Chutney Point.'

Jack, not amused. 'Yes. Very good.' But he still couldn't help himself correcting Juan. 'Corrachadh Mor.'

Flick took the wheel from Venga and followed a course slightly further to the east of Skerryn than he needed to go, but for safety, he wanted to hit the oncoming waves square on. The two friends smiled at each other, enjoying the moment. It was cold and wet but invigorating at the same time. They felt alive.

With Flick at the wheel, Venga gathered his thoughts as they pounded through the rising and falling waves. He'd come a long way with Flick, good times, embarrassingly on his own part, some very bad times too, but the team business had started 26 years ago in the kitchen of their halls of residence one quiet Saturday morning when Venga and Flick were in their third year at Southside University.

It was an innocent comment from Venga. 'We should win this afternoon.'

They both played for the university football team and had a cup semi-final that day home to Ashtown Rovers.

Flick, who played centre-back, wasn't so sure. 'Yes. We *should*. But depends who plays on the right. Lugger we win. Baz we lose.'

Venga, who played centre midfield, hoped it would be Lugger, but knew the manager would probably go Baz. 'Shame. It's so obvious to me.'

Paddy 'Mitz'patrick was a first year and also shared their kitchen. He played in goal for the football team. 'You two are talking shite. Baz is the top goal scorer. First name on the team sheet.'

'You fucking retard Mitz. If it were that simple, you could be manager.' Venga's voice was up an octave.

'If it *were* that simple, you might not have to play in goal.' Flick laughed.

'It is that simple. And you're the retards.'

'Listen Mitz, when Baz plays, he scores, but the team struggles. When Lugger plays, the team thrives and together we score more than Baz. It's all about team. A good team is always better than the sum of its individual parts. Baz is a bad fit. Lugger fits. When Lugger plays, it brings out the best in all those around him. When Baz plays, everyone else has to make up for his weaknesses. He never defends. If we turn possession over quick, he's still standing offside. He gives possession away cheaply. Sometimes in dangerous places. *Team* Mitz. It's a *team* game. It's all about the *fucking* team.'

Mitz laughed. It was quite a tirade. He put his face well inside Venga's personal space and raised his voice. 'It's all about *Baz*.' Then he backed off and laughed. 'Okay Ven, fair point, but I bet the gaffer plays Baz.'

They all sat around the table. Flick poured coffee.

Venga was composed again. 'Beats me why individual performance is so highly prized. The team ethic should be pushed more in schools so people grow up better equipped to contribute in whatever field they are in. Not just sport, but the workplace, or just life in general. It pains me to say it Mitz, but I'm a better person with you and Flick alongside me.'

They sipped their coffee.

'I read something the other day,' Flick, still smiling, 'about a company that built teams.'

'You can buy a team?'

'No. You send your team to them and they give them exercises to help them work better together.'

'Team building company.' Venga raised his eyebrows in appreciation. A great idea. 'I could do that.'

'Yeah. Why not? What else can you do with a sociology degree?'

'Okay. Let's do an exercise this morning. You in Flick?'

'Sure.'

'Mitz?'

'Love to mate, but gotta go round and clean Baz's boots for him.'

'You fucking joking?' Venga took the bait.

Mitz laughed. 'Nah, sorry. Got an essay to finish.'

'What we doin' Vee?' Flick was keen.

'Has to be something we can't do unless we work together.'

They thought about it as Mitz washed the mugs and headed back to his room.

Venga started. 'How about we spray-paint Spurs on the bridge from the library to the sports hall? It's about ten feet high so one of us would have to go on the other's shoulders.'

'No good 'cause you could do it on your own leaning off the top of the bridge… and spray paint costs. And we might get in trouble. And nobody likes Spurs. Maybe we should write Manchester City.'

'Don't think so Flick. You're in the Championship as it is and looks like you're going down. Not the best choice to promote the team ethic. Besides, Spurs is short and snappy, Manchester City would take too long.'

'How about Borussia Monchengladbach?'

Venga couldn't help laughing.

'Okay. Let's just do our names. And maybe carve them in a tree. No cost. And if one of us sits on the other's shoulders, we can do it higher up the tree.'

'Sounds good.'

'And.' Venga had another idea forming. 'How about we do it in town? Go down on our bikes and to make it harder, we can't touch the ground with our feet. So we have to help each other and when we find a tree, we have to lean the bikes against each other, and the tree, and use them as a climbing frame.'

'Alright. Southside Common?' Flick knew that was an easy route with not too many stops.

'Too easy. Let's go down by the river.'

Venga grabbed the sharpest knife from the kitchen drawer and they headed to the bike sheds.

Getting to the river had been tough. Two sets of red traffic lights had seen Flick propped against the post under the lights with Venga leant against him. And making the turn from the road to the slope down to the river had been difficult as they had to wait for a decent gap between pedestrians. Picking a tree had been even harder as they had passed a few contenders but couldn't turn round. Venga made a choice and stopped against the trunk. Flick stopped and fell onto him, then Venga held the bikes together as Flick climbed onto his cross bar with the vegetable knife in his hand. It was slow work. The knife wasn't very sharp and it took him about 20 minutes to carve a large capital M for Mendy.

'This is slow work. Let's swap and you can do a V.'

They struggled for 10 minutes to switch positions on their bikes without either of them touching the ground with their feet. They were so engrossed that they didn't notice a couple of girls who had stopped to stare at them with utter bemusement.

When Venga reached up past the carved M, he noticed the girls and immediately forgot about the team building exercise. Wow. The one of the left was stunning. 'Hello Gorgeous. How are you?'

The one on the right immediately felt left out as soon as her friend was singled out. That's a shame she thought, 'cause the one up the tree was stunning, but she was used to it. Her friend always got first choice. Besides, the one underneath holding the bikes together was nice looking too. Just not quite as nice.

The one on the left was delighted to have been picked out and had rated the two boys the same as her friend. The one up the tree was hot. The one holding the bikes was tidy, to be fair, but the other one was very hot. Be cool.

'What the fuck are you doing?' she smiled.

'Meeting the best looking girl in Southside,' he smiled. Then he remembered his manners, realising that he hadn't even looked at the second girl. 'I'm Venga, by the way. This is Flick.' He gestured below, then held his arm towards the second girl. 'And you?'

'I'm Cindy. This is Mandy. And we recognise *you* with the bikes.'

Flick looked again. Yes he recognised them too. Think.

'First year anatomy.' Cindy told him.

'Yes. That's right. Medical school then? Doctors?'

'Nurses. And you?'

'Doctor.' He then put a hand on Venga's shoulder as they both stepped away from the tree, feet now firmly on the ground. 'Sociologist and the owner of the best team-building company in the country.'

'What's it called Venga?' asked Mandy.

'Mandy's Magic. Was just putting our logo on the tree. Only got as far as M.' His eyes were fixed on Mandy again.

The flirting went on for another ten minutes before Venga took a chance. 'It's time for our coffee break now. Just along the river there's a tea room. Wanna join us for some cake?'

Mandy hesitated, but Cindy cut in. 'Sorry. Would love to, but we have to shoot off. Appointment in town.'

'That's a shame.' Flick accepted the rejection.

Venga didn't. 'Both of you got appointments?'

Mandy's face showed disappointment. 'Sorry. Yes.'

Venga took another chance. 'What about tomorrow Mandy? Meet me here? I'll take you for coffee and cake at the tea room? You and me?'

Cindy and Flick both felt a shade sidelined, but let it go.

Mandy waited, just for effect, she was an instant yes in her head. She tried to sound reluctant. 'Hmm maybe. Just you and me?'

'Yup. Cake of your choice and wonderful company.'

'Alright. Go on then. Noon here?'

'Woohoo.' Venga beamed.

The girls headed off, up the sloping path to the road and right towards Hotel Petra.

The boys sorted the mess they had made around the tree, gathered their bikes and started walking with them along the river, up the sloping path and left for the university.

'Wow. Mandy is hot. And she's into me.' Venga.

It had not been lost on Flick. She was just what he considered to be his type, but he had not got a look-in. 'She is indeed hot, but what about Sarah?'

'Ah yes, Sarah, hmm, well, we're not official.'

'You sure about that? I have a feeling she may see things differently.'

'Maybe. But she's away this weekend.'

'Oh that's okay then.' Sarcasm from Flick. 'And, while we're on the subject, what about Mira? Aren't you supposed to be seeing her tomorrow evening?'

'That's it Flick. That's the key word.'

'What?'

'Evening. So I can see Mandy in the afternoon.'

They rode back to the halls of residence, locked their bikes, and headed to the kitchen for lunch ahead of the big Ashtown Rovers game.

Waiting for them along with Mitz at the table was Brendan Gillies, manager of the Rose And Crown Sunday morning football team.

'Hey Brendan. Alright?' Venga shook him by the shoulders.

'Not really Ven to be honest.'

'Oh right. What's up?'

'Wazza is having his appendix out, Knobby's wife has just had her fourth baby and won't let him out, Tucks is on remand for assault and Polyp is in Hastings, I suspect with Wazza's wife.'

'Ah that's terrible Bren.'

He always had a story to soften up Venga and Flick to try and get them to play for the pub team. Whenever they turned up, there were plenty of players.

'So… Ven… or Flick… or both of you would be awesome, I'm short for tomorrow morning and it's a top-of-the-table clash with The Duck and Fox.'

'You make it sound so appealing.' Flick screwed his face up.

'And. Bren. The usual. The university first team is senior football. You're only allowed one senior player in the side and you've already got Mitz.' Venga said this every time he saw Brendan.

'Shouldn't be a problem Wazza.'

'Bren no. I don't want people calling me Wazza. Or Polyp for that matter.'

'Tucks?' Brendan said hopefully.

Venga looked at Flick for help. He shook his head.

Brendan reached into a carrier bag, pulled out a six-pack of Stella Artois, beyond the budget of most students and plonked it on the table. 'Go on Tucks. You know you want to.'

Venga waited, tried to say no, but gave in. 'Fuck it Bren. Just this once.'

Brendan cheered and shook his hand before turning to Flick. 'How about you Knobby?'

Flick came straight back with, 'No. Sorry. I do have to do some work tomorrow. Much harder course than Vee.'

Brendan reached for the beers and pulled three off the pack.

'Just a fucking minute Bren. I'd have to rethink if you did that.'

He put them back. 'Worth a try.' Apologetic. He stood to leave. 'Excellent Ven, 10am top pitch Southside Common for 11am kick off.'

After he'd gone Flick pointed out Venga's error. 'What about Mandy?'

'Ah fuck.'

All quiet.

Mitz checked his fish fingers under the grill. 'Sounds like you're letting down Team Mandy Ven.'

'Fuck Flick. Help me out.'

'Not much I can do. You've got to choose between the best-looking girl we've met since we started here over two years ago or playing in a crappy pub team in a crappy Sunday morning donkey league. Tough shout.'

'I should have got her number. She'd probably have come to watch. I took the beer. Can't say no now.' He was torn. He'd already agreed to play for Brendan so that wasn't the issue. It was how to save the Mandy situation without letting her down, but he had Mira to see later the same day and Sarah would be back late evening. 'Do me a big favour Flea.'

'What?'

'You meet Mandy, explain, apologise for me, get her number and see if she's free Monday.'

Unusual request to have made, which lead to an unusual chain of events the following day, but, reflecting on his first team-building exercise of Mandy's Magic, which morphed into TV Rush fairly quickly, Venga smiled across at Flick with much satisfaction as he signalled that it was time to make the turn and head towards the beach on the southern end of Skerryn.

'Turn nice and slow. It's gonna feel very different and the pole will stop us riding the waves comfortably.'

'Any rocks we need to avoid?'

'Not until we get close. There's a long stretch of sand with jagged rocks at the far end. That's where the lifeboat went aground. Just avoid that. Don't fight the waves and if we stay on this course, we should hit pretty much the centre of the beach.'

'No problem.'

'Just before we hit the sand, give it a squirt to take us further up the beach, but turn hard right at the same time, so the pole can go past us. I'll lift the engine after that burst.'

He turned to Jack and Juan. 'Could you both jump of the front with ropes when we land and start pulling us up the beach.'

They nodded.

'Boss,' Jack agreed.

They had gone round the island and were now heading in the direction they had come from. The wind seemed stronger but, just for now, the island offered some protection. They all prepared for the landing, Flick squirted the engine and turned hard right, Juan and Jack jumped ashore as Venga lifted the engine. Jack and Juan pulled the boat up the beach, the pole passed the boat and hit the sand.

Venga was delighted, shouted 'dream team baby' and high fived Juan. That was rare for two bickering brothers. Flick and Jack smiled at each other acknowledging the special moment.

Once everything had been safely stored at the top of the beach well above the high water mark and tucked below a sand dune, Venga checked his phone. Jack the only other team member with a phone signal messaged his wife to keep her updated and immediately got a reply frantic about Storm Vicky.

At the same time, Venga called them into a huddle. 'Bad news boys. Thought the wind was picking up and coming more from the land. Friend Baxter was right. Storm Vicky has turned back on itself and is now heading for the bottom end of Scotland.'

'Fuck. Should we ditch the pole and head straight back,' Juan was the most glass half empty.

'We could. But if the storm passes below us and back out towards Ireland, the winds up here will be strong off the land. Basically where we've come from. That makes it much harder than what we just did and growing worse.'

'Options?' Jack.

'Well… I see it as a challenge. We carry on with the exercise. Now we're on land, the weather has far less impact on us. It will get much more windy and it will probably rain, maybe quite hard. The worst of the storm looks like it will miss us. As Baxter pointed out, there is a shack at the foot of the hill where we can stay when the task is complete, ride out the storm and head back tomorrow.'

'Sounds like a plan.' The Wise Old Man.

'Sure.' The agreeable doctor.

They all looked at Juan, who had surprised himself by entering into the team spirit intended by his brother and felt genuine camaraderie and desire to complete the task.

'Game on.'
They all cheered.

Friends reunited

Chapter 6

2025, August 5, Tuesday
Southside Crown Court, trial day 3

Detective Chief Inspector Jon Jordan was the senior investigating officer on the Juan Prost case. He was surrounded by television crews on the steps leading up to Southside Crown Court.

'DCI Jordan, can we expect to see the victim's brother on the stand today?'

'I can't answer that.'

'Why not?'

He tried to hide an embarrassed smile. 'I don't know. Maybe you should ask prosecution counsel.'

'Can you tell us why the two key witnesses Venga Prost and Jack String have been allowed to sit in the public gallery before they have given their evidence?'

He tried to move up the steps but the assembled media were tightly packed.

'DCI Jordan? It's not normal practice?'

'It's not a normal trial.' He waved his arm to indicate the mass of media congregated around the square. 'There has been so much Press interest that sitting in court ahead of giving evidence is hardly likely to add pressure on a witness in either direction. That, as I understand it, was the judge's thinking on the matter.'

'Does that mean the judge took a decision to allow them in.'

'No.'

'He must have done.'

'I'm sorry young man, but that's not how it works. All it means is that he has not made a decision to exclude them.'

'But the judge did make a decision to grant bail to the killer?'

'Alleged killer?'

There was a ripple of laughter. 'With respect DCI Jordan. I don't think there is any dispute there. He is the killer. He's admitted it. We ran the stories. He was a hero. Killed one, saved one. We're only here to find out if the killer is also a murderer. So how did an "alleged" murderer get bail?'

Again, his path was blocked. 'Yes. Agreed. Killer. And bail is extremely rare in a murder trial, but you were at the bail hearing. You don't need me to tell you how onerous the bail conditions were. And we must respect the judge's decision to grant bail. Clearly it was the right decision as the defendant has attended trial, he has not practised medicine since his arrest, not met any of the key witnesses and we still have his passport in a drawer at police headquarters.'

With that he pushed harder and forced his way into the building, where he found his seat only just in time for the start of business. He watched the defendant take his seat in the dock and the jurors arrive in line. He shook his head with disgust as juror number two was still eating what looked like a bacon roll as he took his seat. No respect, and we must trust these people with a massive decision.

Juror number two, 34-year-old lift engineer Bradley Waters, took his seat, still outraged. He would be sitting in court day after day, virtually free, for what could be up to a month, and they tried to take his breakfast off him. No respect. So I'm expected to make a massive decision on an empty stomach.

He looked across to the public gallery where Venga Prost sat. He's the one that started this whole process, went to the police, called it murder. Maybe it was. Maybe it wasn't. And yes, I'm prepared to sit here and play my part in the decision, but surely I should be allowed breakfast.

Venga noticed one of the jurors still eating his breakfast. Couldn't they find 12 people who would take the trial seriously enough to give it their undivided attention? He turned towards the accused, his lifelong friend, well, adult life anyway. How had it all gone so wrong? There had been plenty of chaos through the years, but nothing that cost lives.

Looking back, the watershed day for Venga had been the fateful Sunday morning when his crappy Sunday morning football team lost a dull game 1-0 a day after his university team had won through to the cup final with a dull 1-0 win thanks to a late Baz penalty. At the same time, Flick had been meeting the hottest girl in Southside on Venga's behalf, a mistake as it turns out given that Flick went on to marry her two years later, but only because of the life-changing news he got from his third-choice girlfriend, at the time, moments before he was obliged to end his relationship with his second-choice girlfriend, at the time, Sarah.

He remembered it clear as a bell. Mira, third choice, had invited him round for dinner Sunday evening. She'd been very quiet. Said nothing all the way through the meal, barely given him any eye contact and Venga had started to think woohoo, it's over, I'm free to pursue Mandy and Sarah. This could turn out just fine. Any replies to his questions got lame one-word answers. Arctic roll for dessert was total silence. They both finished. Then Mira rested her chin on her hands.

Her elbows on the table and she looked him in the eye. He returned her gaze. They stayed like that for at least two minutes before she spoke.

'I'm pregnant.'

Venga's jaw metaphorically dropped. His appearance didn't actually physically change much. There was nothing. What the fucking fuck? He was 20. She was 19. How? Stupid question. They'd been careful. Or, at least, as careful as you can be when the girl is Catholic. Fuck. Catholic. She's gonna want to keep it. He said nothing. His mind was racing. He maintained eye contact. He was looking straight at her, but all he saw was Mandy. No chance. Then he saw Sarah, but not as clearly as Mandy. Now he saw Mandy again, partly undressed. Fuck it. Focus.

'I'm pregnant.'

'Yes.' He had nothing.

She raised her eyebrows, expecting some reaction. 'I think your silence has told me everything I need to know.'

More silence.

He opened his mouth. Nothing came out.

'Don't you dare ask me if it's yours.'

'I didn't.' But his eyes had already asked.

'Yes.'

'Congratulations?' It came out wrong. The stress was at the end of the word.

'Okay Venga. That was a question and I'll answer it, along with all the others you don't have the balls to ask me. Yes. It's yours. You're the only person I've ever slept with. Yes. I'm keeping it. I'm Catholic. I have no choice. No. You don't have to be involved. If you walk away, I'm still having it, but it makes no difference. I'm too young to be a mother. I've got too much life to live. I'm giving it up for adoption.'

She got up and cleared the plates, washed the pots, changed the music, topped up their wine glasses. Venga still hadn't moved and she sat down and faced him again.

As before, she raised her eyebrows. She wanted something. Anything.

His head was scrambled. He didn't know what he wanted to do, but he'd made a decision that, for now, he would say and do the right thing. Then see where it took them.

This time he got the intonation right. 'Congratulations. That's fantastic. We should keep it. Forget adoption. I graduate next year. I'll be working, we can get a place together. We can make it work. It's wonderful news Mira.' He got up and hugged her.

She didn't hug him back. It was hard to believe. Venga, she suspected, was a player. He was too good looking not to be. Especially at the age of 20. But you never know. Maybe.

Later that night, when Sarah got back from her weekend away, he told her it was over. He found Flick, thanked him for filling in with Mandy, but explained that he couldn't see her anyway moving forward as he was gonna be a daddy. They talked about it with disbelief for hours before Venga remembered to ask, 'How was it with Mandy?'

'Not gonna lie, she was disappointed when I showed up instead of you, but she joined me at the tea room and we got on really well.'

'Did you ask her to meet me tomorrow?'

'Sort of.'

'Sort of?'

'Well. I mentioned you'd like to meet her for a meal in town.'

'And?'

'I asked her how she'd feel if you couldn't make it and I showed up.'

'Wanker.'

'Sorry.'

'She say yes?'

'Yes.'

Venga laughed.

'I quite like her Vee.'

'Well. She's all yours now.' He laughed again. 'Be funny if you married her. She'd be Mandy Mendy.'

They laughed together.

Two years later she became Mandy Mendy just a few days after Mira walked out on Venga leaving him as a single father to a baby girl. Flick was on placement at Southside hospital and Venga had joined a company offering team-building activities. They had played football for the university, but after Venga graduated, they both joined Southside YMCA Football Club where Venga's brother Juan played and, despite being well into his 30s, Jack String, a sub-editor on the Southside Gazette played.

Venga's friendship with Flick was strong until he messed up five years later. He overstepped the mark with Mandy. Flick's response was swift and three months on, he was working in a hospital in Manchester, far enough away from Southside to make sure there would be no repeat of Venga's indiscretion with Mandy. They lost touch. Hardly surprising, but ten years on, Flick was back in Southside as a GP and surprisingly got in touch suggesting a beer together. Venga was over the moon. A chance to make a proper apology.

Venga stood at the bar of The Wanderers' Rest with a pint of lager, his back to the door. Flick walked in. Saw him. Stopped. Soaked up the atmosphere. There was his old friend, part of the reason he had left town 10 years ago. It was a long time. He hadn't seen him or spoken to him since he left for Manchester in a hurry. He walked quietly up to the bar. 'Vee.'

He turned and smiled broadly. 'Flea mate. How are you? You look great.' His normal greeting used to be to lift him off the ground, but he was unsure. 'Cider. You still on that girly drink?' He waved the barman over and ordered without waiting for an answer. Then shaking his hand warmly, he looked him in the eye. 'I'm so fucking sorry mate.'

Flick nodded, accepting the sincerity. 'Divorced now. Year ago.'

'No shit. What happened?' Venga bowed his head. 'Apart from me?'

'You were the first of many.' He shook his head. 'Or maybe not. There could have been others before you. So, in short, you weren't directly to blame. She just had an appetite for men that I couldn't satisfy.'

'Wow. So sorry Flick.' He couldn't help a smile. 'She was a babe though.'

Flick wasn't ready to smile. 'And the other old problem. I wanted kids. She didn't.'

Venga put his hand on his friend's shoulder.

Flick thought how *Sliding Doors* things had been. 'If only you'd said no to Brendan, I wouldn't have met your date. *Turn a different corner and we never would have met.*'

They talked more about his failed marriage and Flick's return to Southside.

'A lot has changed in 10 years mate.'

'Everything changes. Nothing changes. Manchester City rose from the third tier of the pyramid to win the Premiership. Spurs are still there or thereabouts and have still won nothing.' Flick was slipping back into the banter more easily than he expected. The drinks flowed.

'You playing any football Vee?'

'I could. Still fit enough. Just. But too many jobs fall on weekends.'

'Doing any other sports?'

'Clay pigeon shooting now and then. You ever tried it?'

Flick shook his head. 'Nah. Doesn't appeal.'

'Destroying clay discs with a 12-bore shotgun. What's not to like?'

'Not for me. Does it clash with work?'

'Can go any time.'

'Not your thing though. Surely? Not a team sport.'

'S'pose. But work's busy so I do what I can?'

'Still with that Woking firm?'

'Nope. On my own now. TV Rush.'

'Ahh, well done. That was the dream. Why TV Rush and not Mandy's Magic?'

Venga smiled. 'Yeah right. TV is Team Venga and Rush is adrenalin rush.'

'Oh right. Cool. Making money?'

'Yes. Plenty. Got a nice detached place on The Crescent. You should come over. Gonna have a barbecue some time when there's better weather.'

'Sure. Sounds good.'

'How about you? Doctors make a pretty packet don't they?'

'Not too bad. Steady. Divorce costs though. Mandy had expensive tastes and most of my money is tied up in the house she still lives in.'

'Gonna sell it?'

'I know we should, but she likes it. Don't want to push her. The split was a mutual thing by the way. There's no friction. We're still good friends, so as long as she's happy there, I'll let it go.'

'Wow. Don't think I'm friends with any of my old girlfriends.'

'And there's a lot of them.' Flick laughed. 'How about now? Anybody?'

'I'm sort of seeing someone at the moment, but I'm pretty sure I'm one of a few. We've not had any conversations about being exclusive or anything.'

'She nice?'

'Alright… I'm not selling her am I?'

'Okay. Is she normal? Is it a vanilla arrangement?'

Venga smiled, now he understood the question. 'She's normal.'

Flick raised his eyebrows and Venga added, 'ish. Mostly normal.'

Then he was lost in thought for a moment.

'I did have an odd one just prior to this one though.'

Flick groaned. 'Go on then.'

'Well… She was into bubble wrap and baby oil.'

'Ah right?'

'And role play.'

'Interesting.'

'One time I borrowed a van off a plumber, wore some overalls and went home. She opened the door pretending I was a plumber, invited me in, made me a cup of tea, then spread bubble wrap all over the kitchen floor, drenched it in baby oil, undressed and lay in the oil waiting for me to fix her sink.'

Flick laughed. 'Jesus Vee. Why does it always happen to you?'

'I'm just lucky mate. Or unlucky, depending on how you look at it. Would be nice to have a steady woman for once.'

Flick nodded.

'If you divorced a year ago, you must have been back on it. Anybody?'

Flick thought about Tasha. It was like Titanic. A brief, but incredible meeting of mind and body. In many ways so much better than his doomed marriage. There was no glass slipper and he couldn't find his Cinderella. He'd tried everything. In years gone by, Venga would have been the first person he'd have teamed up with in his search, but not yet, he'd best hold that back. Gotta rebuild the trust first. And apart from Tasha, there had been nobody.

'Nothing Vee. No energy for it. Focussed on work.'

'What is work at the moment? You up at the hospital?'

'No. GP at All Saints' Surgery. Know it?'

'Course. Only round the corner from my house. I'm with a doctor miles away. I was gonna switch anyway. How about I register at All Saints'?'

'Sure. Sounds like a plan. Your brother is already registered there.'

'Cool. Enjoying it?'

'Yes. Lovely staff. Some odd patients, but mostly good. I have some other work too.'

'Ah right.'

'I'm a consultant with the army over at Aldershot, spend the odd day there. Helping them develop equipment for the battlefield.'

'Wow. How'd that happen?'

'I specialised in haematology in Manchester, and when I left, they put my name forward and the Army got in touch.'

'Sounds good. You gotta get your mojo back though. Find a woman.'

'Maybe. Gotta get settled in first. GPing is new. Giving it my all for a while.'

'Gotta get back in the saddle.'

'I will.'

It was a long time ago. Venga shuffled in his seat and turned back to the jury box. Juror number two had finished his breakfast and was staring at the judge.

Bradley had finished his bacon roll and was still hungry. Don't suppose they'd let him get more food. No chance. The judge was in place now and looked determined to get started. He savoured the smell of bacon still on his fingers. Behind him juror number eight Jon Frazer, a 60-year-old university professor leant forward, his seat squeaking as he moved. Bradley's mood took another dip as he realised the juror's chair behind him had not been the source of the squeak. The smell of bacon was gone.

Great expectations

Chapter 7

2024, October 8, Tuesday
Skerryn, ten months before the trial

'The weather is kicking off. This must be the front edge of Storm Vicky. Let's get going. Lift on three… one, two,' Venga wanted to get moving as fast as possible. The weather was worsening rapidly and he wanted to know if the shack at the foot of the hill was going to be good shelter for the night.

They lifted the pole onto their shoulders and headed along the overgrown track. Slow going but could have been a lot worse, the exposure to the weather had kept the growth down on what used to be the main road through the island, albeit little more than a stony path.

After a hundred yards the heavens opened. They were soaked. Strong head winds driving the rain into their faces.

It was the start of October, but this weather was far worse than Flick had expected in early autumn, although they were a long way further north than Southside. Global warming he told himself. Extreme weather events. Venga was leading the march, Flick immediately behind. On the car journey up the two friends had agreed, as always, no secrets, but there was a big one. Massive. Flick thought back to another extreme weather event, a warm sunny day in Southside five months after his interview for the GP job, two months after he started the new job and a month after he had rekindled his friendship with Venga following ten years without seeing each other. It was a barbecue at Venga's house on the patio in the large manicured gardens and the first social gathering for Flick since his move back from Manchester.

He lacked motivation. Small talk was hard work. He had tried and failed to find Tasha and he had no interest in meeting anyone new. But soon after arriving and handing Venga a four pack of lager and another of cider, he was delighted to bump into Jack String, The Wise Old Man, finally retired from playing football for Southside YMCA veterans football team, and his wife Lisa.

'Doctor Flick. Great to see you. How are you?' Jack shook his hand warmly.

'Wise Old Man how are *you*?' He beamed and then hugged Lisa with a kiss on the cheek.

'You visiting or back for good?'

'Back for the foreseeable future,' was as far as Flick would concede. 'Working as a GP at All Saints' Surgery.'

'We should switch. Ours is crap.'

'No it's not Jack. You do come out with rubbish sometimes,' Lisa berated him.

Flick laughed. 'Still bickering eh?'

'Yes. Nothing changes. You must come down the football club. I'm chairman now and we've got a great side.'

'Sure. I'll catch a game some time.'

'Not as good as our team back in the day though.' Jack patted him firmly on the back. 'Have you seen Juan? He's here somewhere.'

'He was in the garden.' Lisa grabbed Flick's arm and lead them out.

Juan was by the barbecue with his wife Megan. He turned as they approached. 'Flick Mendy. How are you? Venga said you were back in town. Great to see you.'

Flick shook him warmly by the hand, hugged and kissed Megan.

'Great thanks. Good to see you. It's been a long time.'

'Far too long my friend. Far too long.'

Half an hour later the catch-up had only scratched the surface. Ten years was a long time. When it was just Flick and Juan they got deeper.

'Juan, gotta be honest, I was desperately hoping to see youngsters running around your feet. Still no luck?'

'None. And we can't afford the IVF any more. We had two starters but both miss-carried. It destroyed Megan. The second one we knew was a girl and I painted the nursery pink, had a cot set up, bought a mobile, silver stars on the roof. It just wasn't meant to be.'

Flick hugged him.

'Thought you might have had some yourself, but Venga told me about the divorce. So sorry.'

'Same thing Juan. Just wasn't meant to be.'

They both looked down into their drinks… defeated.

Juan tried to pick up the mood. 'You're a handsome fella. You must be fighting them off. Doctor. Mid thirties. There must be a queue around the block. Onwards and upwards.'

Flick thought about Tasha. He *had* found someone. But he'd lost them again. Maybe Juan could help. 'I did meet someone recently.'

'Ah cool. Go on. Fill me in.'

'When I came down to interview for the GP job in the summer. Stunning girl. A female version of me but way nicer.'

'Where is she then? We must meet her.'

'Bit of a problem there. I went back to Manchester the day after I met her and didn't take her phone number.'

'So you've not seen her since?'

'No.'

'Right.' Juan was rubbing his chin in thought and couldn't help asking the most useless question he could have come up with. 'Why didn't you get her number?'

Flick's grimace answered that.

'Alright. Look her up in the phone book.'

'Only got a first name.'

'Mate you fucked up.' Juan shook his head. 'Go on then. What's her name?'

Venga interrupted. 'Caught up with everyone Flea?'

'Mostly.'

'Jack and Lisa are here somewhere.'

'Yeah. Saw them.' Flick laughed. 'Still bickering.'

'Jack's finally stopped playing football.'

'Shame. He was quality.'

'He's been clay pigeon shooting with me a couple of times.'

'Ah right. He any good?'

'Rubbish. Not a natural.' Venga looked over Flick's shoulder at a new arrival, with poorly disguised disapproval. 'I, on the other hand, am extremely good with a shotgun, which may come in handy when I deal with a certain young man.'

Flick resisted the temptation to look round.

Venga regained his composure. 'You seen my daughter yet?'

'No. How is she? Must be an adult now. What was she when I left? Six? Seven?'

'Seventeen now and, sadly, very much an adult.'

'Sadly?'

'You'll see. Here she is, with her menace of a boyfriend.' He waved her over. 'Natty. Come see uncle Flick.'

Now he turned round.

It was Tasha.

In a maternity dress.

Pregnant.

About five months.

Oh my fucking god. What have I done?

The rush of blood to his head left him dizzy. Close to fainting, but he kept it together. People were speaking. He heard nothing. People were moving. He saw nothing. He felt enormous physical pressure. Like he was going to explode. Or implode.

'You okay Flick?' Juan held his shoulders.

He stared into her eyes. She stared back. Once again, they were the only two people on the planet. It felt like minutes went by. Longer. But it can only have been a fraction of a second.

'Mate. You okay?' Juan was worried.

Flick tried to rally. 'Sorry Juan. Turned round fast. Too much cider. Can't take my drink any more.' He stepped forward, hugged Tasha and kissed her cheek. 'Wow. You've turned into a beautiful young lady. How are you?' He felt like he'd got away with it.

'Good thanks uncle Flick… uncle Mendy… Doctor M.'

Flick turned to the young man by her side.

Tasha grabbed his arm gently. 'This is my boyfriend Denzil.'

Flick shook his hand. He definitely wasn't a dog. 'Pleased to meet you.'

'And you.' He nodded respectfully as he shook hands.

Flick's eyes looked down at Tasha's bump then back up. 'Congratulations.'

'Now you know why I need my gun.' Venga was half joking.

Denzil was nervous. 'Thank-you doctor.'

'Thank-you uncle.' Tasha smiled.

Flick resisted the temptation to ask when the baby was due. 'So what you up to these days Nat?'

'Just finishing my A-levels at sixth form college.'

'Going well? Do you know what you're going to do?'

'Very well thanks. Expecting all As. Wanted to be a vet, but things change.'

'Life ruined by bad judgement in my opinion.' Venga glared at Denzil.

'I wouldn't say that Dad. Not ruined at all. Just different.'

'You're being too kind.' Venga had known about the baby for about a month now and had not yet calmed down. If he thought he'd get away with it, he'd have gladly used the shotgun on Denzil. The foolish young man had destroyed his daughter's future. Stolen her life.

Tasha was losing patience with him. 'Listen Dad. Don't you think you're being a hypocrite? You were a dad before you finished university. Do you regret having me? Have I ruined your life?'

It was calm. Well presented. Venga felt slightly foolish. As if he had been told off. He had. But he would be having a word with Denzil in his drawing room some time soon.

'So, Doctor M, maybe instead of a vet, I could work for Vicar Insurance.'

'Big employer. Plenty of opportunities. You could do well.'

'I think so. I did a week of work experience there a few months back. Was fun. Lots of friends from my netball team work there.'

The conversation flowed. They ate burgers. Drank beer. And cider.

Juan cornered Flick. 'You feeling alright now?'

'Yes thanks. Don't know what came over me. Maybe I should see a doctor.'

Juan laughed. 'So, Flick. This girl. How we gonna find her?'

He hesitated. 'Not going to be easy. Think I've tried everything, but may get deeper into social media.'

'Good shout. What's her name?'

'Ella,' Flick replied. As close as he could think of to Cinderella.

Tasha joined them. 'Doctor M. Do you remember that tree you bought me for my sixth birthday? It's matured nicely. Wanna come see?'

There was no tree. 'Yes. Lead the way. Excuse us Juan.'

She led him to a quiet corner of the garden.

He tried to hug her.

She backed off. 'Better not. We could be seen. Denzil is 21. Dad wants to shoot him because he's four years older than me. Imagine what he would do if he knew about us.'

'You're right. Sorry.'

He took a step back. 'I've been looking everywhere for you. Why do you have to be Natty Prost? Natty Wilson, Smith, anything but Prost. And how can you possibly be 17? Mid twenties. I was certain.'

'Late 20s for you I thought… or early 30s. You're my uncle fucking Flick.'

They frowned at each other. The frown melted into a smile. The magic was still strong, but it could never happen.

'Now I know you are 17 and my best friend's daughter. Everything has changed.'

'Same.' She nodded agreement.

'But I'm still drawn to you.'

'Again. Same.'

'I know I shouldn't be. It's wrong.'

'Not necessarily wrong, but probably a bad idea. What's the worst that could happen?'

'Venga shoots me. He goes to prison. You miscarry the baby with stress.'

'Fairs. What's *more* likely?'

He couldn't think of anything. 'Nothing good.'

'We should leave things as they are. I would love to be with you, but we can't. See how things go.'

He couldn't stop himself. He hugged her tight. Didn't kiss her. Just hugged her. 'See how it goes.' He stepped back again, looked down at the bump. 'It is mine isn't it?'

'Denzil thinks it's his.'

'But it's mine?'

'He's determined to stand by me.'

'I know it's mine and I know you won't be able to live with yourself if you let him believe it's his indefinitely.'

'You know me well. If there's anything to tell, I'll find the right time.' She smiled. 'How'd you like the tree?'

'Impressive.'

They rejoined the others hoping their absence hadn't been noticed.

Flick adjusted the pole on his shoulder. It seemed heavier than before they put it in the water back in Tobermory. Must have soaked up a lot of water on the trip. The road reached the end of the beach where it met a rocky headland. Sat alongside the road was the wrecked lifeboat from the 90s. It was big, with a massive hole carved in the hull by the rocks. It had been dragged safely away from the water. All the colour now faded. The bright orange was soft peach and the dark blue much lighter.

They turned away from the beach and the visibility improved as the rain stopped. The shack slowly got bigger as they approached and they were ready for a lunch break when they lowered the pole to the ground and tried the front door. Open.

Jack lead the way. 'Gonna be tough to give it a five, but I've stayed in worse Airbnbs.'

'Looks good to me.' Venga was impressed. 'Was expecting dirt floor and boarded up windows. This is great.'

There was glass in the windows, one smashed and boarded up at the back, but that kept the weather out and there was plenty of light. There was one big room with a bathroom through the only door. No power. No water. But there were a couple of single beds at the far end. No bedding. There was a wardrobe, with a few blankets. That'll do. They could feel the building shake as Storm Vicky gathered pace.

'Okay boys, we're about 400 yards from the top of the hill.' He checked his phone. No signal. He'd had one on the beach. Must be the hill blocking the signal from the mainland. 'Here's the situation.'

They gathered round.

'Firstly, Storm Vicky is getting closer. We're not getting off the island today. Gonna have to make the best of this place. Beyond that there are three choices. One, we stay in this shack until the storm passes and go home tomorrow. Two, we go outside the shack, lift the pole, raise the flag, then kip in here for the night, or three, we carry on to the top of the hill, where we'll probably have a phone signal again, by the way, raise the pole and flag at the highest point of the island. Job done. Dream team.'

Juan looked at the horizontal rain through the window. The wind was loud on the roof and the building was still shaking around them. He was exhausted and his legs were aching. Clingy wet jeans didn't help. If only somebody with more experience had shown the good sense to advise a change of clothing.

Jack, as always, went first. 'My vote is top of the hill. Storm Vicky can fuck off.'

Flick was still keen. They were already exhausted and soaked to the skin. Why not make one final push? 'Top of the hill for me.'

Nothing happened unless Juan was in. As always, all eyes were on Juan, and on this occasion, there was no hesitation. 'I'm with Jack, Storm Vicky can fuck right off.'

They cheered and Venga reached for the equipment bag to sort the flag and ropes. Most of the baggage was stored in the shack. They would take the bare minimum to complete the task. With the equipment prepared they huddled together in a tight circle, much the same as they had years ago before they played a football match. Venga lead a chant of *together we are stronger* and they headed out into the storm.

On the count of three, they lifted the pole and marched slowly up the incline. There was steady progress, with a couple of steeper sections, but nothing beyond them. It only took 15 minutes to complete the climb. At the summit, about 200 feet above sea level, Venga checked his phone. A good signal again. The wind was horrendous, but they had found a gap in the rain. The terrain beneath them was mostly smooth lumpy rock, some loose sharper rocks, very short grass in places and other weeds. The highest point was a ridge of about 30 feet with the land sloping down on all sides, gently towards the beach where they had come from, a little steeper to the rocky north coast.

Venga attached four ropes to the end of the pole without metalwork. Best to keep that safely close to the ground. He then chose a small indent to plant the end of the pole. It was a 35 foot pole so Venga wanted each person at about 50 feet from the pole to improve control, but the steeper slope to the north became much steeper after only 20 feet, so they placed two coiled ropes north east and north west at about 20 feet with the other two forming a cross but about 35 feet from the base of the pole. Again, further would have been better but the ground was firmer at 35 feet. Venga was opposite Juan and Flick was opposite Jack. They placed the end of the pole in the indent and lay it on the ground between the two longer ropes. Juan and Jack held the foot of the pole in its slot as Venga and Flick started to pull it vertical. When it was halfway, Juan and Jack went to their coils so all four of them took the strain. Venga and Flick pulled slowly as Juan and Jack released their ropes until it was upright with the flag horizontal in the relentless wind. It was tough to keep it in place as ferocious gusts whipped it.

'What now?' shouted Flick.

'We need a picture. Jack. You're best placed. Down wind and on a longer rope. And apart from me, you're the only one with a phone that works.'

They were struggling to hear each other, exhausted and holding on desperately to the ropes, all totally dependant on each other.

'Left it in the shack. Sorry. You said *only what we need* and I didn't know we needed it.'

'Fuck. I'll have to take it then.' He knew that was risky as he was on a short rope, on the steepest ground and taking more weight than any of the others as the wind was directly behind him. At that point, his experience should have told him to forget the picture. Too risky, but he was one photo away from finishing the job against all odds. Thirty seconds. He was too close. His judgement was compromised. And he was about to make a catastrophic mistake.

He wrapped the rope around his waist and loosely secured it with a quick-release bow, which he held onto with one hand. With his other, he unzipped and reached into his pocket for his phone, set it up, pointed and took the picture. As he dropped it back in his pocket, a gust pulled him slightly off balance. One hand on the rope wasn't enough to stay in control of the rope and he fell forwards. The pole was falling and dragged him almost to the foot of the pole before he was able to release the bow. He screamed at Juan to jump out of the way and waved his hand frantically but the gust carried his screams away.

Juan heard nothing. He had fleetingly looked away at the same time as the gust hit Venga, a seagull flying by distracted him. It was very unlucky. The timing was unfortunate. By the time Juan looked back the end of the pole was almost on him. It thumped into him before he had chance to react. It was a glancing blow, but 600 pounds of wooden pole, probably 700 with the metalwork and all the water it had soaked up, ripped into his flesh.

Worse was to come. Venga had been dragged to the base of the pole. As the top end smashed into Juan, the bottom end pivoted on an extruding rock and whipped back up with all the metalwork raking across the side of Venga's body.

Juan was screaming, the pole pinning him to the ground. Flick took a closer look before deciding that Juan's chances were greater with the pole removed. It hadn't impaled him. 'Okay, Jack, on three.' They lifted it off Juan and lowered it slowly to the ground, conscious that they could be causing more harm to Venga at the other end.

The injuries were shocking and Flick saw blood flowing fast. He showed Jack how to press firmly on the wounds to slow the bleeding so he could get to Venga and see how bad his injuries were.

They were different but equally horrific. The metalwork had ripped through his clothes and flesh. The amount of blood suggested arterial damage, but he couldn't immediately tell where it was coming from. His chest, hip and leg were all damaged. Most of the blood was below his hip, so he used some of the rope to tourniquet his thigh and the flow eased.

He reached into Venga's pocket for his phone, pressed the screen against Venga's finger to unlock it and dialled 999. He quickly summarised their perilous situation and urgent need for help, but the response wasn't what he was hoping for.

'We can probably get a helicopter to you, but not for another 24 hours. Storm Vicky is a big problem for us. Visibility is almost nothing with the rain and that's a tough island to land on.'

'I'm a doctor. Most of my experience is in haematology and these two men will be dead long before 24 hours is up.'

'I understand what you are saying but trying to land a helicopter on that island, which is difficult at the best of times, is too dangerous. We can't risk lives to save lives. I'm sorry. And it would be harder for the lifeboat. They said 24 hours too. At best.'

'From what I can see, they will bleed to death in a few hours. Their injuries are different but equally life threatening. There is shelter a quarter of a mile away. We'll try and get them there and stabilise them. Get a closer look at the injuries, but please, talk to anyone who may be able to help, perhaps the military have different equipment.'

They were struggling to hear each other with the howling wind and the rain had started again.

‘We always work with the military. The problem isn’t getting to the island, it’s landing. I’ll do what I can, but you’ve got to proceed on the assumption that you’ve got a 24 hour wait.’

Flick realised that he had to accept what she was saying and do what he could for the brothers. He hung up.

‘Jack,’ he shouted. ‘We’ve got to get them to the shack.’

Denzil

Chapter 8
2025, August 6, Wednesday
Southside Crown Court, trial day 4

Juror number five 36-year-old teacher Vicky Mather couldn't choose. Flick Mendy was good looking, but his eyes were dull. He looked washed out. Who wouldn't facing a murder charge? His body language was apologetic. He looked guilty. Venga Prost, his accuser, on the other hand, was also good looking, but in a different way. He was raw. His eyes were bright, more switched on. He was the aggressive player in this trial though. He had chosen to accuse his best friend of murder, even though his best friend had saved his life. That detail had been in doubt, but expert medical witnesses confirmed that Flick Mendy's intervention had been the key action in keeping Venga alive. They had also confirmed that Flick Mendy's assessment of both brothers' chances of survival and the timings related to the expected arrival of the air ambulance on the island, were correct.

Witnesses from the emergency services confirmed they had initially advised Dr Mendy there was no chance he would get any help until at least 24 hours after the hilltop accident. The first three days of the trial had not helped Vicky choose between Flick and Venga. And, however seriously she took the trial, and that was very seriously, she couldn't stop her mind wandering. If she were one of two people who survived a nuclear holocaust, would she rather be left with Flick or Venga. It was a tough one.

It was day four of the trial and she hadn't made a choice yet. She looked around the courtroom for other contenders. There were a few she had seen in the papers. DCI Jordan, the senior investigating officer, not exactly a friend of the accuser, but, according to the papers, they belonged to the same shooting club. Sounds a bit masonic, helping each other out regardless. Why does that put me off the police officer but not Venga? Weird.

Juror number four Joe Wareham immediately to her right had to be a contender. He said he was a swimwear model. Not sure if he was making that up. Who knows? Nice looking young man, but how useful would a swimwear model be in a nuclear wasteland? Nah.

The other obvious choice sat at the end of the public gallery on the back row, 31-year-old Denzil Penhale. He was also a teacher. Vicky knew of him, but he was at a different school. He wasn't directly involved in the trial, but he'd been in the papers, sharing his opinion of those involved, because he used to go out with Tasha Prost, Venga's daughter, and, according to the papers, was the father of her son Zac.

She watched him. Handsome. Very. But there was something missing. His body language was downbeat. He looked like he was hiding. There was no confidence. Wonder why? Maybe his brush with the Prost family had gone badly. It certainly didn't go too well for Flick Mendy.

Denzil sat on his own in the public gallery. He wasn't involved in proceedings and didn't need to be there, but his fascination with Tasha was unrelenting. They were still friends and he wanted to show support, but he didn't want to intrude too much so he kept a respectable distance. From the back row, he could see Tasha, and looked over now and then. More than now and then. Too much really. He tried not to. She was next to her father Venga. Denzil didn't look at him at all. He daren't. Bad memories.

When Tasha had been pregnant with Zac, there had been a barbecue at Venga's house on an unusually warm sunny November day. Venga, angry about the pregnancy, had made jokes about using his shotgun on Denzil and two weeks later, he arrived early for a date with Tash. She was still in the bathroom and Venga invited Denzil into his drawing room for a 'chat'.

'Have a seat Denzil.'

Venga walked slowly across the room. Closed the door. Locked it. Walked slowly back behind his large desk. He hadn't looked at Denzil and said nothing. Instead of sitting down, he reached for his 12-bore shotgun leaning in the corner. He placed it on his desk, sat down in his seat, looked straight at Denzil. Still silent. No smile. A neutral expression. Giving nothing away. They both looked at each other. This lasted about a minute before Venga stood again, picked up his double barrelled weapon, cracked it open, checked it wasn't loaded, then went about the task of cleaning both barrels. Solvent, cleaning rod, copper brush, oil. Closed it up, stood it back in the corner and sat back in his seat.

The effect on Denzil had been just as Venga had probably intended. His mouth was dry, he was physically trembling, probably unable to speak, if he tried, and he had broken out in a cold sweat. Did he really want to have anything to do with this family? Was Tasha worth it? Well. Yes. She was worth anything. He knew he was punching. She was out of his league and he couldn't believe it when she agreed to date him just over a year ago. He hadn't realised there was an age gap at all. Let alone, four years. She was so assured. Her father had been cool about the age gap until the pregnancy. Venga had floated the idea of an abortion with Tasha, but she had closed him down straight away. The suggestion had horrified Denzil.

Apart from the passive threats from Venga, Denzil was over the moon at the thought of a family with Tasha and he would probably have his first teaching job soon after the child was born, which would give them chance to set up their own family home. But he had to get through his current ordeal with Venga.

The gun was safely back in the corner, but the intimidating stand-off continued for another half a minute or so before Venga opened the conversation.

'You should join me for a clay pigeon shoot Denzil.'

'Love to. That be great… That'd be great.' He half stammered.

'You ever fired a shotgun?'

Denzil shook his head.

'Lethal weapon.'

'I can imagine.'

Venga waited again, eyes on Denzil. Still a neutral expression.

'If I were to shoot you across this desk, the spray of lead would take your head off.'

Denzil's eyes widened.

The awkward silence returned, both men unwilling to look away, or even blink.

'I'm disappointed.'

That seemed like the understatement of the year to Denzil.

'Natty was forecast straight As, the university of her choice and a rewarding life as a veterinary surgeon.'

Nothing from Denzil.

'Way I see it… you've taken that from her.' He shook his head very slowly. You could hardly tell it was moving. 'Stolen her life.'

Still nothing.

'But, young man. Yes. There is a but. She sees it differently. And that is why I'm not going to plaster your head all over my drawing room wall.' He laughed. 'Joking of course.'

Denzil wanted to speak, but had no idea what to say.

'She wants to keep the baby and she wants to keep you.'

'I qualify soon and will…'

'So Denzil,' Venga cut him off. 'Tasha will stay here. She will have the baby, complete her studies and, with a few words in the right direction, embark on a career with Vicar Insurance.'

Denzil nodded.

'And you, young man, will move in with us and provide all the moral support she needs.'

Denzil was mortified. Living under the same roof as Venga was not how he saw his new family's future. He would have no control. Conceding control to Tasha was just about acceptable and probably unavoidable, but conceding control to her father was horrific.

'Mr Penhale… Do we have an understanding?'

It wasn't a question. It was a statement. The only offer on the table.

'Yes sir.' He'd never addressed Venga as 'sir' before, but he felt obliged on this occasion.

Sat in the public gallery, Denzil shivered as he relived the unpleasant memory, but it was nothing compared to the trauma that followed two weeks later after date night with Tasha in the car as they were driving home to her father's house. When they turned into The Crescent, Tasha asked him to pull over so they could have a chat without her father intruding.

He went in for a kiss. She pulled away.

'Give me a minute Denz. We need to talk.'

Oh no this doesn't sound good. She held his forearm with both hands. Their faces were half in shadow, street light spilling into the car.

'I am very fond of you Denz. You are so important to me. I'm certain we'll have a wonderful life together.'

'Same,' he agreed hoping it was true. All the time waiting for a 'but'.

'I know you don't like living in my dad's house. It's not ideal, but it makes sense for now. I appreciate you've given up a lot, certainly mentally anyway, to accept this situation, and it's hard on you. I am so grateful for your commitment.'

'Goes without saying Tash. I love you. You're my world and I can't wait to be a family. Can't wait to have our own place.'

'I share those dreams.'

He could almost feel it coming.

'But.'

'Not gonna lie Tash. I saw the "but" coming. I've no idea what it is, but if there's any chance we get to stay together, I don't care what it is. I'd rather not know. Then again, you might be ditching me, so you'd better tell me.' He was shaking again, grateful that his face was in shadow. She hadn't said anything yet, but he was already fighting the tears.

'I'm not dumping you Denz, but when I've told you what I absolutely *must* tell you, you may want to dump me.'

'No chance Tash. That's never going to happen.'

She squeezed his arm. 'Denzil.'

Now he braced for the impact.

She waited, knowing she would shatter his world. Eking out the last crumbs of harmony, then letting it go with her crushing news.

'You're not the father.'

Denzil instantly pulled away. 'Fuck… did *not* see that coming.' The change of mood was massive. Suddenly there was anger. Who was the father? That's what he wanted to know. He wanted to ask. He didn't think she'd tell him. Probably be as angry as him. Don't ask. It won't help. Say something. Anything.

'Who *is* the father?' He couldn't stop himself.

She expected it to be the first question and she had rehearsed the answer in her head. 'I will never tell you. It makes no difference. I haven't told him. I don't want him to have anything to do with the baby. I don't want to be with him. I want to be with you Denzil.'

'*Who's* the father?'

Silence. She'd already answered that. She never repeated herself.

He wiped away tears, faced forward, staring aimlessly in the distance, focussed on nothing. Lost for words and utterly deflated.

Ten minutes later, he was ready to talk some more. 'Okay Tash, why do you want to be with me instead of the father?'

'It's complicated and you must choose to trust my judgement. Or not. I won't blame you if you walk away. But, in short, and you won't like hearing this, you are more *suitable.*'

Now Denzil laughed. 'I would have preferred you to tell me you love me rather than tell me I'm more suitable.'

'Same Denzil. I'd prefer to be saying that now. And I'd prefer to feel that way, but I don't. I had to tell you. I don't want you with me for the wrong reasons and you deserve the truth.'

The anger had passed and Denzil had moved on to a new emotion and it wasn't the cliché denial that is often talked about. It was total hopelessness. Denial came before the shattering news on this occasion. He had believed Tasha was falling in love with him, but that now seemed stupid. Delusion, denial, whatever it was, he had been so besotted that he allowed himself to think Tasha was the same. He'd sat through torture with Venga only two weeks previously because she was worth it.

'Does your dad know it's not me?'

'No… and I'd prefer it to stay that way.'

'He locked me in his office the other day and sat cleaning his gun because he thought I had got you pregnant. Did you know that?'

'No, but it doesn't surprise me. He can be volatile.'

'No shit.'

It was quiet again for a few minutes.

'Okay Denzil. Drop me off, don't stay tonight, go home and think about it.'

Denzil twisted in his seat in the public gallery and found himself saying the word out loud. 'Suitable.' Oops. This time he repeated it in his head. Suitable. Fucking suitable. Really? He looked over at her again. Stop doing that.

He had done as she suggested, but he only stayed away until 7am the next day, when he knew her alarm would go off. He accepted the news and moved forward as if the child were his. He had no choice. He loved Tasha and desperately hoped that one day she would love him, which took his thoughts to the next major blip in the Tasha story. It happened during Zac's first birthday party after considerable planning and investment.

It was a Friday evening party, March 24, 2017, a date etched on his memory. The venue was YMCA FC's clubhouse and there were a few other younger guests from Zac's baby club, but most of the guests were friends from Denzil's school, Vicar Insurance, family and old family friends, Jack and Lisa String, Venga's brother Juan and his wife Megan, Dr Flick Mendy, alone, as always, and, of course, Venga with yet another girlfriend, this one rather inappropriately wearing a see-through shirt with no bra under. The only reason you couldn't see her nipples was because they had fluorescent pink bunny stickers covering them. About 40 guests.

After they'd all had a go on the karaoke, the younger guests, with parental help, began a game of pass the parcel, Denzil operating the music using the karaoke equipment. He made sure each toddler/baby had a go, stopping the music for their parents to remove a layer of the parcel until it got to the last package.

Megan Prost had a friend's baby on her knee. She took the paper off the parcel. It was a jewellery box with a note. 'Tasha must open this box.'

She read it out and there was a collective intake of breath. Excitement. She handed it over.

Before Tasha opened the box, the karaoke started up again. It was Bruno Mars and Denzil sang.

It's a beautiful night, we're looking for something dumb to do

Hey baby, I think I wanna marry you

Then he left the song playing at lower volume and walked over to Tasha with everyone cheering and clapping him. He went down on one knee.

'Natasha Prost, you are my world. I love you and want to be with you always. Will you marry me?'

The cheers grew louder.

Tasha opened the box. A classy and very expensive-looking ring.

It had cost Denzil a month's salary.

Tasha, for once, was flustered. 'It's beautiful Denz.'

One of the babies started crying uncontrollably. His mother headed for the exit. As all eyes followed the retreating mother, Tasha looked fleetingly in Flick's direction. His eyes gave nothing away. She knew he wasn't an option. She'd stuck with Denzil. He was a teacher now, they had bought a house together. Happy family. But she didn't love him. She so wanted to say yes. But she didn't love him.

The cheers were fading. A few guests had noticed. She hadn't replied.

Denzil reached for the jewellery box, pulled out the ring, and, smiling, asked, 'Is that a yes?'

They faced each other, ignoring the crowd. Denzil saw her smile melt into anguish. Her eyes said no. The tiniest of movements, only Denzil noticed, she shook her head.

Rock and a hard place

Chapter 9

2024, October 8, Tuesday
Skerryn, ten months before the trial

Venga's worst injury was his leg. After applying the rope tourniquet, Flick moved his injured friend so he was lying with the damaged leg on higher ground, then rushed back to Juan.

Jack was pressing firmly on the deepest wound, just above Juan's elbow. 'Shit Flick. What now?'

Flick tied rope around Juan's arm under his armpit. He screamed in agony. The arm was broken, but Flick's priority was to stop the bleeding. How to carry him? Don't wanna touch that shoulder. He tied another length of rope around Juan's waist and injured arm to limit the movement and with Jack's help, lifted him over his shoulder in a fireman's lift.

The wind was howling on the hilltop, but the rain had eased as Flick carried Juan steadily down the hill with Jack following. Exhausted and relying heavily on adrenalin, Flick shouted instructions. 'Go back and tell Venga we'll be ten minutes.'

'Optimistic.'

'Yeah. Tell him anyway. And grab the TV Rush flag. I might need it for dressings.'

He set off. 'Wait.' Flick had another idea. 'Then get to the shack before me and set up both beds. Then break the bathroom door off.'

Jack set off back up the hill and five minutes later, raced down past Flick to the shack. When Flick struggled in with Juan whimpering uncontrollably over his shoulder, he was grateful for Jack's help easing the older brother onto one of the beds. Without stopping to catch his breath, he threw open his battle bag, ever so grateful that he had equipment specially prepared for the battlefield. That's what it felt like now. First thing, a shot of morphine. Then a quick temporary job with dressings and a proper tourniquet to replace the rope. He slipped a second tourniquet into his pocket and signalled for Jack to pick up the door and join him on a half jog back up the hill, where they loaded Venga onto the makeshift stretcher, applied the proper tourniquet and headed for the shack.

Jack had told Venga they would be back for him after 10 minutes. It had actually been 16 minutes, but it felt like 16 hours. There had been no pain when the accident happened, just shock. He couldn't believe he'd made such a school-boy error. He couldn't believe he'd been badly injured and he couldn't believe he'd been responsible for someone else being badly injured, especially his brother.

The pain followed, almost as soon as the rope tourniquet had been applied, he suddenly became acutely aware of every mangled inch of his battered body. The pain came from so many sources in so many different shapes and sizes. Different intensity. Throbbing, sharp, dull, burning, a paralysing cocktail of agony that stretched every second well past breaking point. He had never known anything like it and desperately steered his thoughts onto happier times; the birth of his daughter, the cup-final-winning goal he scored, the birth of his grandson. Wow, didn't realise that was a good thought.

But then there was a new level of pain, being lifted onto a bathroom door and carried down a hillside in storm-force winds and, yet again, heavy rain.

He looked up at Flick, his best mate, the man trying to keep him alive and felt an enormous wave of guilt. This lovable doctor, who joined him on his first team-building trip so many years ago and was still by his side, had tolerated him despite Venga having wrecked his marriage. Yes, he moved away to Manchester for ten years, but when he came back, there had been forgiveness and the friendship continued where it had left off. Now his life was in the hands of Doctor Flick Mendy and all Venga could think about was how much he had betrayed him two decades ago for no good reason other than his own insatiable appetite for women.

It was a hot summer night in 2005. Friday. End of a busy week. Venga had planned to meet Flick in the pub for a couple of beers, but his child minder for six-year-old Tasha had let him down. Never easy for a single parent. He was running late and thought he'd try Mandy Mendy. If she was home alone, with Flick at the pub, maybe she'd watch Tasha.

He parked on the drive and told Tasha to keep the doors locked. No answer at the front door, so he went down the side path to the back. Nice big garden with a few trees, shrubs, patio and a brick path leading down to a wooden workshop at the bottom of the garden next to an old Victorian greenhouse. Venga followed the path, saw movement in the workshop. Must be Mandy.

He stood in the open doorway. She hadn't noticed him. She was working at the other end of the large, high-roofed building, sun streaming through a row of Velux windows as she transferred small geraniums into bigger pots. She was wearing white tennis shoes, a peach-coloured short summer dress and a lightweight royal blue cardigan. She looked stunning. She always did. If only he hadn't agreed to play football for the Rose and Crown all those years ago, he would have dated her. It could have been so different. She still left him breathless.

'Hello Gorgeous. How are you?'

She turned with a beaming smile. 'Mr Prost. Thought you were supposed to be in the pub corrupting my handsome husband.'

'Nah. That was just to get him out of the way, so I could sneak round to his house and corrupt his beautiful wife.'

They always flirted.

Venga walked over to her and gave her a peck on the cheek in greeting. It was ever so slightly more than a peck, and he held onto her just a little bit longer than normal. He remembered being given advice many years before about how to avoid being nervous at a job interview. *Just imagine the interviewer naked.* He wasn't in a job interview at the moment and he wasn't nervous, but he was taking the advice, and enjoying it very much.

'Venga, I'm probably mistaken, but did I just notice your eyes look me up and down.'

'Guilty. Gotta be honest, you're looking hot today.'

'Naughty Venga. You'll get me in trouble.'

He stood a little closer, testing. He was in her personal space, looking for reaction.

She held her ground. Then reached a hand out. Placed it on his hip.

He put an arm around her waist and gently pulled her towards him. No resistance. Their faces were close now, almost touching. He could smell her perfume. She breathed in his aftershave. She ran her lips softly over his cheek.

He had imagined this moment so many times. He was confident she had too. Then he gave in to his urges, grabbed her hips and swivelled her around so she was facing away from him. He reached around her and swept the workbench clear with his arm before pushing her forward. His eyes danced around the array of tools and he grabbed a staple gun, stretched her cardigan down to the bench and shot a staple through it, connecting it to the bench. No protest. Encouraged, he pushed her down on the bench and added more staples, both sides of her body, so she was pinned to the worktop.

Now she joked. 'Stop Venga, stop,' playful resistance. She laughed.

He stretched her arms out either side along the bench and applied more staples. Then, looking around he saw a hammer and box of six inch nails. He grabbed them and fell to his knees, pushing her legs open before sliding a nail down the side of each tennis shoe and hammering them into the wooden floor. She couldn't move. Venga pushed the hammer and nails to the side and grabbed her calves, he ran his hands up to the backs of her knees and higher until he reached the bottom of her cotton peach dress. He lifted the dress up and over her rear and rested it on her restrained body.

He reached over the bench for a pair of scissors and cut away her white lace panties. He was encouraged to see she was short of breath. She wanted this as much as him. Seven years of anticipation. It was primal. The Discovery Channel.

Ten minutes later, her phone vibrated. A message from Flick. 'No sign of Venga. On way home.'

Venga read it. 'Shit. Shit. Shit. He's only two minutes away. Tasha's in the car on the drive. I'm gonna have to run.' He headed for the door.

'Fuck Ven. Don't leave me like this.'

He was already halfway to his car, jumped in and pulled away as fast as he safely could. He saw Flick arriving from the other direction in his mirror. 'Shit. What have I done?'

Now he looked up at that same man. The man he betrayed. The man now doing everything in his power to save his life. The guilt was as unbearable as the pain.

Flick held firmly onto his end of the bathroom door, working hard to make sure his friend didn't fall off during what was a horrendous 400-yard decent through the worst weather imaginable. He had no energy left, his whole body ached, but he would do whatever it took to keep Venga and Juan alive. That's what doctors did. All the time. And now, that's what best friends did.

That friendship had certainly been tested through the years though. The obvious low point being when he had come home from the pub to find his wife naked from the waist down, bent over and stapled to his work bench with six inch nails hammered through her shoes holding her legs open.

Didn't need to be Sherlock Holmes to realise it was the work of Venga, and Mandy didn't deny it. She promised it had never happened before and would never happen again. Let's move away and start again she said. They did and three months later Flick was pursuing a specialisation in haematology at a hospital in Manchester.

Yes. Their friendship had seen ups and downs, and Venga shagging his wife was the deepest low, but Flick was still carrying the biggest secret. And it must always stay secret. He remembered back to a different hospital at a different time. Southside Hospital two days after Tasha had her baby.

Flick sat in his car waiting for Denzil to leave. Took longer than expected, but he wanted Tasha and her new baby alone when he made his first visit. He nodded and smiled at the receptionist as he walked in with a bunch of purple tulips.

Arriving on the ward, he smiled as he realised he had them to himself. Tasha smiled warmly as he gave her a kiss on the cheek and fussed over a vase for the flowers.

'Good to see you Doctor M.'

'Likewise Natasha. He's a bonny wee lad and you are blooming.' He looked around theatrically. 'Was hoping to see Denzil. How is he?'

Tasha laughed. 'No you weren't. Bet you waited outside till he'd gone.'

Flick smiled. 'Okay. You got me. But seriously, how is he? You gonna get your own place soon?'

'Offered on a house today. Accepted.'

'Congratulations.' Flick frowned playfully. 'Although you could both move in with me right now if you prefer.'

'Please Flick. Don't joke. You know I want to.'

'If only.' He looked at the baby. 'Can I…'

'Go ahead.'

He lifted him up and cradled him in his arms, gently rocking him from side to side. His tiny hand gripped Flick's little finger. 'Strong fella.'

'Wonder where he gets that from?'

'Denzil I'm guessing, although you're stronger than him Tash.'

'Aww Flick. Don't be mean.'

He thought he'd try again for an honest answer. The baby had to be his. Surely.

'He's got my nose hasn't he.'

She waited before answering, making sure there was eye contact.

'Yes Flick. You know he has.'

He said nothing in reply, but she watched as a tear ran down his cheek. They said nothing for a while. Enjoying the moment. It was special for both of them. And rare. They knew how rare, and savoured it.

'Got a name yet?'

'Nothing agreed. Some contenders.'

'Go on.'

'Cameron. Haydn. Alain, no chance.'

Flick laughed.

'If *you* could choose,' Tash asked. 'What would you go for?'

'Zac.' No hesitation. 'I've always thought, if I ever have a son, I'd go for Zac.'

Venga must never know. It wouldn't just end their friendship, it would destroy the magical relationship he had with his daughter.

With both injured brothers safely in the shack, drugged up and wounds dressed, they stopped to think about their next move. Venga and Juan were both light-headed, holding grimly onto consciousness, hearts racing and enormously thankful for the pain-killing injections.

Taking quick breaths and with very little energy, Venga, almost whispering, berated himself. 'I'm so fucking sorry boys.' He took more breaths and waited for his strength to return. 'I'm an idiot. The photograph was stupid.'

Flick barely heard. He was planning ahead. The brothers were both alive, but he knew they didn't have long. Certainly not long enough to wait for help from the mainland. He was going to have to give them the news, warts an' all. And in this case, far more warts than all.

Juan, bickering forgotten, the situation well past trivial differences of opinion, reassured his younger brother, also softly, not much more than a whisper. 'Bro. Don't beat yourself up. Shit happens.' He waited for another burst of energy. It never came, so he struggled on. 'No blame. Besides, we've got Flick. All good.' He looked at Flick now wanting confirmation. 'All good?'

Flick knew he had bad news. Hesitated. Struggled for the right words and, instead, opted for a factual update before giving the unpleasant conclusion. 'You are both a mess to be honest.'

'Fucked then?' Jack tried to joke.

Flick didn't say no.

'Equally bad.'

'We'll be okay though…' pause for breath, 'won't we?' Venga wheezed.

Flick didn't say yes.

Now they were all looking at each other fearful of what Flick would say next.

'Venga.' Another awkward pause. 'I've got to be honest, if I'd taken another minute to tourniquet your leg, you'd be dead already. I've had a closer look at your wounds and the one on your leg has nicked your femoral artery. Hard to stop the bleeding.'

Venga would have nodded if he could. His eyes said he was following.

'You have multiple lacerations on your hip, stomach and chest, mostly superficial and none of them a major problem on their own, but they all add to the blood loss, so, like I said on the 999 call when they told me a 24 hour wait, we're looking at a best case scenario of a few hours. Up to five maybe. Not much more.'

'Before I pass out?' Venga asked.

Flicked looked him in the eye before answering. 'No Vee. Before you die.'

If it weren't for the savage winds and rain hammering on the roof, the shack would have been silent. They were all lost in their own thoughts for a moment, trying to accept the gravity of their situation. It didn't seem real. An hour ago, they were marching up the hill on the final furlong of an epic adventure. Four hours ago they were singing football songs as the spray hit their faces from the waves. And now, Venga had five hours to live, at best. Could it get any worse?

Yes.

'Juan, you have a broken arm. Unfortunately, that's the least of your worries. You also have a couple of broken ribs, which, I suspect, have pierced your lung, which could collapse any moment. Whether it's your lung or something else, I'm quite certain you have internal bleeding. You also have a badly damaged brachial vein. Again, to be brutally honest, without Jack's immediate pressure on your wound, you would have died on the hilltop too.'

Silence again, before Juan reached an arm out towards Jack. 'Thanks mate.'

Flick wasn't finished. 'But, sadly, again, I think we're looking at about five hours.'

This time the silence and the tension was broken by Venga. 'Five hours then boys. Let's crack open the beers and score some morphine.'

No laughs. A couple of half smiles. But they all appreciated the attempted humour.

'Now we know more clearly what we are looking at, we need to plead with the emergency services. Our most urgent need is blood, just to keep you both alive, win back enough time to get you to hospital.'

'I can do that,' Jack volunteered. 'Hilltop is the nearest good signal. Beach is further, but flat all the way with the hill a good windbreak. If I go the beach way, I'll have a look in the lifeboat wreck, see if there's anything that can help us.'

'Sounds like a plan. Before you go though, do you know what blood type you are?'

That took him by surprise. His eyes widened. 'No. Why?'

'We need blood. I have all sorts of gear in this bag,' he waved his hand in the direction of his military battle bag, 'and could do a transfusion. If you had the right blood, I could take some and keep the brothers alive.'

'Shit. I've no idea. I could call my doctor from the beach.'

'Chances are they wouldn't know either. Not unless it's been an issue at some time. Or if you've ever given blood, the transfusion service would know.'

'Sorry. Never done it.'

'Shit.' Flick was clutching at straws. 'No worries.'

Venga would take anything he could get. 'I'll take some of Jack's blood. Got to be worth a risk hasn't it?'

'It's a massive risk. The wrong blood could kill you faster than your injuries.'

'How about you mix yours and Jack's? Would that work?'

Flick grimaced. 'No. That definitely wouldn't work. I know I'm not compatible. You and Juan are both O positive and I'm B negative.'

Venga had a moment of Deja Vu. He never knew what his own blood type was, but realised Flick, as his and Juan's doctor, with his history as a haematologist, would likely have the information, but he had heard something about B negative blood some time recently. 'Is B negative dangerous?'

'Potentially to you or Juan, yes.'

'Is it rare?' Venga whispered.

Surprising question, Flick thought. 'Yes. Very. Only about two per cent of people have it.'

Juan's mind had been working things out. 'So me and Venga are the same blood?'

'Yes.'

'So we could give blood to each other?'

Flick laughed. 'Yes. But we'd be no better off, obviously. You'd both still be short of blood.'

Venga followed Juan's thinking. 'Right. I'm with you bro. Just one-way you're thinking aren't you?'

'Makes sense. If we're both gonna die before help arrives, at least one of us would survive if we used the other for spare parts.' Juan half laughed at his own joke.

When they had all absorbed the idea, Flick confirmed. 'Yes. It could work. In theory it is achievable and I have the equipment to do it. As long as I can keep everything clean enough in these conditions and avoid infection or blood contamination.'

'What's stopping us then?' Venga was up for it.

Flick wasn't. 'What's stopping us is the donor would die straight away. Much sooner.'

'But whoever the donor is would die anyway.' Juan was up for it.

'Probably, but not definitely. I have absolute confidence in my assessments, but there is still some speculation in there. Like Juan's internal bleeding and the severity of the nick on Venga's femoral artery. It's guesswork. Good guesswork, but it *is* guesswork. You're asking me to kill someone.'

Jack thought he should contribute. 'And the weather might change. What if Storm Vicky suddenly evaporates and a helicopter lands on the beach in the next hour?'

'We all know that's not gonna happen. We should give this idea some serious thought.' Venga was prepared to talk about it.

Juan agreed.

Jack headed off towards the beach to call the emergency services with an update.

Naked nuns

Chapter 10
2025, August 7, Thursday
Southside Crown Court, trial day 5

Juror number eleven 28-year-old commercial solicitor Emily McGovern struggled to concentrate on the evidence. She had seen the most bizarre opera the night before in London and Tasha Prost, the niece of the 'alleged' murder victim looked just like one of the cast members. It had been hard enough to get the opera out of her mind without the lookalike, sitting alongside her father Venga Prost, only 30 feet away.

It was Florentina Holzinger's Sancta, which featured roller-skating naked nuns, mutilation, real blood, and surprisingly 18 members of the audience had needed medical treatment as a result of what they had seen. Three ambulances had been called. And Tasha Prost looked just like one of the naked roller-skating nuns. It was a tough image to get out of her head.

Tasha sat next to her father in the public gallery. They said very little to each other. The relationship was strained. It had been ever since Venga went to the police suggesting wrongdoing after the disastrous Skerryn trip. Juan had died on the island. When the other three returned home, Dr Flick Mendy was hailed a hero in the national Press for having made the agonising choice of saving one brother when it had looked very much like both brothers would have died. A few days later, Venga visited the police and Flick was arrested. News of the arrest had not come from her father, instead, she had seen it on the BBC news website. She drove straight round. Zac waited in the car on the driveway as she banged on the front door. Venga opened it.

'Lost your key?'

'No dad. Lost your fucking marbles?' She glared at him. '*WHY*?'

She pushed past him and marched into the lounge.

He followed, but had no answer.

She had a copy of *The Sun* in her hand folded open on page three. She'd marked her dad's quotes in bright yellow. She read them out almost shouting.

'I was dead. I'd already said goodbye. Flick saved me. Yes. He's a hero.'

She slapped the paper with her free hand.

'Let's read a bit more Venga.'

She only called him Venga when she was angry.

'He's always been my best friend. Top bloke. I owe him my life.'

She looked daggers at him.

'That was five days ago. *Five* days.'

Still no reply.

'What changed? What changed in the last five days?' Shouting now.

They both stood. Face to face. Couple of yards apart. Explosive tension.

She suspected he had found out Flick was Zac's father and gone straight to the police in a vengeful rage. But she couldn't ask him that. Could be wrong, and she would give herself away.

Tasha was the centre of Venga's universe. She was livid. It hurt him to see. He had an answer ready but was waiting for the initial anger to pass its peak.

He went to the kitchen and made them both coffee. He handed her a mug and the intensity of fury in her eyes showed the peak had not passed yet.

She ignored the coffee.

'Tell me dad.'

Ooh, back to dad. Peak gone. 'I will. Please though. Let's sit. Have your coffee.'

She sat on the edge of her seat.

He leaned back in his. Not because he was relaxed. He just wanted to appear relaxed, believable.

'It was an intense trip. A lot to take in. The papers had Flick on a pedestal before I'd even had chance to collect my thoughts and then I was carried along with the flow of their narrative.' He stopped to think through his prepared answer.

'Go on.'

'I didn't actually say those things. They asked me stuff and when I didn't say no, they took that as yes and used it as a direct quote. You know what papers are like. But when I got home and had chance to think about it. Well. It all added up differently.'

'How?' Still very animated.

'And, by the way, I talked to Jack a lot to make sure I was remembering right.'

'And, no doubt, you talked to Flick, because dad, he is your best friend, and he is the one you are accusing of murder. You talked to him didn't you?'

Another awkward silence.

'Well…'

'Well what dad?'

'Well… no. It was about him, so no.'

'That's shit dad. Keep going.'

'What it boils down to is this. The transfusion idea. One dies, one lives, was sort of my idea. And Juan. We came up with it together, but it was just an idea. We talked about it. All four of us, but Juan did not agree to be the donor.'

'And you only remembered this a week after it happened. Five days after Flick is a hero in the papers? And then suddenly it's so clear you want to see your best friend, who incidentally, saved your life, behind bars for the rest of his life because he couldn't perform two miracles on the same day?'

'Natty.' He was much more assured now. 'I am absolutely certain Juan did not agree to it. I swear on your life and mine, he did not agree to be the donor.'

She shook her head, but the aggression was reducing.

'And what that means in the bigger picture is so fucking hard to get my head round that, yes, it took me a week to realise I had a duty to act. I couldn't let my friendship with Flick stop me doing what I knew I had to do.'

Tasha started to have doubts now. Maybe he hadn't found out. Maybe he hadn't gone to the police in a reckless act of revenge. Shit. I just don't know.

And sat alongside her father in the public gallery, she still wasn't sure whether her father knew Flick was Zac's dad. But she did believe, with total certainty, that whatever happened on the isle of Skerryn a year ago, Flick would have crawled on his hands and knees to the moon and back to keep her father and uncle alive.

Tasha glanced over at the jury. Juror number 11 had been watching her, but quickly looked away.

Emily still couldn't shake the opera images, the naked nuns were roller-skating endlessly across the stage, but she had to stop looking at the public gallery. Focus on the evidence.

The judge signalled lunch and chatter filled the courtroom as some stretched their legs, others discussed what they had heard and others headed for the door.

Denzil caught up with Tasha and Venga on the steps outside.

'Hey Tash, how's it going?'

'Denz. Not so bad. Joining us for lunch?'

'Sure.'

Denzil nodded in her father's direction. 'Venga.'

'Denzil.'

They grabbed a table in the coffee shop opposite the courthouse, which was filling fast as the court house emptied.

'Not looking good for Flick.' Denzil thought he was on safe ground. After all, it was Venga who triggered the police action.

'I wouldn't say that.' Tasha, quick to defend him. 'All the medical evidence has gone his way. He called it right. As far as he knew, help would arrive too late. Confirmed.'

'S'pose, but there's more to come.' Venga was less certain.

The coffee shop was packed by the time their food was served and the conversation dried up. Tasha and Venga both reluctant to be drawn into much beyond small-talk.

Tasha watched Denzil eat. He didn't always close his mouth and she saw his food sloshing around. It had been a pet hate since their first date. And eventually became an 'ick' that she fought against. As time passed, more of his traits added to the 'ick' list. He farted in bed and found it funny, he wore socks for three days in a row, then left them on the floor wherever he took them off, he apologised too often. The more she thought about it, the list grew longer. It had peaked on Zac's third birthday, held at Venga's house, it was bigger than their two-bed-terrace, when Tasha had tried to drown the 'ick' feeling with Martini, followed by white wine when the Martini ran out.

Her speech was coherent and she was walking straight but her head was starting to spin when the cake was cut and handed around. Denzil took a mouthful and the washing machine started. By the time he reached the spin cycle, Tasha lost patience.

As always with Zac's birthday, there were a lot of guests. A number of toddlers from the playgroup, their parents and many others from Denzil's school, Vicar Insurance and some of Venga's TV Rush customers. They were stood in the lounge enjoying the cake.

Tasha tried to discretely tap her partner on the ankle to gain his attention. It was a little harder than intended.

'Oww.' He almost yelped. 'What?'

She nodded towards his mouth hoping he would catch on.

He didn't.

'Close your fucking mouth Denzil.' It was louder than intended. One or two noticed, and looked over briefly, before turning away, not wanting to intrude on a domestic.

'So sorry Tash. I'm so sorry.' He gushed apologies.

She was more discreet this time and leant into his ear. 'I don't want apologies Denzil. I just want you to close your mouth when you eat. It's disgusting.'

Now he looked deflated. Chastised.

She saw his sulking schoolboy look and couldn't help rolling her eyes. It was on the 'ick' list.

He saw the eye roll and nudged her gently away from the others. 'You okay Tash? Want me to make you a coffee?'

'Oh right. You eat like an animal. I mention it, so I'm drunk.'

'Well. You did kick me rather hard. And you are talking quite loud.'

Now she was angry. She raised her eyebrows in astonishment, held out both hands, a gesture of defeat, and walked away, past the gathered cake eaters, along the hall and into her father's drawing room. She sat at his desk, going through her 'ick' list, occasionally glancing at her father's shotgun leant in the corner of the room.

Fifteen minutes passed. No good. Still angry.

The door opened. One of Denzil's teacher colleagues. A bit older than Denzil, not by much. Average. Not handsome. Not ugly. She knew he was single and she'd caught him checking her out, but she'd never spoken to him.

'Oh. Sorry. Thought this was the bathroom.' He started to close the door, but stopped. Opened it again. 'You okay?'

The Martini and wine clouded her judgement and fuelled by her anger, she walked round the desk, reached past him, pushed the door shut, then pulled him close and kissed him.

He couldn't believe his good fortune and the kiss went on. And on. He tried his luck now and his hands skated over her body, enjoying her curves. He pulled up her skirt a little and reached for her blouse buttons with his other hand. Then it was over.

She took a step back.

'Next on the right.'

He looked that way, and back. 'What?'

'Bathroom.' She went back behind the desk and sat down.

He didn't move, hoping it wasn't over.

It was.

'Shut the door on your way out.'

He did as he was asked.

It was another fifteen minutes before she was calm enough to rejoin the party. Avoiding Denzil, she began the kids' games, refusing to let them play pass the parcel, just in case, but she was miserable, listening to the happy voices around her, the smiling mums and dads, lots of laughter and a crying toddler every now and then.

Only when she watched Zac did she feel motivated and happy. He gave her the mojo she needed to keep going, but Denzil dragged her down. Her father was some help now and then, but she felt that he leaned on her more than the other way round. He was reactionary and very alpha. Quick to act. Unable to look at the bigger picture before he was bouncing along pumped up on testosterone following his nose. No wonder he struggled so badly to make a relationship work. She felt like she was carrying Venga and Denzil when she should be the one propped up by them. She was too young to have such a heavy burden.

Then there was Flick. He was always there. Was he the love of her life? Her soulmate? Maybe. Dunno. She knew he would drop everything without question if she gave him the nod. He'd take his chances with Venga to be with her, but she held back. She held back for her father's sake. She felt responsible for him, like a parent. She didn't want to crush his world, so she kept Flick at a distance. There was also the fear of what Venga might do if he ever found out. Something stupid. That's for sure.

She saw Flick arrive, very late, but he had explained. Double booked. Her mood immediately improved. She felt a warmth just seeing him enter the room, watching him greet everyone warmly, always with a smile, a hug, a kiss, a handshake and always a question? Genuine interest. How's your ill brother? How's the new job? Was the Paris trip a success? She had to wait a good hour before she got him on his own. Chance to down a few black coffees.

'Tasha. You look beautiful. And Zac is full of beans. Has he enjoyed his day?'

'Loved it. And he loved your gift. Thanks. How was your other commitment?'

He screwed his face up. Uncertain. 'Good. I think. Went on another date with Lara.'

Tasha felt a pang of jealousy, but maintained her cool. 'Ah right. Is that the one my father refers to as "that crazy bitch from the hospital"?'

Flick laughed. 'Yes. That's the one.'

'Go well?'

'As well as could be expected.' His smile was replaced with concern. 'I'm thinking of making her my girlfriend. She's been kicked out of the hospital accommodation and I thought it may be a good idea moving her in with me.'

Wow. The jealousy pang was almost painful. 'You must be keen. But only thinking about it. What's stopping you?'

He smiled and reached for her hand. 'The usual, of course.' He squeezed her hand. That warmed her heart.

She needed that. 'You don't need my permission.' Confrontational words, but they didn't come out that way.

'I know. I know. But, I've said so many times, I would drop everything in an instant if I thought we could be together. I know you have to protect your father and I love him, but… well… you know what the but is.'

'Move in with Lara, Flick. You deserve some happiness.'

They hugged.

'How are you and Denzil? Played pass the parcel yet?'

'We rowed.'

'Oh shit. What happened? Did he do something?'

'This is so stupid. You're gonna laugh.'

He laughed anyway. 'Let's hear it.'

'He ate with his mouth open.'

'Fair enough. That's gross.' Slightly sarcastic.

'I told him I wasn't happy. It escalated.'

'Oh dear.'

'Then I walked away and sat sulking in my dad's drawing room for half an hour.'

'That's not so bad. You'll be alright.'

'There's more.'

'Go on.'

'When I was in the drawing room, one of Denzil's mates came in looking for the toilet.' She stopped with a guilty face.

After a short pause, Flick's eyebrows shot up with surprise. 'You kissed him didn't you? Shit Tash. Why?'

'It was only a kiss.'

Flick couldn't help replying, '*Now I'm falling asleep and she's calling a cab.*'

'Jesus Flick. Take this seriously.'

He smiled. 'Sorry Mrs Brightside.'

'I really don't know why I did it.'

'Sounds like a cry for help.'

'Maybe. I'm just so sick of Denzil. So many things he does irritate. They shouldn't. They're trivial. If I loved him, they wouldn't, but I don't.'

'You want to knock it on the head don't you?'

'Yes. It's too much. I'm gonna end it. He's great with Zac and he adores me, but it's not working.'

They hugged again.

Two hours later, Tasha and Denzil were back in their own house, Zac asleep upstairs. She was sober. Very sober, knowing what she planned. They sat opposite one another in the lounge, Denzil on the sofa, Tasha in an armchair. Denzil felt the gloom, half knew what was coming.

'Denzil.'

'Tash.'

'You have been nothing but good to me, and Zac, and I love you for it.'

The seconds ticked by.

'I know… but you don't love *me*.'

It was quiet. A car went slowly past on the road outside. A baby cried next door. Thin walls. Tigger came in through the cat-flap, walked past them both and settled on his bed in the corner.

More seconds ticked by.

She looked at him.

'I'm so sorry.'

He looked sad. Waiting for the axe to fall. Then it fell.

'It's over.'

Chapter 11
2025, August 8, Friday
Southside Crown Court, trial day 6

Juror number six 60-year-old business owner Lesley Regan had spent the whole week listening to the prosecution case and today they were given numerous character references for Venga. She was trying to understand why. Venga was not the defendant. He's the accuser. It was starting to look like the prosecutors were building up Venga Prost in advance of the defence building up the defendant. This may be heading for a clash of personalities and if the evidence conflicts, we're going to be left choosing between the two men.

Lesley had three children and four grandchildren. Her family life was everything. It revolved around her grand-kids. Dr Mendy, charged with murdering a close friend, was 47. No kids. It shouldn't effect her opinion of him, but it did. She tried to put it out of her mind, but how can a good-looking 47-year-old doctor be single and childless. Maybe he's just been unlucky. She had read the Press coverage and there was mention of an ex-wife. He probably cheated, and that's why she left him. Same old, same old.

Venga, on the other hand, had a stunning daughter and a larger-than-life grandson. Single parent as well, unusual for a dad. The mother must have been trouble. Poor Venga. Seems like such a nice bloke. I hope it doesn't turn into a choice between them. Venga is streets ahead at the moment.

Tasha's phone vibrated and she checked the message. Zac's child minder had an emergency. Shit. She showed Venga the message.

'I'll go pick him up. Watch him till lunch, then swap.'

'Thanks Dad.'

He worked his way along the row excusing himself, briefly attracting a look of contempt from the judge. He had volunteered straight away to avoid a row. Or rather, another row. It had been a bone of contention ever since Tasha split up with Denzil. It led to a massive row that had been building for years.

It started when his daughter had a conference to attend with a 'colleague'. Not exactly a colleague, she was always very vague about her relationship with him, but he was ten fucking years older than her. Paedo should be shot. She had started seeing him about a year after ditching Denzil, and he never, as far as he knew, had anything to do with Zac. At least Denzil was a good dad. And with an old man dating Tasha, he was starting to think Denzil's four-year gap wasn't so bad. Zac should be with his real dad. Tasha should have found a way past their differences.

During the conference, Venga had agreed, reluctantly, to take Zac. The reluctance was nothing to do with Zac. He doted on him and loved every minute they spent together. Venga just felt like he was facilitating an opportunity for a paedophile to groom his daughter. And all Tasha ever said on the matter was, 'It's just a number dad. Why does it matter so much to you?' Stupid question. Yes. I know it's not illegal. Lucky for him it *is* against the law to shoot him in the nuts. On the bright side he had a whole weekend with his six-year-old grandson.

'Zac my boy. Shall we put some finishing touches to the tree house today?'

'Yup granddad.' He copied his phrases. 'Yup. Can we have a swing?'

They stood in the garden surveying the large timber shed on legs against a tree that Venga had spent most of his spare time putting together, often with Flick's help.

'Yes to a swing, but not today.' Venga slapped his hand down on an old washing machine sat against the base of the tree. 'What do you think this is Zacster?'

Easy question. Zac smiled. 'Washer machine.'

'Exactly, that's what I want you to think.'

Zac looked confused.

'We're going to use my angle grinder to cut off the front and use it as a back door in the tree house.'

'Why?'

'Other people, just like you did, will think it's a washing machine, so it'll be a secret door. And window. Only you and me will know it opens.'

Zac smiled. 'And uncle Flick?'

'Yes. If you want. And uncle Flick.'

'It's a small door.'

'Exactly. Again. It's for special people like you, who can fit through.'

'But not you granddad?'

'No. I'm too big.'

'And not uncle Flick? He's too big for his boots.'

Venga laughed. 'Just you. And your friends, but only your best friends 'cause it's a secret door.'

Venga had already prepared the frame and hinges and just had to cut the front of the machine off. He made Zac stand well away as sparks flew from the cutting disk. The boy's eyes opened wide with awe.

When it was ready, Venga tried it in the frame. Perfect fit. He just had to hold it in place and fix the screws in the hinges. Not gonna be easy. The screws went on the outside while the door needed holding in place on the inside. Zac could do that. He didn't need to take any weight. The door would sit in place. He just had to stop it falling over. Venga lifted the boy into the tree house and talked him through the job, adding, 'I wouldn't be able to do this without your help Zac. You're the key man here.'

Zac smiled.

With the boy inside stopping the door toppling, Venga climbed the ladder outside with his electric drill and screws.

'Ready Zac?'

'Yup granddad.'

Venga lined up the first screw, held it in place with his left hand and inserted the driver bit. As he pulled the trigger the screw turned slowly, but it didn't bite into the wood. He'd been unlucky and the hinge fell at the same point as a knot in the wood. He pressed harder. No luck. He pressed harder again. The screw had not bitten into the wood at all. The firm pressure on the drill toppled the screw and Venga's electric drill shot forward and sideways, at the same time, slamming into the cut-off washing machine door. The door flew inwards pushing Zac to the floor of the tree house. His arm, which had been up holding the door, was pushed back.

The newly-cut sharp metal edge of the door scraped over Zac's wrist, cutting deep and severing his radial artery. There was about five seconds silence before Zac started screaming. In that five seconds, Venga jumped to the ground, lifted the ladder to the open end of the tree house and climbed up, horrified to see blood pumping from his grandson's injury.

He carefully lifted the boy, carried him swiftly to the kitchen, wrapped his wrist with paper kitchen towel and ran Sellotape around it a number of times, before racing to the hospital on the other side of town, running two red lights and nudging dangerously over the speed limit a few times.

There was a six-hour wait in the A&E department, but Zac sailed straight through.

Sat in the waiting room, Venga called Tash and explained what had happened.

'I'm on my way.' She hung up.

An hour later a doctor came out with an update.

'He's gonna be fine Mr Prost. He's all stitched up. Good as new. Should be no long-term damage. Still a bit woozy though. We're working on that. Will take a bit longer.'

'Okay. Thanks doctor. His mum's on the way.'

'We'll keep you updated.'

Another hour later, he'd heard nothing and a nurse stepped out of the operating theatre. It was *that crazy bitch from the hospital*.

'Ah hi Venga. Thought I recognised Zac.'

'Hi Lara. How is he?'

'All good. He'll be fine.' She hesitated, uncertain whether she should say more. 'We're still waiting but it won't be long.'

That was a red flag.

'Waiting for what?'

'Zac lost a lot of blood. He needs a transfusion. We're waiting for the right blood.'

'I know it's a big hospital, but it's been two hours. Is it lost?' Venga knew sarcasm wouldn't help, but he wasn't happy.

'We didn't have the right blood here. It's coming down from London.'

'Really?' Venga hadn't meant to sound aggressive, but he took a step back aware he was being unkind.

'Your grandson has B negative blood. It's very rare. We can give him O negative too, but that's also rare. We were expecting more but an emergency up in London this morning hit our stocks.'

Venga wanted to stay calm. Not easy.

Lara tried to reassure him. 'Zac is not in any danger. The delay won't harm him.'

There was movement. More staff.

'Here it is. I'd better get back.' She headed off.

Tasha arrived soon after. Zac made a full recovery and by the following evening they were all home again. Venga visited Tash to check on Zac's progress. He was asleep upstairs.

'I'm sorry Natty. Total accident, but, yes, it happened on my watch.'

'Lucky you got him to the hospital so quick. Thanks Dad.'

She hugged him.

He couldn't resist a dig. 'Of course, if you hadn't been away with the *Paedo From Vicar*, it would never have happened.'

She rolled her eyes. 'Okay Dad. I'm going to ignore that. It's an old issue and we're not getting anywhere with it. Me and Dean are an item and will be for a long time.'

As it turned out, the argument lasted longer than her relationship with Dean, and it came to an explosive conclusion two years later on the day of Jack String's YMCA Gala charity dinner.

Tasha had been helping set up the football club function room with Jack String, Lisa String, Juan Prost and Flick Mendy, while Venga looked after Zac, playing in the tree house. Towards the end of the afternoon, she had gone to collect Zac so she could go home and get her new dress on for the ball.

'Function room looks great Dad. Jack says we've got about 120 guests and he's thinking of giving most of this year's takings to cancer research as the football club is doing quite well.'

'Sounds good Natty. I've had my Tux dry cleaned and my plus-one has something "special" to wear.'

'Ah cool. Who you taking?'

'You probably know her. She works at Vicar.'

'Ah right.'

'Marija Brankovic.'

Tasha's face dropped. Hackles up. What the very fuck. 'Venga. She's not much older than me.'

Venga was caught off guard. Should have seen this coming. Didn't. 'She's 36.'

'Okay. 36. Age gap of ten. Same as me and Dean were?'

'Well. There you have it… *were*. Obviously a mistake.'

'For fuck's sake. The main reason we didn't work was the constant grief you gave him. He eventually decided I wasn't worth the baggage I came with.'

'He ditched you?' That surprised Venga.

'Well… no. But you were still the main problem.' She raised her voice. 'Stop deflecting. Ten fucking years. Can't you see what a hypocrite you're being?'

'No, to be honest.' He was indignant. '46 and 36. No problem. 31 and 21. Paedo.'

'Jesus Dad. I thought you were smarter than that. You're just a strutting alpha pecking at anyone that takes an interest in your daughter. I was 26 when I stopped seeing Dean. 36 and 26. No problem. 21 and 17. No problem.'

'Not how I see it.'

'Dad. 25 and 15. Problem. Why? Because the age of consent is 16. 16 Dad. I'm 26 now. Nobody who takes an interest in me can be referred to as a paedo.'

'Natty. You must see that life experience makes a difference. Not in the eyes of the law, but in reality it does. Morality matters. Unwritten rules matter. Marija Brankovic is middle aged. Same as me. Not much difference in life experience. In fact,' he laughed. 'She's probably got more than me. Wait till you see her dress.'

Tasha felt beaten. He wasn't going to change. His values were set in stone.

'I know what this is about Dad.'

'Oh. Enlighten me Natty.' The sarcasm always crept in when he was on the back foot.

'You didn't like Dean because he wasn't Zac's father.'

He grimaced a half acknowledgement.

'I don't think you were as fussed about his age as you make out… Marija's inclusion tonight tells me that. Especially as my protest took you so much by surprise… Yes. I noticed. You didn't like Denzil to begin with because you thought the age gap was too much, but when he stood by me, and Zac, he was the best thing since sliced bread.

'So much so, that you'd have rather I'd stayed in a loveless relationship with Zac's father, than find someone who was my Mr Right.'

'And Dean was your Mr Right?'

'No,' she shouted. 'But I deserve the opportunity to find out one way or the other.'

Venga wasn't backing down.

'You are wrong this time and should accept the benefit of my experience.'

She laughed at the irony. Couldn't help it.

'Denzil would have been there for you whenever you needed him. He loved you. It's not old fashioned. It's just good sense. Dumping Denzil was a mistake. Dean was a mistake. You should have stuck with Zac's father.'

It went quiet.

Tasha couldn't stop herself.

'Denzil is *not* Zac's father.'

She grabbed Zac from the tree house and headed for the door. 'See you later Dad.'

The annual gala dinner hosted by Jack String, chairman of YMCA Football Club, was one of the biggest social events of the year in Southside. There were 12 large round tables with roughly 10 guests each, depending on who had booked and group size. There was space set aside for dancing and the top table included club chairman Jack String, his wife Lisa, Flick Mendy, Tasha Prost, Juan Prost, the club secretary, the manager of St Day Football Club Joff Mallaber, near neighbours, his wife Gemma, and two empty seats waiting for Venga Prost and Marija Brankovic. Venga enjoyed being last to arrive when he had a trophy plus-one to show off. He liked to make an entry and this one was going to be up there with the best.

There was a quiet moment between songs as he walked in wearing an all-white Tuxedo. Alongside him was Marija Brankovic. Most heads turned. Those that hadn't saw that everyone else had, and joined them.

Lisa String whispered to Jack. 'Wow. Do you remember that Versace dress Liz Hurley wore, just after *Four Weddings And A Funeral* premiered, held together with gold safety pins?'

'I do,' replied Jack, not facing his wife. His eyes were still on Venga's plus one.

Tasha leaned across. 'Earlier this year Miley Cyrus wore a dress for the Grammys that was entirely gold safety pins.'

Gemma Mallaber had seen it. 'Yeah, I saw that. This is either a step up from those or back to square one.'

'Hard to say.' Lisa.

'Zac could have made that at school.' Tasha.

'I bet it's designer though, and cost hundreds.' Gemma.

Marija was a short curvy girl of Slavic origins, short blonde hair, probably bleached. The dress was daring, revealing and butchered. It was translucent, orange satin, long enough to brush the ground, even wearing six inch stilettos, but split up her left side to her waist; her hip and buttock spilling out. The briefest navy blue G-string protected her dignity. It had a reverse halterneck, so the top of her back was covered but breasts exposed. No bra. Instead she had a thin necklace with two navy blue discs that covered her nipples. There was speculation, but nobody could tell how they stayed in position. The most striking feature, however, which had prompted the Liz Hurley comment, was the back right of the dress opposite the split. It looked as if a child had taken a pair of scissors and cut a jagged, frayed line from top to bottom, which had been rejoined with a line of large blue safety pins, which looked very much like nappy pins.

Under the see-through dress, she had drawn or printed circles on her body of different sizes and shades of blue. She had elbow length blue silk gloves and a small blue hat, very much like cabin crew, with a blue veil that covered her eyes.

The ripple of murmurs collectively said 'seriously, this is Southside, not Paris or Milan', but Venga nodded greetings to guests as he lead Marija to the top table where two empty seats waited. He pulled her chair out for her and made introductions.

Tasha knew Marija from work. She was adventurous in her selection of office attire, but nothing had prepared Tasha for this. 'Wow Marija. That's some outfit.'

'Thanks Nat.'

Jack was editor of the Southside Gazette. He'd spent many years as a reporter and had asked a lot of difficult questions, so he was first to ask the tough one. 'Wonderful outfit Marija. Hope you don't mind me asking. How do the blue discs on your chest stay in place?'

She laughed. 'Mr String. Nip clips. Like bulldog clips, but smaller, less pressure.'

He winced and attempted to move the conversation past Marija's dress.

'So, Venga, looking very dapper. How's work?'

Venga was still fired up after his 'unfinished' discussion with Tasha. He also had testosterone flowing, thanks to Marija, and he was in a mood to strut. Impress his partner.

'I have a new idea to help the wealthy successful Square Mile high fliers to part with their money, and I need your help.'

He had the attention of the whole table, which was quite a feat considering the competition from Marija.

'It's the ultimate team-bonding exercise. Can't be done without total cooperation from every team member.'

Jack nodded encouragement.

'A thousand miles in 48 hours including ferry trips and a boat ride to a deserted island to plant a flag on a pole weighing the same as the combined members of the team.'

Jack smiled. 'Ha. I was expecting something more difficult. That sounds very achievable.'

Lisa didn't agree and was worried Jack would get roped in to a dangerous and reckless trip. 'Sounds impossible Venga.'

Marija was impressed. Job done. 'Wow Baby. Cool trip.'

'So Jack. Does that mean you're in?'

'Maybe.' He looked at Lisa, already shaking her head.

'Ten would be a good number, but I can scale it down to five for a trial run. Gotta make sure it works before I load it on the website.'

'When were you thinking?' Flick knew he would be expected to join.

'Two months. End September or start of October. Before the weather breaks.'

Flick nodded.

'So I need Jack, Flick, Juan and Joff. All paid for by me. I just need 48 hours of your time and a commitment to the team ethic. Flick?' He was the easiest. Flick would never let him down.

'Probably. Have to check work when you have definite dates.'

'Jack? Can we turn that maybe into a yes?' Next easiest, but not so easy with Lisa sat next to him.

'Sure. Count me in.' Lisa kicked him under the table.

Venga notice him flinch. 'He'll be alright Lisa. I don't take uncalculated risks. And I'm always ready to pull out if need be. Juan?'

'I'll check work when you have dates.'

Wow. He expected Juan to resist. 'Joff?'

Gemma answered. 'We have a holiday booked around those dates.'

Venga looked at Joff.

'Mate. I would, but work is manic at the moment and, like Gem said, we got a holiday. Sorry.'

'No worries. Could work with four. I'll do all the calculations for four and get you some dates.' They raised their glasses to TV Rush.

Tasha stood. 'Drinks anyone?' She took a couple of orders.

'I'll help.' Flick joined her.

Away from the others it was easier to talk.

'You don't look happy Tash. What is it?'

'Big row with Dad.'

'No change then. Why's it bothering you?'

She leant in closer so her voice didn't carry. 'I told him Denzil wasn't Zac's father.'

Flick wasn't sure how to react to that. Delighted if it meant she had gone on to say it was Flick. It would be ugly, but there would be some chance of getting together with Tash. But if she hadn't, it was the *Sword Of Damocles* hanging over his head. Either way, Tash needed words of comfort. He squeezed her shoulder. 'Stay strong. Don't let it get you down. I know Vee means everything to you, but you have to put yourself and Zac first. If I can help, just ask. Anything.'

'Thanks Flick.'

She told him the details of the argument, the age gap with Marija, no different than her and Dean. 'Such a hypocrite. Ten years is okay for him, but not me.'

'Why did you ditch the *Paedo From Vicar*?' It was four months ago and Flick hadn't had chance to ask.

Tasha laughed. 'I told Dad it was because he was gobbing off about the age gap all the time.'

Flick smiled. 'But it was?'

'Don't laugh. He had a small dick.'

Flick laughed. They carried the drinks back to the table.

Flick was sat between Tasha and Lisa. He always got on really well with Lisa and they caught up on news through the meal before he turned back to Tasha.

'I have news.'

'Ooo go on.'

'*The Crazy Bitch From The Hospital* has finally gone. She's moved to Brighton, so I'm free.'

'Woohoo. Congratulations.'

'Thanks.'

'Why, by the way, do we always refer to people with the bigoted unkind phrases that my Dad makes up. Let's stick with Dean and Lara.'

'To be honest, she was a crazy bitch.'

They both laughed.

Tasha's face lit up. 'This is the first time since we met that we have both been single at the same time.'

'Fuck. Yeah.'

'I so wish we could be together.'

'Say the word.' Flick almost sung. He said it so often.

The next song to play was *Tender*.

Tasha reached for his hand under the table.

Lisa had got up to dance with Jack. Venga took her seat and leaned aggressively across Flick towards Tasha.

'Who the fuck is the father?'

Chapter 12
2024, October 8, Tuesday
Skerryn, ten months before the trial

Jack was exhausted. The beach was a mile down the overgrown track, but the wind was behind him and not nearly as strong as it had been on the higher ground. The hill was protecting him, and the rain had stopped again. It was late afternoon and it seemed a little brighter. He could have been imagining it, but could the weather be losing some of its force?

It gave him encouragement. Keep going. I'm probably on a doomed mission, but failure isn't an option. Juan and Venga had less than five hours. And the last thing Jack wanted was for Flick to be bullied into trying some wacky idea about using one man for spare parts. He checked his phone. Still no signal. He could see the beach in the distance, the wrecked lifeboat beside the track, a reminder of how treacherous the rocky bay could be.

He ate a Mars bar as he walked. Against his usual diet rules. He needed energy. Rules suspended. Another look at his phone. One signal bar. Nearly at the lifeboat. Wait for two bars. He could see the waves crashing on the beach now. Wow. So glad we're not trying to launch in this. Wave after wave rolling in from the far end of the beach. Their intensity strong along the whole beach. Most of the beach anyway. The waves weren't as bad as you neared the jagged rocks at the near end, where the lifeboat had perished.

Now he was close to the boat. The damage to its hull caused by the rocks was brutal. Jack imagined it must have been a day like today. Maybe the crew had died. Who knows? The boat lay partly on its side, and Jack could reach just above the hull. He pulled himself up and looked around. Nothing. When it was hauled up on the beach, anything that wasn't screwed down would have been taken away. The door was unlocked and he checked below. Same. Anything of use had been taken. Checking through all the cupboards, he found a chart and a set of flares, a couple of damaged fenders and a tin mug.

Then he saw a white metal can, like an old one gallon container he remembered his dad using for the car when he was a boy. No writing on it. Picking it up, it was heavy. Full and unopened. He turned it round and someone had written on it in black paint 'storm oil'.

Back up top he checked his phone. Two bars. The extra height probably helped. He found the quietest spot he could in the boat and called Tobermory lifeboat station, reiterated the urgent need for blood and pleaded with them for help. He got the same message as Flick.

'We could safely get as far as Skerryn and probably within about 200 yards of the beach, but landing is the issue. We are doing everything we can to help you and will get there as soon we can. A helicopter arrived on Mull from the mainland and we have a doctor, and the blood packs, ready to go.' The line went quiet for a moment. Jack heard talking in the background.

A different voice came on the line. 'Hi Jack.'

He sounded familiar. 'Hi. I heard talking in the background. Got any ideas?'

'Maybe. I know the island well. Have you seen the wrecked lifeboat?'

'I'm on it right now.' He glanced at the white can. 'Found a can of something marked storm oil. Any use?'

Again there was talking at the other end.

'I've just come on shift. Getting up to speed on this. You're inside a Waveney-class lifeboat. Was built back in 1964, faster than the boats it replaced but badly exposed propeller.'

'Wow. You know your boats.'

'I was on her when we perished. Prop hit the ground, no steerage and we were blown on the rocks.'

'You must have lost some colleagues.'

'No. All rescued unhurt.'

'Wow. How'd you do that?'

'Well. Here's the thing. Can you see where the waves are breaking on the beach?'

Jack looked out of the window. 'Yes.'

'Whole length of the beach?'

'Yes.' He looked again remembering the intensity dropped off towards the rocks. 'Apart from this end, I guess 'cause of the rocks.'

'It's not the rocks causing the flatter waves.'

'No?'

'Have another look. Do the lower waves follow the rocks right out to sea?

He looked again, feeling a rush of optimism. 'Yes. Right through the breakers.'

'That's a rip current Jack. There's a sand bar right across the bay. Stops just before the rocks. The rip is how we got off the lifeboat after it hit the rocks. We threw the life raft in the rip, jumped after it and it sucked us all out to safety.'

'Wow. And this could help us now?'

'Maybe. I know the island well and there's a rip every tide for about an hour running up to low tide, peaking in about…'

Jack heard him making a few checks.

'40 minutes time. Then it stops for the slack. We have a D-class rib available at the moment. Very fortunate. It's on loan, but it's fast and manoeuvrable.'

Again Jack heard them discussing things.

'It's blowing about force seven at the moment. Just beyond normal safe operation for the D-class, but the wind is off the land so the seas aren't so big. Also, the beach you are on is protected from the wind by the island. That's quite a hill at the top end.'

Jack was pumped now. Starting to believe help was a possibility. 'You think you can land?'

'Listen Jack. That white can could help.'

He looked at it again. 'Yeah?'

'Every lifeboat used to carry one. Empty it in the sea and it softens the waves. Changes the viscosity or something, but if you pour it in the sea where the rip starts. Don't get sucked in mind. The oil would be pulled out along the rip and, with the sea further reduced along the rip, that would give us a safe channel to punch through. Wouldn't get out again. The oil would only give us a couple of minutes and the rip stops pretty quick. It's all about timing.'

'Let's do it.'

'If we set off in the next five minutes, we'll be with you when the rip peaks. I'll burn a red flare when you need to pour the oil in the sea, and we'll see if it opens up a channel.'

'Thanks. I'm good with that.'

'It's all about the timing. See you soon.'

'Thanks very much. You're a star. What's your name, by the way?'

'Baxter. See you soon. Bye.'

Jack felt an echo of his embarrassment from earlier in the day, but it was soon replaced by euphoria. Game on. Then he remembered Juan and Venga's transfusion idea. Shit. I've got half an hour to get to the other end of the island, and back, to tell them help is on the way. It would be terrible if Flick used one brother's life to save the other when help is less than an hour away to save them both. He climbed down from the lifeboat and started running, now feeling pain in his legs, lungs, feet, hips, back. Everything really. If he didn't get back in time for Baxter's flare, the window of opportunity to land the fresh blood supplies would be gone. He fought the pain and kept up a steady jog.

He was running into the wind. The rain was falling again, light, but it made his clothes heavier, obscured his view. He wiped it from his eyes constantly. After so many years playing football, and a broken ankle ten years ago, his doctor had advised against running at all, in favour of swimming and cycling for exercise, but now he was hammering along like a man half his age.

He thought he heard the sound in the distance of a boat engine. Not possible. The rescue boat would be miles away. But perhaps the strong wind carried the sound further and faster. He was feeling pressure. He felt sick but pressed on. A minute later he stopped and vomited at the side of the track, took a few deep breaths, wiped his eyes and carried on. The shack was getting closer. Please be in time. Make it a quick turnaround. No time to explain everything to them. Just let them know help is coming and get back.

With 50 yards to go, he slowed his jog to try and get his breath back. He heard what must be the lifeboat engines again, coming and going with the gusts of wind. The pressure was building. Almost in a panic, he threw open the door of the shack and saw his three friends at the far end of the single room, both brothers now wired up to drips and Flick, with his back to the door, tending their wounds.

No time to spare. He shouted, 'Blood on the way. Lifeboat coming.'

Flick, still with his back to him, raised his arm in acknowledgement. Jack turned, pulled the door shut and ran. With the wind behind him again, and the rain easing, he fought the pain and kept up a jog, albeit a little slower. Again he heard the sound of an engine with the gusts of wind. Getting closer. He made steady progress and could now see the lifeboat out to sea, still heading south giving the island a wide berth, much the same as they had done on their approach. Presumably for the same reasons, to hit the large swell head on before making a turn toward the beach and the shelter of the island.

Jack reached the beach as the rescue RIB made its turn and headed towards him. He grabbed the oil can, moved towards the breaking waves, and waited for Baxter's flare. He could make out three people on the boat now. One driving, one keeping low, must be the doctor, and another towards the front holding something in the air. It started burning red. The flare.

He unscrewed the can lid and waded into the sea as far as he felt safe. He could feel the suck of the rip current. His feet sank further into the sand. He held the can upside down and waved it from side to side to spread the oil over as large an area as possible. He couldn't be sure, but the waves did seem to soften. He could see a channel. Not quite the parting of the Red Sea, but a definite calmer path through the breakers towards the rescue boat.

The revs built up and the orange RIB gunned it's way through the gap, fighting the current and gusting winds, turned towards a rapidly retreating Jack, another slight turn and up onto the beach.

Jack cheered, but then felt his eyes fill with tears as a gush of relief filled him. He ran to meet them and shook Baxter firmly by the hand.

'Looks like the forecast was wrong.'

Jack had expected a bit of 'told you so', but still hugged him. 'Thank-you. Thank-you. Thank-you.'

Baxter introduced the doctor. 'Jack, Dr Sarah Bruce and this is Donald. You both go ahead while we make the boat safe. We'll all be staying in the crofting hut tonight.'

Sarah and Jack set off at a brisk walk.

Chapter 13
2025, August 11, Monday
Southside Crown Court, trial day 7

'The winner gets his wife's weight in cash and five times his wife's weight in beer,' juror number ten, 49-year-old chef Alister Wilson, explained to juror number nine, 69-year-old retired telephone engineer Roger Temple.

The jury was waiting to be called in to court on the seventh day of the trial and Alister was telling Roger he had missed the annual wife-carrying championship in Maine, USA, to take his place on the jury.

'Sounds random.'

'Well. It's based on a 19 century Finnish legend about a Viking and his gang who attacked villages and carried away their women.'

'Didn't you say USA?'

'Yes. They used the idea I suppose.'

'How far do you carry them then?'

'There's a course with hills, slopes, mud, ponds and all sorts of obstacles. Probably about the same distance as running round a football pitch. And some do it in fancy dress. I was gonna be an ice cream cone and Kirsty, my wife, was gonna wear an all-white "onesie" with a brown scarf.' He laughed in anticipation of his next line. 'Our entry number was 99.'

Roger smiled. 'I'm not gonna lie Alister. Think I'd rather do jury duty.'

The call came to head for court.

'I heard Venga Prost will be in the witness stand today.'

'Hope so. Nothing's happened yet. Really. Wanna hear what he's got to say.'

Judge Faith Haydn, at 59 years old, was experienced enough to know her way around a murder trial, and young enough to appreciate the effect social media and the wider media in general was having on Dr Flick Mendy's trial. Like the majority of people in the country, she had followed the story since the doctor had been hailed a hero in the Press for saving a man's life, then later accused of murder for killing the same man's brother. It concerned her that the current jury, and any future jury, should they have to go to a retrial, would not be able to ignore the media sideshow, and focus entirely on what they were hearing in court.

She felt that the current trial was following the pattern set in recent years in American politics, where the president was supposed to be elected after selling a more trustworthy set of policies than his or her rival, but in fact, it was only ever a popularity contest between two charismatic personalities. It was a choice between two people, when it should be a choice between two sets of policies. Her court was heading that way and this trial was starting to look like a choice between two people, Mr Prost and Dr Mendy, when it should be a choice between the prosecution case and the defence case.

On top of that, she was distracted by the young woman sat next to Venga Prost. She was the spitting image of a roller-skating naked nun she had seen the previous Wednesday in a bizarre opera in London. And on top of that, she thought she had seen one of the jurors in the audience at the same event. She concentrated on the lead prosecutor Botic van der Sar, who had called Venga Prost to the witness stand.

'Would you say Mr Prost, that Dr Mendy ran his finances with an unhealthy regard for what he could afford?'

'Objection Your Honour.' Defence counsel Petra Patel was on her feet. 'That requires speculation.'

'Sustained. Please stick to the facts Mr van der Sar.'

He hesitated, unruffled, checked his notes. The seed was planted with the jury, ahead of the key issue of the money Flick borrowed from Juan to buy his house.

'Have you ever been a passenger in Dr Flick's car?'

'Yes.'

'What model is it?'

'VW Polo.

'Year?'

'2002 I think.'

'Any idea on the mileage?'

Petra Patel was on her feet again protesting about the relevance of Botic van der Sar's questions.

He responded calmly with assurance. 'Your Honour, I wish to paint a clear picture of Dr Flick's finances to establish the vital importance of his off-the-record £100,000 loan from Juan Prost.'

The judge nodded. 'Proceed.'

Petra Patel was not happy. Objection overruled and the jury had been reminded, once again, of the debt hanging over Flick's head.

'Where was I? Ah yes. The mileage Mr Prost?'

'Dunno, but it was on its second time round the clock.'

'What was its value?'

Petra couldn't resist. 'Objection Your Honour. Venga Prost is not an expert on the used car trade.'

'Sustained.' Judge Haydn raised her eyebrows in warning.

Botic shuffled his papers again.

'Do you know how much he paid for the car?'

'£700 cash. Bloke down the pub.'

Botic looked at Petra as he asked Venga his next question. 'Would it be fair to call the car a cheap runaround Mr Prost?'

Petra Patel bit her tongue and kept quiet.

'Yes.'

'Not the sort of car most people would expect a 47-year-old doctor to drive around?'

Judge Haydn didn't wait for Petra's objection this time.'

'Can we stick to the facts please? We're not here to establish "most people's" driving preferences.'

'Sorry Your Honour, just trying to show that Dr Mendy was short of money.'

Flick was squirming in his seat. His divorce had been expensive, his ongoing generosity to his ex-wife had been a burden and he had never been one to splash out needlessly. A cheap runaround was all he wanted, all he needed.

Botic hadn't finished. 'Do you know what model of mobile phone Dr Mendy uses Mr Prost?'

'Think it's an old Nokia 3310.'

Petra was on her feet. 'Your Honour. If Mr van der Sar is going to go through every item Dr Mendy owns, we're gonna be here all week. Can we concede that Dr Mendy was careful with his limited resources and fortunate to have modest tastes?'

Judge Haydn agreed. 'Please move on Mr van der Sar.'

Papers shuffled. 'Mr Prost.' Now he raised his voice a little and faced the jury as he asked Venga the key question. 'Did Dr Mendy borrow £100,000 from your brother Juan four years ago to help with the purchase of his house?'

'Yes.'

'Did your brother tell you about the loan?'

'Yes.'

'Did anyone else know about the loan, perhaps a solicitor or a finance company?'

'Just Juan, Flick, me and Flick's ex-wife Mandy.'

'Why was Dr Mendy's ex-wife in the loop?'

'She still lived in the marital home. That's where Flick was gonna get the money to pay back Juan.'

'Where does she live now?'

'Same house.'

'Is it on the market?'

'No.'

'How long has she lived in it since the divorce with Dr Mendy?'

'Eleven years.'

A few eyebrows were raised in the jury box.

'Doesn't sound like a trustworthy source of funds to pay back the loan? Were there any time limits written into the loan contract set up between your brother and Dr Mendy?'

'There was no contract.'

Botic van der Sar's face took on a theatrical shocked look. He waited to allow the jury to take in the reckless nature of the loan.

‘Good practice would dictate such a large and unconventional loan should pass through the hands of solicitors. Was Dr Mendy in the habit of breaking with convention, cutting corners, going off script? Would you say he is something of a maverick?’

Petra Patel was torn. This was absolutely speculation, but she didn’t want to score another indirect hit with the jury.

Judge Haydn knew it was speculation but felt that some kind of opinion on the defendant’s thinking was, in part, relevant, in the context of what happened in the final moments of Juan Prost’s life.

Flick was aghast. Fair enough, he was cautious with his money and had a very old phone, but why was Venga allowing his barrister to infer that Flick had scant regard for rules and convention when it was clear that he had devoted his life to the service of others? But, thinking about it, maybe he had a point. Flick was okay with rules if they worked for him, but he wasn’t slow to sidestep them if he felt they were wrong, too onerous and ill-fitted to any given situation. Okay. Venga did have a point, and it had been well made by Botic van der Sar.

During the Covid lockdown, there had been a vast array of rules applied to the whole country and Flick had been on the front line, saving lives 24/7, constantly putting his own life at risk and as the lockdown appeared to be nearing its end, there had been an incident where he had put the rules to one side and made his own judgement.

A week before lockdown ended, the rules were; stay in your family bubble, outdoors for exercise only, wear face masks in public and two metres social distancing. Flick had not seen Tasha much at all through the pandemic, his work commitments and the strict rules had limited their connection to social media. He didn't have a smart phone, so it had all been through Facebook Messenger on his laptop. Not enough, but she'd agreed to bump into him 'accidentally' under the M tree by the river.

It was a Saturday morning, not raining, but no sun, or wind, and very few people about, just the odd dog walker and runner. They both wore masks and stopped a couple of meters apart. They were beaming at each other. It was such a treat to see each other face to face, even with half of their faces covered. She told him her news, how Zac was coping, how Venga was coping. The three had formed a family bubble. Flick talked her through his news, but didn't say too much. There were horror stories and he didn't want to kill the mood.

Flick had seen the *crazy bitch from the hospital* during work, but nothing outside, as she had thrown one of her moving-out dramas just before the latest lockdown and couldn't return. Flick wasn't worried. It was a pleasant break.

Tasha hadn't seen much of the *paedo from Vicar* for similar reasons, apart from Zoom meetings for work. She was equally relaxed about the forced time apart.

As the conversation bubbled along, the two metre social distancing dropped to one metre and, before long it was half a metre.

'You were one of the first to get the vaccination weren't you Flick?'

'I was. Perk of the job.' He smiled.

'I had it last week. Did some volunteer shifts at the care home for Juan. Bumped me up the list.'

'Great news.' Flick smiled. 'You tested since?'

'Yesterday. All clear. You?'

'This morning. All clear.'

Flick reached for her hand. 'Both vaccinated and clear.' His eyes were bright. Longing.

She squeezed his hand, tugged off her facemask and pulled him towards her.

He tore off his own mask and they hugged, tight. Intense. It went on for minutes. They had been starved of each other's company for over a year. They had been starved of intimacy for nearly six years now and it was too much. The hug morphed into a kiss. Passionate. They had held back for so long, and the damn burst. For around five minutes the Venga issue was suspended and it was beautiful.

'I so want to rip the band aid off. Tell Dad and hope for the best.'

'I'll ring him now.'

She hesitated. Grimaced. Knew it would destroy him. Same old argument. Lost the impetus and backed down.

'No.'

'Flick. Tash. How are you?' Lisa String and her dog were walking along the path towards them. She had her facemask on.

They both turned, startled, hoping it didn't show.

'Hey Lisa. How are you?' Tasha bent down to cuddle Montgomery.

Lisa kept the two-yard gap. 'Naughty, naughty, where's your facemasks? Oh no. Sorry. You must be in the same bubble.'

Flick didn't correct her and, gambling that she hadn't seen them arm in arm, slipped seamlessly into their usual banter.

'How's the Wise Old Man? Must be itching to be back on the football field.'

'Flick. You know he stopped years ago.' She laughed.

'When he's 80, he'll still be worth his place in the team.'

She slapped him on his arm. 'Well best get going. People will think we're having a party.'

She headed off leaving Flick and Tasha looking at each other with enormous relief.

'That was close.'

Too late

Chapter 14

2024, October 8, Tuesday
Skerryn, ten months before the trial

As they neared the shack, Jack String and Dr Sarah Bruce picked up the pace almost to a jog. He'd filled her in on why they were on the island and everything that had happened. Jack gave her a summary of Flick's assessment.

The wind was in their faces. She raised her voice to be heard and spoke in short bursts. Short of breath from the half run.

'I have blood Mr String, but, from what you've said, we could be too late.'

'Dr Mendy said five hours, but he was guessing. Wasn't sure how bad the bleeds were.'

'Gotta hope for the best. What meds did he have?'

'Morphine. Flick is a consultant with the army. Had something called a "battle bag".'

'Ah right.'

'Developed for front line emergencies.'

'Sounds like they're in good hands.'

'He had a kit for transfusions.'

'Yeah I heard they were looking at that.'

Jack was struggling with the brisk walk, half run. When he finally stopped, he would sleep for a week.

'The brothers had a crazy idea.' Jack forced a laugh.

She nodded.

'They knew help was 24 hours away.'

Fifty yards to go.

‘Knowing they both had only five hours left, they suggested a transfusion from one brother to the other.’

‘Wow.’

‘One lives, one dies.’

She thought about it as she jogged. ‘You say crazy, but… better than both dying.’

‘S’pose.’

‘Wouldn’t want to be Dr Mendy. What a choice.’

Jack reached for the door, a wave of relief almost dropping him to his knees. He’d done everything in his power, and it was down to the professionals to finish the job. Dr Bruce followed him into the shack.

At the far end of the room, Flick turned with a look of absolute horror when he saw Jack had company.

Flick fell instantly into a catatonic trance. His stomach fell, he could not breath, speech was impossible. What cruel trick was being played on him? He looked up to the heavens. A million unanswered questions. They were racing around his head. He felt faint. He didn’t fight it. Unconsciousness would be a welcome relief.

The woman next to his friend was a doctor. She had supplies, equipment, and, undoubtedly, blood. She had what would be needed to keep Juan and Venga alive until the storm cleared and the air ambulance arrived.

Jack’s wave of relief was replaced with nausea when he saw his friend.

Flick’s face was full of anguish and pain. It was as close as Jack had ever seen to Edvard Munch’s scream

Looking past his devastated friend he saw the TV Rush flag had been placed over Juan and pulled up over his face. They were too late. Jack’s eyes filled with tears again and he crossed the room to hug Flick.

Jack held him firmly.

Flick was lifeless, drained.

Jack could feel Flick's heart beating.

Flick's body was present, but his mind had timed out. Flick stared aimlessly into the distance at nothing.

'You did your best.'

Flick didn't reply. The shock filled the whole room, bursting out through the open door, and then his tears started.

Jack held him firmly as he started to sob uncontrollably.

The turmoil in Flick's head was pure emotional pain. He wanted to swap places with Juan. He wanted to be lying on the makeshift bed under a TV Rush flag, while his good friend, who deserved life so much more than Flick, was hugging Jack.

His thoughts went back in time to another patient. Someone else he had not been able to save. Five years ago he had been coming out of the village bookshop in Wickstead and headed across a busy car park, busier than normal on carnival day, and he had heard a woman scream. A chilling scream that left him cold. With others, he raced over. The woman had been backing her car into a parking space against a low wall and did not see her own six-year-old son. She'd pinned him fatally against the wall, and now stood by the back of her car, fixed on the horrific scene.

Other stunned onlookers had physically lifted the car off the child and pulled him away. Flick had been first on the scene and did what he could but the child died in the ambulance on his way to the hospital. Flick remembered the mother's face. She had killed her own child. He couldn't come close to imagining her pain.

Until now.

The pain was suffocating him. He had killed Juan. The emergency services had reached the shack. With blood. Juan could have been saved. But Flick had killed him.

Jack was still hugging him. When he finally pulled away, Flick stood, walked to the door, opened it, closed it behind him and walked out into Storm Vicky. After 50 yards, he turned into the wind, held his arms aloft, faced the black clouds and screamed 'no' with all his remaining strength. Exhausted he took a deep breath and did it again. Then again.

Back in the shack, Jack and Sarah turned towards the door. Despite the howling wind, they clearly heard Flick's tormented cry.

Dr Bruce checked Juan's pulse, to be sure. No chance of revival. She checked on Venga, out of it but stable. She studied the equipment arranged by Dr Mendy. It was for a transfusion. It looked used. Looks like he did it. Dr Mendy had followed the 'crazy' plan. She understood his pain. What a choice he had been forced to make. If only they could have got there quicker.

'I need to know what action Dr Mendy has taken so far, before we can move forward. Looks like he did the transfusion from one brother to the other. Sorry to have to ask, but can you go get him?'

Jack internally did a double take. I'm pretty certain she just said the transfusion had been done. Surely not? I told Flick help was on the way. Juan and Venga must have deteriorated rapidly if Flick went ahead. 'Sorry. Yes. Of course.'

Confused. Conflicted. Compromised. Jack headed for the door. Flick would only have done the transfusion if he had no choice. Surely? And, he's a doctor. He must have lost other patients. Not friends, I know, but he was calm when we arrived. The shock only took over when he saw the doctor with me. He didn't expect to see her. And when he did, he flipped. What is going on? Jack walked down the overgrown track to his friend and reached an arm around his shoulder.

'Flick mate. You did the transfusion?'

Flick was staring into the distance. Unfocussed. Blank. He slowly turned to Jack.

'I killed him.' He nodded slowly. 'Jack. I killed Juan.'

They looked at each other. Flick had avoided his direct question. He tried again. 'Did you do the transfusion?'

'Yes.'

Soft. Jack barely heard it.

'Why didn't you wait?'

Flick didn't roll his eyes, but Jack felt as if he had. Flick's expression said we talked about this Jack. You know they weren't going to last 24 hours.

'Would half an hour really have made such a big difference?'

Now Flick looked confused. His expression more stern. Almost irritated. 'Probably not Jack. Easy to say with hindsight, but before help arrived, I was convinced that we had a 24 hour wait. Venga and Juan talked about it. We agreed a plan and… and Juan gifted Venga his life.'

Jack didn't know what to say now. One of his good friends had needlessly killed another of his good friends and seemed unaware that he had been told that help was on its way before he took a fatal gamble. He clearly remembered seeing Flick from the door of the shack and shouting to him, 'Blood on the way. Lifeboat coming.' He saw him raise his arm in acknowledgement.

'But Flick… I told you the lifeboat was coming. I told you there was blood on the way.'

Flick looked surprised. No reply.

'You raised your arm. You acknowledged me when I told you.'

Flick was shaking his head in disbelief. Still said nothing.

'You did hear me didn't you?'

Flick thought back. Going over everything. Looking for clarity.

'Yes Jack. Course. I remember you popped your head round the door. Said something about the lifeboat. I knew you'd been to check out the lifeboat.'

'What did I say Flick?'

He thought about it. Unsure.

'Dunno.' Shook his head. 'Something lifeboat. Dunno. I was about to kill one friend to save another, with an untested process in extreme conditions. I was concentrating.'

'But you put your arm up. You must have heard me.'

'Yes. I heard something.' He shook his head. 'Not sure what.'

'Why'd you put your arm up then?'

'Gotta be honest. Sorry Jack. You were breaking my concentration. I didn't want the distraction.'

'Fuck it Flick. Juan might still be alive if you'd heard me.'

Flick fell back into his trance. What had been a disaster had just become dramatically worse. He had needlessly killed his friend and now he knew he had been told, in good time, that help was imminent. Juan died for nothing.

Jack shook his shoulders. He needed him to get a grip.

'Listen Flick, Venga still needs you.'

Flick focussed on Jack.

'Doctor Bruce needs you. She sent me to get you. Needs to know what has happened so far. Let's go.'

He put his arm around his shoulder again, and got him moving towards the shack, covered the ground slowly, opened the door and ushered him in. Then he turned towards the voices he heard coming up the track.

'You help Dr Bruce. I'll go and meet the lifeboat men. Be right back.'

He walked to greet Baxter and Donald.

'Boats nice 'n' safe alongside yours. All ready for the morning.' Baxter was upbeat. 'How's it going in the croft?'

Jack stopped to break the news. 'Not good.' He shook his head respectfully. 'We were too late for the older brother Juan, but Venga is stable.'

Despite the horrendous wind, both lifeboatmen took off their hats, held them across their chests and offered sincere sympathy.

'I did hear some shouting.' Baxter.

'Doctor Flick. Venting. We were so close to saving Juan, but, too late.'

Baxter genuinely shared their pain, and suppressed a joke he was embarrassed even passed though his mind regarding Flick's cries and humpbacked whales. He felt some guilt for his thoughts. He also felt guilt that they had held off on launching the lifeboat. But it was only his detailed knowledge of Skerryn that had made the rescue attempt possible and they set off as soon his shift started. Nothing more could have been done. He tried to put a positive spin on the situation.

'Sounded like both brothers were bad though. Lucky one survived.'

Jack explained how Flick had done the transfusion to use one brother as a donor to save the other. He didn't mention that he had run the length of the island twice before the lifeboat arrived to make sure Flick didn't do the procedure. He wasn't sure how to deal with that going forward. For now, it seemed reasonable to keep it to himself, but if anyone asked a direct question, he would feel obliged to give an honest answer.

Baxter was impressed. 'Respect to your pal. Tough shout.'

They entered the shack. Jack made the introductions, noticing that Flick's head was starting to clear.

Baxter and Donald offered Flick their condolences for Juan and asked after Venga.

'Thank-you. And good to see you again Baxter. We should have taken your weather advice.'

'No worries pal. You trusted the forecast. Due diligence. Can't expect more than that.'

Flick smiled appreciation of his understanding.

'Sounds like you're a hero pal. Would have lost them both without your quick thinking.'

Flick appeared extremely modest, having none of it. Praise not needed. He's a doctor. Doing his job. But he was thinking, you're actually wrong. Without my warped quick thinking, or, at least, my cavalier response to Juan and Venga's warped quick thinking, they'd both be alive.

‘The Media call our station all the time looking for stories. They’ll be all over this. You ready for all the attention?’

Jack knew Baxter was right. He had his reporters calling the emergency services every day without fail. It was a major source of stories. And following a storm, lifeboat stations would be top of the list. Doctor kills one brother to save another. This would be everywhere in no time.

Chapter 15

2025, August 12, Tuesday
Southside Crown Court, trial day 8

Venga Prost asked the two police constables to leave his bedroom.

'We can't leave Mr Prost. Our car is blocked on your drive.'

'That's nothing to do with me.'

'Yes it is Mr Prost. Your garden, driveway and the whole street is blocked with half-naked women, all wearing see-through orange dresses waiting to take their turn at mopping your fevered brow.'

'Like I said, nothing to do with me. They want to help. I didn't ask them.'

The constables looked at each other unable to comprehend how Venga Prost was so incapable of accepting any responsibility for the traffic chaos outside his house.

'Venga darling, can I get you anything to drink?' One of the girls asked with a Russian accent.

'Could I have some water please. Bit of a headache.'

'Mr Prost. Something to eat?' asked another.

He didn't answer. He'd been distracted by another woman trying to lift him to make him more comfortable with an extra pillow.

The constable tried again. 'Mr Prost. Do you remember waking up?'

'Sorry. Could you repeat the question?'

'Do you remember waking up in the crofting house following treatment?' repeated his barrister, Botic van der Sar.

It was a tough question. He remembered half waking up. Confusion. Everything was fuzzy. There was so much going on in his head. Almost random. And he couldn't distinguish between reality, fantasy, past, future and present. And he was so weak, he didn't have the energy to get his head straight. It was dark outside. He was sure of that. There were more people than he expected to see.

'Sort of.'

'Can you talk us through it?'

'Dark. Definitely dark. Incredibly weak. So confused.'

Botic waited for more.

'There were some people asleep on the floor and a doctor sat by my bed, who I now know was Sarah Bruce. Can not thank her enough, I must say.'

Again Botic waited.

'I reached for her arm. She woke straight away. So quick with kind words. She reassured me. Told me I'd lost a lot of blood.'

Juror number twelve Kate Ellis was a nurse. At 53 years old, she had seen a lot of trauma. She felt Venga's pain. Many years before she had watched a young mother bleed to death after giving birth to healthy twins. As a Jehovah's Witness, the mother's faith had not allowed a blood transfusion and the maternity team had been given clear written instructions to respect her faith. They had pleaded with her family to overrule the mother's wishes, but they held firm. Kate had watched a perfectly healthy mother die needlessly. There had been no doubt a transfusion would have saved her. Her family said afterwards that she had died with her faith intact. Watching the witness tell his story, Kate could imagine his panic and fear after Dr Mendy had told him, and his brother Juan, they would die without urgent blood supplies. Venga had been so lucky. Juan hadn't.

'Then I asked Dr Bruce how my brother was.'

Botic let the silence stretch out. It was pulling the jury in his direction.

Reliving the moment was hurting Venga. He stared beyond the jury, lost in his memories of Skerryn.

'She reached for my hand and faced me. Sad eyes. Then she told me, we had lost him. He was gone.'

Botic nodded encouragement.

'The fuzziness grew stronger, I closed my eyes and I sank back into confusion. Think I asked for morphine, hoping it would soften the emotional pain as well. It didn't. Should have been me. It was my poor judgement that got us in that mess. Juan didn't deserve what happened. It should have been me.'

Venga lowered his head into his open hands. For a moment he was back on the island reliving the nightmare that cost Juan his life.

The next time he remembered regaining consciousness was the dawn sunrise next day. Glowing red sun rays creeping through the gaps around the front door, the floor full of sleeping strangers, Jack stood by the window looking out at the new day. A bright day. The storm had gone and the weather was sunny, a gentle breeze and no rain. The others stirred, and before long, Sarah Bruce was checking his pulse, blood pressure and dressings.

Flick followed her and sat on the edge of the bed.

'I'm so sorry Vee.'

Venga's expression stayed neutral as he looked his friend in the eye.

'So am I Dr Mendy. This is not how it was meant to be.'

Flick reached out to grip Venga's arm, a gesture offering comfort.

Venga rolled out of his reach and closed his eyes.

Next came the sound of the helicopter passing over the shack, hovering, looking for the safest spot to land, as close as possible. It was almost as far as the beach. Sarah explained he could only take one of his friends in the helicopter, the other should stay on the island and help get Juan's body ashore with the lifeboat and the hired RIB.

'Jack. I want Jack in the chopper.'

Sarah beckoned him over.

'You okay going in the helicopter with the patient?'

'Sure,' he replied to Sarah. Then he turned to Venga. 'What about Flick? I'm fine staying here.' He bowed his head. 'Making sure we get Juan home.'

'I want you with me Jack. We need to talk.'

There was a lot of action and Venga was soon on his way to the helicopter. Before he left the shack, Flick offered Venga a word of encouragement. Venga missed it. He was 'asleep' again.

The helicopter was too loud for conversation and by the time they landed at the hospital in Oban, there was another problem to deal with. The Press. News had already travelled fast and reporters wanted quotes from Venga, Jack, Dr Bruce, the helicopter pilot, the porter that wheeled Venga into the hospital, the nurse that watched the porter wheel Venga into the hospital. Anything really.

Jack as a former reporter, and current editor of the Southside Gazette, considered their options. The stories would run, with or without their approval. If they said nothing, there would be gaps. The media would find a way to fill those gaps and the story risked distortion. After a quiet word with Venga, they agreed Jack would speak to the gathered Press before selecting one trustworthy journalist, based on Jack's first impressions, to interview Venga after he was settled in his hospital bed.

Jack saw Venga safely to the ward before facing the media.

'Did Dr Flick kill Juan Prost?'

'It's Dr Mendy. Flick is his first name. And yes. In a roundabout way. In order to save his brother Venga. The alternative was they would both have died.'

'But the lifeboat arrived sooner than expected?'

'It did. But not soon enough.'

'How long did Juan Prost die before the lifeboat arrived?'

'Hard to be accurate. Fifteen minutes, half an hour?'

'Would the surviving brother have died without Dr Flick's emergency transfusion?'

Jack corrected the reporter's inaccurate use of Flick's name to win some time. Tough question. He didn't want to mention his failed warning that help was on the way. Omission was not a lie.

The correct answer was 'probably', but he knew they'd adjust it to suit their needs, so he stuck with something that guaranteed a consistent outcome in the Press.

'Yes.'

Then for good measure.

'They would both have died within minutes of the accident if Dr Mendy hadn't acted swiftly to stop the bleeding from their wounds.'

'Whose idea was the transfusion from brother to brother?'

'The brother's came up with it themselves when we talked about their options. Dr Mendy was against it.'

'Why did he change his mind and how did they choose which brother would die?'

'I don't know, to be honest, I left them talking about it and went to the beach where phone reception was better, so I could beg the lifeboat crew to help us.'

'When will we be able to ask Venga Prost about that final conversation?'

'Later today, but I can only allow one reporter in for a brief interview.'

There was a collective groan.

'Any chance we can get Dr Flick's phone number off you?'

'No chance for you sunshine, because you've got his name wrong three times now,' Jack came back fast.

'Could we get some contact details, Mr String, for the hero of the hour, Dr Mendy?' another reporter asked smoothly.

'What's your name young lady?'

'Ginger Green, freelance, Mr String.'

'He is a GP at All Saints' Surgery in Southside, near London. Their number's in the book.' He then wrapped things up before beckoning Ginger Green over. 'I'll take you for the interview with Venga. What's your number? I'll text you when he's ready. Be about an hour. Good with that?'

'Thanks Mr String. That's great.' She handed him her card.

Jack retreated and found his way to the ward. Venga was settled, his dressings redone. Surgery on his damaged artery and chest lacerations was scheduled for later that morning. Otherwise the prognosis was good, and, with rest, he was expected to make a full and swift recovery.

His strength was building and his whisper a little louder.

'Jack. I have questions.'

'Fire away Ven.'

'Firstly I want to apologise again. The photograph I took caused all this. It was wrong. Poor judgement. I should know better. I'm sorry for everything that has happened to you.' He stopped. His eyes filled with tears again. 'Juan… I can't believe Juan is dead.'

'The reporter is going to ask you about the conversation after I left the shack.'

'Fair enough.'

'They want to know why Flick changed his mind and how you decided who would be the donor.'

Venga sidestepped the subject and switched it back to Jack.

'I've been thinking about your trip to the beach and your call to the lifeboat station. What happened?'

Jack explained about Baxter coming on shift at just the right time, his experience of the island, his knowledge of the wrecked boat, the rip current and the storm oil.

'Wow.'

'Yes. Wow. He's the one they should be writing about. Probably will be I expect.'

'I just assumed you'd been very persuasive.'

'Same outcome.'

'S'pose. But what's been bothering me, and, again, this is the same whether you'd been persuasive, or what actually happened, is the time gap.'

'What time gap?'

'Between Baxter saying they would attempt a rescue and you all walking through the door with a cute doctor and a bag of blood.'

He's on the mend, 'cute doctor'.

'Even in a high speed RNLI RIB, in heavy seas, it's gonna take 45 minutes to an hour to get from Tobermory to Skerryn.' Venga was putting the pieces together.

'It was about 40 minutes.'

'Wow. Fast.' Venga nodded. Impressed. 'Here's the problem. You knew Flick had suggested a transfusion that would kill me or Juan. And you had 40 minutes before they arrived to run to the shack and stop him doing it.'

'I didn't know he was going to do the transfusion.'

'I know.' Venga almost shouted. 'But you knew it was a possibility. And you're a fit bloke. I know you could run two miles in 40 minutes in any conditions. And if you thought there was the remotest chance that Flick would do it, you'd have made that run.'

Jack said nothing, unable to keep eye contact.

'Tell me I'm wrong mate, but you told Flick help was on the way.'

Jack was torn. What difference did it make now? It wouldn't bring Juan back and it could spoil a very special friendship. It was probably part of Venga's grieving. Looking for someone to blame other than the obvious… himself.

'He was distracted. Concentrating on saving you. It worked. He did save you. The lifeboat might have been too late. But, yes. I told him help was coming.'

Venga was shaking his head.

'But I had to race back to pour the oil in the rip. He didn't hear me. He raised his hand in acknowledgment, but, and *he* told me this, he hadn't heard me, needed to focus and just waved me away. I was distracting him.'

Venga shook his head. He was thinking. The cogs were whirring.

Jack was worried. He thought back to the shack before they headed for the helicopter.

'Why did you ask me to go through Flick's bag? What do you need his toothbrush for?'

Venga was lost in thought.

'Yes Jack. The toothbrush? That's another matter. Let's talk to Ginger Green. Wanna give her a call.'

Jack texted her knowing she'd be staring at her phone ready for the scoop of the year.

She started by expressing sincere apologies for Venga's loss. Then got down to the detail.

'Did you think you were going to die on the island?'

'Yes. Without a doubt. I was as good as dead. In fact, I'd already said goodbye. I knew I was going to pass out and I didn't expect to come round again.'

'And your friend saved you?'

'Without Flick I would not be here today.'

'Is he your best friend?'

'I've known him nearly 30 years. We've been through a lot together.'

Ginger wasn't sure. He didn't sound convincing. Must be the grief.

'Top bloke then? Fair to say you owe him your life?'

Venga half nodded and looked at Jack, the same neutral expression.

Ginger's instincts told her she was missing the real story, but she pressed ahead with the hero narrative. Venga gave her the quotes she was looking for.

The nurse arrived with a porter to take Venga for his surgery. Ginger shook his hand and tried for a phone number. She already had Jack's from his text and was delighted that Venga also gave her his number.

Jack watched as Venga was wheeled away. Something was wrong and it wasn't the grief playing tricks. It was more than that.

Two hours later, following successful surgery, Jack and Venga shared small talk. He's clammed up. Jack couldn't get anything out of him and when Venga suggested he go to a hotel, Jack accepted and headed off, noticing that Venga was quickly onto his phone.

Tasha answered on the second ring.

'I'm so sorry Dad. I just can't believe it.'

Jack had called earlier with the news.

'I know. Who am I gonna bicker with now? Just doesn't seem real.'

'Dad I just want to give you a hug.'

'How'd Zac take it?'

'Hard to say Dad. Who knows what's going on in an eight-year-old boy's mind?'

'Jack mentioned a photo. You shouldn't blame yourself…'

'I don't.' Sharp from Venga.

Tasha was taken by surprise. Jack had been quite clear that Venga *did* blame himself, for trying, unwisely, to take a photograph at the top of the hill.

'Okay Dad. Just an accident. Jack was devastated, holding it together, but I could feel the tremble in his voice. How's Flick? What a horrific ordeal for him too.'

'Dunno. Haven't talked to him today. He stayed on the island after the helicopter arrived.'

'You not rung him?'

'Not had chance.' Venga quickly changed direction. 'We're gonna have to start thinking about a funeral.'

They chatted for another 10 minutes before Venga got tired and wound things up.

Tasha's phone immediately rang again. It was Flick.

'Has your dad called?'

'Yes. And Jack earlier.'

This time Flick was offering heartfelt sympathy for Tasha's loss.

It came back, with interest. Juan and Flick had been such good friends.

'What a trip. It's so good to hear your voice Tash.'

'Same Flick. I can't imagine how you must have felt. Take a life. Save a life. Who'd be a doctor?'

Flick had no words in response.

Tasha still had a bad feeling from talking to her dad.

'Just spoken to Dad. Said he hadn't talked to you today. Everything alright?'

'I think so.' Flick was worried now. 'I tried a couple of times. To be honest, he blanked me second time. Short answers the first.'

'Odd.'

'Maybe… I put it down to survivor's guilt.'

'Yeah. Maybe.'

Chapter 16
2024, October 12, Saturday
Southside, ten months before the trial and four days after Skerryn

'Good morning Southside. It's 10am and this is Ned Ferris bringing you the news from Radio Razor.'

The tinny little radio was on in the background as DCI Jon Jordan and his wife Jo enjoyed a continental breakfast during a lazy Saturday morning. Jo had been following the Flick Mendy story and held up a hand to silence Jon before the morning report.

'Heroic GP Flick Mendy was back at work in Southside this morning after his life and death choice between two brothers.'

Jo took a sip of orange juice. 'It's all happening in Southside Jon. Hard to believe.'

Jon couldn't help correcting her. 'Think it was up in Scotland actually Jo.' He smiled to himself.

'Knob.' Jo tutted and rolled her eyes. 'What a choice to have to make. What would you have done babe?'

'Stayed at home until the weather got better.'

She shook her head. 'I should have married a doctor.'

They tucked into their croissants, Jon thinking about what choice he would have made in Flick's position, Jo thinking about how it would feel to be married to a national hero, with a crowd of paparazzi camped outside the front door.

'I would have done what I presume Dr Mendy did.'

'Which is?'

'Talk about it with the brothers and let them choose.'

'Fairs. Think I read something along those lines.'

Jo's thoughts moved on to the older brother. 'I have a friend who worked at Juan's care home. Pinefields. She posted something on Facebook. Said he was a lovely man. Loads of pictures of him with the other staff and the residents. Such a shame.'

'Them's the breaks Jo.'

'Was shared 14 times and got 250 likes.'

'That's a lot is it?' DCI Jordan had no idea. His relationship with social media was limited.

'Yes babe.' Slightly condescending. 'Lots of comments too. Apparently his wife died during the pandemic.'

'Not a lucky fellow then?'

'No.'

DCI Jordan hesitated before his next comment, fearful that anything he contributed may find its way onto Facebook, but he didn't like keeping things from his wife. 'Had a call yesterday from Venga Prost.'

'What?' Shocked. 'The younger brother?'

'Yes.'

'Why didn't you tell me?'

'I'm telling you now.'

She seethed. He had priceless gossip and kept it from her. 'Do you know him or was it just a general call to the police?'

'I know him.'

'You're friends with a media celebrity?'

'He's not a celebrity. He's just a normal man suffering his 15 minutes of fame. And I wouldn't exactly call him a friend. He's an acquaintance. Clay pigeon shooting.'

'You shoot with him?'

'I have done. A few times.'

'What did he want?'

'No idea. Probably wants to know how he can get rid of the paparazzi outside his house.'

'Good morning Southside. It's 10am and this is Ned Ferris bringing you the news from Radio Razor.'

Flick sat at the desk in his consulting room at All Saints' Surgery struggling with the burden of sudden fame. He'd had to run the gauntlet of reporters to get into the surgery.

'Heroic GP Flick Mendy was back at work in Southside this morning after his life and death choice between two brothers.'

He turned it off. He didn't feel like a hero. He'd killed one of his best friends and if he'd been just a little bit sharper, he might have heard Jack's warning and kept Juan alive. The pole could have fallen on any of them, but it fell on Juan.

Flick's guilt was more than survivor's guilt. He knew he had made a mistake. Yes, doctors make mistakes, but this was a big one.

He still hadn't talked to Venga since leaving Skerryn and wanted to know if their friendship was still strong. He feared not. He tried his number again. Let it ring 20 times. No reply. He'd already left messages. Nothing to add. He left it.

Maybe Jack could help. He dialled his number

'Flick. How's it going?'

'Not too good bud, to be honest. Can't stop thinking about Juan and still haven't talked to Venga. Won't answer his phone. I need help Wise Old Man.'

'Wish I was as wise as you all think I am, but I told you everything I know on the drive down. He pretty much cut me off as soon as we'd dealt with the Press, sent me off to a hotel, then asked me to help you make the arrangements for Juan's body, sign off the paperwork and drive his car home.'

'He's home now. Yes?'

'Yes. Flew down. Didn't want a bumpy ride.'

Flick thought for a moment. 'He just didn't want to be in the car with us. Well, me.'

'Maybe Flick. We all grieve differently.'

'Listen bud, I think it's more than grief. He's not thinking straight and I'm worried about what's coming next. We've seen how volatile he can be.'

'You know I told him about the lifeboat warning. And I told him you didn't hear me.'

'Yeah?'

'Maybe, and I know this can't be true, but maybe he's got it in his head that you did hear me and went ahead anyway.'

'No.' Flick dismissed that straight away. 'I know he can be a dick, but I can't see him thinking that.'

They both considered it for a moment. Both thinking the unthinkable.

It wasn't possible. Flick knew it wasn't possible. 'No Jack. Gotta be something else.'

'You're right. If I hear anything, I'll let you know.'

'Thanks Jack.' He paused. 'S'pose I'll see you at the funeral.'

'Good morning South…'

Venga slammed his fist on the off button. Not listening to any more of that hero crap. He lay back down on his sofa, head on the armrest, focussed on the toothbrush in his hand. Flick's toothbrush.

Every time he thought about Juan, his anger towards Flick grew. Venga should not have woken up in the shack. He should have died. Not Juan. Venga had the reckless idea for the trip, Venga carried on despite the pole being covered in metal fittings, Venga carried on in poor weather, and Venga chose to take the ego picture to confirm they had succeeded against all odds. It was vanity. Alpha-male vanity and it had cost Juan his life.

Venga knew he was hurting and looking for someone to blame, but he firmly believed Flick *was* to blame. There was so much pointing to him.

Flick was short of money. His ex-wife was still in the home they jointly owned ten years after the divorce, Flick still making payments. He'd struggled to buy Juan's house and fallen short by £100,000… a verbal loan from Juan sealing the deal. With Juan gone the debt was gone.

And Jack told him help was on the way. Flick waved his arm. He heard him. He knew help was coming and killed Juan anyway. Debt gone. Everyone trusts a doctor. Who'd ever know?

But, and this is the clincher, Juan never agreed to be the donor. The three of them had talked about the transfusion, joked about it really. It was never a serious suggestion and Juan absolutely did not agree to be the donor.

Venga convinced himself that Flick had chosen to kill Juan.

But Venga also considered that maybe he had reached these conclusions for the wrong reasons. Why didn't he make these claims to the police as soon as he woke up on the island, or as soon as Jack confirmed that Flick had been warned about the lifeboat coming? Not an easy question to answer considering the second line of thought that was now haunting him. Was Zac linked to Flick?

On the day of the gala dinner, Natty told him Denzil was not Zac's father.

When Zac cut his arm on the washing machine door *the crazy bitch from the hospital* told him his grandson had very rare B negative blood.

In the shack, as Juan, Venga and Flick discussed the transfusion idea, Flick explained that his own blood was no use because he had very rare B negative blood.

Flick spends a surprising amount of time with Zac considering he is just an old friend of the grandfather.

Flick had to give the hospital in Manchester three months notice before he could start work in Southside. That meant Dr Mendy would have visited Southside for interview five month's before Venga's barbecue, the day he saw Natty for the 'first time' in ten years, the day she was five months pregnant.

Venga had Flick's toothbrush for a parental DNA test. He'd made arrangements online with a clinic in London to do the test for him. Now he needed a DNA sample from Zac. Better pay Natty a visit, then he could submit the test and start work on the funeral arrangements. There must be a date when Flick would be unable to attend.

'Good morning Southside. It's 10am and this is Ned Ferris bringing you the news from Radio Razor.'

The Google Nest played in Tasha's lounge while Zac worked on a dinosaur model on the kitchen table.

'Heroic GP Flick Mendy was back at work in Southside this morning after his life and death choice between two brothers.'

'Mum, Mum.' Zac ran to the bottom of the stairs and shouted up. 'Uncle Flick on the radio.'

She came down the stairs, arms full of washing, and loaded the machine in the kitchen as they both listened to the news report.

'Is he coming to see us today Mum?'

'Hopefully. But he's at work this morning. He'll have a lot of paperwork to catch up on.'

Zac got back to his dinosaur. 'Can you help me with this? Think there's a piece missing.'

She read the instructions. No help. And 'read' was probably the wrong word. It was just a series of pictures and related to many different dinosaur kits, not just this one. She pushed them to one side and studied all the parts hoping the answers would show themselves.

Following her nose worked well and ten minutes later, the model started to look like a dinosaur.

The doorbell rang.

Zac raced to the door.

'It's Granddad.'

Tasha came through.

Zac held out his arm. 'Here Granddad. Let me take your coat.'

He took it to the row of hooks along the hall. No free hooks so he placed it over his own favourite green beanie hat.

Tasha and Venga hugged. More tears. Few words. Then Venga hugged Zac.

'Wanna see my dinosaur Granddad?'

'I'd love to,' he replied, with genuine enthusiasm.

'Coffee?' Tasha asked.

'Please.'

Venga 'read' the instructions. 'Impressive job Zac, considering these instructions are a joke.'

'Mum didn't need them. Maybe it's a man thing granddad.' Zac borrowed one of his mum's phrases.

Venga and Tash smiled at each other. She handed him his coffee and emptied the washing machine into a basket. 'Be right back.' She headed to the garden to hang it out, always optimistic with the weather.

Zac 'read' the instructions. 'I'm sure there's a piece missing Granddad. These instructions are a joke.'

With Tasha out of the room, Venga slipped away and reached for Zac's green beanie hat from the same peg as his own coat. He slipped it in his coat pocket and hung it back up.

Back in the kitchen, Zac let his frustration get the better of him and screwed the instruction sheet into a ball and threw it towards the bin. 'Joke.'

Venga smiled. Got his granddad's temper.

'Here Zac, I've got a proper joke for you.'

Zac's eyes lit up. He always enjoyed Granddad's jokes.

'What does DNA stand for?' His subconscious was setting the agenda.

'Dunno. Go on.'

'National Dyslexia Association.'

Venga smiled.

Zac looked confused.

Venga tried to explain and gave in as Tasha returned.

'Not sure these instructions are helping,' Venga said as he reached for the ball of paper by the bin and smoothed it out.

As soon as he finished his coffee, he stood and headed for the door. 'Gotta shoot Natty. Got a million things to do. See you later.'

'Ah right. Okay. Short and sweet.'

They hugged and he was gone.

'Wow. That was quick Zac.'

'Grief Mum. We're all different.' More borrowed phrases.

'Quite right Zac. Quite right.' She locked the back door and picked up her phone and keys. 'Shopping next my boy. Grab your coat. Might need your hat too. Bit chilly.'

He came back with his coat on. 'Wanna hear a joke Mum.'

Oh no. What rubbish has he told him now? 'Go on then.'

'What does NDA stand for?'

'I dunno Zac. Tell me.'

'National Detoxic Association.'

'Oh.' Odd one. 'Don't really get that to be fair.'

'Nor did I.'

They headed for the door.

'Got your hat?'

'Couldn't find it Mum.'

An inspector calls

Chapter 17
2025, August 13, Wednesday
Southside Crown Court, trial day 9

Botic van der Sar needed to put Jack String on the witness stand. His evidence was damning and vital to his case, but he called him with reluctance. He was a close friend of Venga *and* Flick and, as such, would be something of a character witness for the defence. That said, he could not do without him, the defence could have called him anyway, albeit not in the middle of the prosecution case, and he'd kept him towards the end in the hope that he had already won over the jury.

'Mr String. While you were in the shack, did you hear talk of a blood transfusion from one brother to the other?'

'Yes.'

'Did Juan Prost consent to be the donor in this proposed transfusion?'

'No.'

'And was it made clear by Dr Mendy that such a procedure would kill the donor patient?'

Jack looked over at Flick, then Venga. He didn't like the nature of Botic's questions. In the heat of the moment in the shack with Storm Vicky battering the tired old building, nothing was as black and white as Botic was implying. Jack had been invited to prepare his answers with prosecution counsel but had refused. If he were to give evidence it would be organic and real, nothing choreographed.

'I wouldn't say that.' Jack was vague.

Botic had wanted a clear yes and regretted not having the chance to prepare his witness. In cross examination he would have forced a yes or no, but that wasn't a good look in front of a jury with his own witness. He needed to tread carefully.

'Was it made clear by Dr Mendy that such a procedure would shorten the life of the donor?'

Much easier. He should have opened with that question instead of being a clever dick.

'Yes.'

'Did the doctor give any time frame?'

Not such an easy question. Flick had said the donor would die 'straight away'. How do you quantify 'straight away'? It wasn't clear cut and Jack didn't want to repeat the line, especially as Venga hadn't remembered the exact phrase when he gave evidence earlier in the week. On top of which, the jury would take 'straight away' as instant, in which case they'd assume I had avoided saying a clear 'yes' to Botic's first question.

'He didn't give a clear time frame, but the inference was that it would be a matter of minutes.'

'And you had already been told by Dr Mendy that without help from the mainland, specifically blood supplies, both brothers would have died within five hours, an assessment made by the doctor, which has been confirmed as trustworthy by medical experts earlier in the trial?'

'Yes.'

'At that point, you headed for the beach to call the lifeboat in Tobermory to reiterate the urgent need for blood?'

'Yes.'

'A successful call?'

'Yes.' That irritated Jack. Trivialising the fact that the lifeboat had only agreed to try a rescue due to an outrageously unlikely succession of good fortune.

'How long was the expected wait for help to arrive on Skerryn?'

'About 45 minutes.'

'So Mr String, knowing there was fresh blood on the way and knowing Dr Mendy had talked about a potentially fatal, and rather desperate, blood transfusion, you chose to alert the doctor that help was imminent?'

Fuck you Botic. I'm not answering a question loaded with the phrase 'rather desperate' and you've not mentioned the pressure on the time scale caused by the need for calming storm oil to be poured in the rip current at a specific state of tide to facilitate the lifeboat's safe landing. It was chaos. We were in the middle of a named storm. None of this is as simple as Botic is making out and he's throwing in facetious comments like 'rather desperate'.

'If you want me to answer that question, you need to remove the inflammatory phrase "rather desperate".'

Jack kept a straight face.

Botic cursed himself. He was pushing his own witness away.

'Did you return to the shack before the lifeboat arrived on the island?'

'Yes.'

'To ensure that Dr Mendy knew blood was on the way?'

'Yes.'

'With the intention of removing the need to consider the one-way blood transfusion that could lead to the death of the donor patient?'

Jack hesitated. Looked at Flick. Very reluctant and softly. 'Yes.'

'Do you remember what you said to the doctor?'

Jack remembered clearly, as if it were yesterday. He'd thought about it so often since. 'Blood on the way. Lifeboat coming.'

'Did Dr Mendy acknowledge what you had said in any way?'

Again, Jack wasn't happy. This gave Flick no chance. He was at the far end of the room in a storm with his back to him and Jack knew he should have got closer, been clearer and got more clarity in his response. He almost felt as if he should be on trial himself, not Flick. If he'd been clearer, Flick would definitely have heard, and Juan would still be alive.

'He raised his arm.'

'And you headed back to the beach to meet the lifeboat?'

'Yes.'

'When you returned with Dr Sarah Bruce, the blood transfusion had already been completed and Juan was dead?'

Jack looked over at Venga in the public gallery, head in hands. Flick looked equally devastated. Jack couldn't understand why their collective pain needed to be shared with the whole nation. Nothing would bring Juan back. Mistakes had been made. Shit happens, as Juan himself had said from his bed in the shack.

'Yes.'

Botic had what he needed from his witness and worded his next line with the jury in mind, knowing he no longer needed to keep Jack on board.

'Medical experts have already confirmed that the arrival of Dr Bruce with blood could have saved Juan, if the reckless and ill-conceived transfusion had not been performed, by a doctor who had an off-grid loan of £100,000 from the patient and ignored information that made it clear the transfusion was not necessary. That sounds like a desperate doctor taking advantage of an opportunity.'

He waved an arm in the direction of defence counsel Petra Patel.

'Your witness.'

She stood. Looked at the jury. They seemed hostile.

'Mr String. Can you be certain that Dr Mendy heard your warning?'

'No.'

'What makes you unsure?'

'There was a howling gale. It was hard to hear anybody say anything. I was in an open door, with Flick at the far end of the room with his back to me, about 20 feet away.'

'Did you leave straight away because you were sure Dr Mendy understood the message?'

'No.'

'Can you tell us why you left so quickly?'

Now Jack had the opportunity to explain the horrific demands of the weather, the rugged nature of the island and the need to cross it twice, rapidly, at the age of 60 after an exhausting and testing day, following a virtually sleepless night due to a 500-mile car journey. The desperate need to be back at the beach in time to pour storm oil on the waves to help calm the rip current at a crucial state of tide ahead of low water, to give the lifeboat a once-only fleeting chance to land safely.

Petra felt the hostility of the jury lessen very slightly.

'Did you ask Dr Mendy later that day if he had heard your warning?'

'Yes.'

'And how did he respond?'

'Said he didn't hear me. He was mortified that his error had been costly. He was concentrating, heard me say something, but wasn't sure what, and waved me away.'

'Have you any reason to doubt that?'

'None whatsoever. I've known Flick, Dr Mendy, 25 years, played football together for Southside YMCA, went to his wedding. He's a decent man and I'd trust him with my life, just as, I'm sure, Juan did.'

'Thank-you Mr String.'

Venga watched Jack leave the witness stand. His memories of the shack seemed different, not necessarily different factually, but different. Cloudy. Blurred. Injuries and morphine had muddied the water. During Jack's testimony, Venga noticed the senior investigating officer DCI Jon Jordan smiling at Jack's awkward answers to Botic's tough questions. It was a boyish smile, Venga remembered it from their time clay pigeon shooting. It was a smile that betrayed him. Venga thought at the time he'd love to play poker with the detective, must be easy to read.

DCI Jordan had the same smile when they met at the very start of the investigation following Venga's emailed results from the DNA laboratory. Venga had been unsure of the results, presented in a high-brow scientific table, so he called them asking for a simple summary. The sarcastic technician replied, 'Toothbrush is the father of green hat.'

Venga saw red. Fury filled every nerve of his body, a primed and charged cannon ready to fire a horrific broadside if anyone crossed his path.

'Are you absolutely certain?'

'I'd bet your house on it.'

Venga hung up and immediately called DCI Jordan to arrange a meeting as soon as. He felt an enormous sense of betrayal. His best friend, the same age as him, was the father of his daughter's son.

Zac had been conceived when Tasha was 17. He pictured Flick standing at the far end of the room while he loaded both barrels of his shotgun and took aim, like a firing squad. Just before he pulled the trigger, Juan stepped into the firing line.

'Are you thinking straight Venga?'

Fuck off. What's it to you? She's my daughter and he was my friend.

'What's it to me mate? You've just called the police. You're gonna tell them your best friend murdered me. Really? You ask what's it to me?'

It's nothing to do with you Juan. Nothing.

The image of Juan disappeared. Venga had a clear line of fire, took two steps closer to be sure of a kill, and fired. Flick disintegrated, and plastered the far wall. Venga was angry that there was so little left for his second cartridge. He needed more. He fired at what was left of Flick and the bloody mess filled the wall above the fireplace, dripping onto the mantelpiece, where he kept his football trophies, many won in the same team as Flick. There was even a blood-soaked picture of Venga with Tasha, Zac and Flick. He strode over grabbed it and threw it to the floor, stamping on it repeatedly.

He grabbed his keys, phone, jacket and stormed out of his house slamming the front door behind him. He marched into police headquarters and asked for DCI Jordan.

In the interview room, he started talking before he'd even sat down.

'I want to make a statement about my brother's death in Scotland.'

DCI Jordan couldn't help his boyish smile, giving away his glee at an opportunity to be involved in something that was all over the media.

'You okay if we record this?'

Venga nodded with irritation.

'I think it was murder.'

DCI Jordan's eyebrows shot up.

'Okay Mr Prost. I'm all ears.'

'You've read what happened?'

'I've got a rough idea.'

'So you're aware of the brother to brother blood transfusion that killed Juan.'

'Yes.'

'Right. Well. Flick didn't need to do it. Help was on the way and he knew it. Jack told him.'

'Jack String told Dr Mendy blood was on the way before he started the transfusion?'

'Yes.'

'You heard him say that?'

'Jack told me. You can check with him.'

'Okay. Well that changes things. So why did he still go ahead?'

'He owes Juan £100,000.'

'Right. Have you seen the contract?'

'There isn't one. So the debt died with my brother.'

'Can anyone else confirm this?'

'Probably the solicitors that handled Flick's purchase of my brother's house, less the borrowed sum, and you can get a look at bank statements. Also,' Venga remembered, 'Flick's ex-wife Mandy Mendy knew about it.' Venga scribbled her number on a piece of paper. 'But the final thing.'

'Yes.'

'Juan did not agree to the transfusion. There was no consent. We talked about it, but it was banter. Nobody expected Flick to actually do it. He owed money, and he saw an opportunity.'

DCI Jordan was delighted that he was now involved in such a high profile alleged crime, but he had one burning question.

'Why has it taken a week for you to come forward with this information Mr Prost?'

Venga had been tripping over his words. He was in such a hurry to get his story out. He spoke fast, but now he paused. Thought carefully.

'Fair question Jon. Flick's my best friend. Has been for nearly 30 years. I gave him the benefit of the doubt, to begin with, but as the red flags accumulated, I eventually had to put our friendship aside and accept the truth. And I felt it was my duty to come forward.'

DCI Jordan nodded. That seemed reasonable.

They dotted the Is and crossed the Ts before Venga stood to leave.

'Flick will be at work now. All Saints' Surgery. You gonna arrest him?'

DCI Jordan rubbed his chin. 'Well Venga, we certainly have enough to bring him in for questioning.'

Sat in his car before driving home, Venga texted freelance reporter Ginger Green.

'Just met with DCI Jon Jordan from Southside CID. They'll be questioning Dr Flick Mendy in the near future. Charges may follow for the murder of my brother Juan.'

The reply was almost instant.

'Many thanks for keeping me in the loop Mr Prost. Are you okay to talk if I call for more detail?'

They chatted as he drove home.

Five hours later an unmarked police car pulled up outside Flick's house in Milo Road and DCI Jordan knocked on the door, made introductions, stepped inside and explained why he was visiting.

The word 'murder' felt like a punch in the face. The horror of losing Juan a week before had already knocked Flick sideways. He knew his mistake had been fatal and the guilt he felt was suffocating everything he did, everything he thought and he hadn't slept since Skerryn. He was exhausted and couldn't believe the word murder had been used in a sentence that included his name.

But he felt he should be punished. Not for murder, but definitely punished. He was already punishing himself, every minute of every day. Not physically, but mentally chastising himself for the critical error that caused Juan's death.

Venga had still not spoken to him and it seemed clear that his friend, possibly former friend, had put two and two together and come up with murder. He agreed without fuss and drove to police headquarters with DCI Jordan.

News travels fast, especially when it's given a push, and later that evening online news sources had changed their hero stories for 'alleged murder' stories.

Venga sat at his laptop feeling like he had done something for his brother, something to right a wrong. He couldn't get the horror of Juan's death out of his head and the trip to the police, although it helped, was a drop in the ocean. He needed a distraction.

He logged on to Doting.com and viewed his inbox. Leanne had left two messages.

'Sorry to hear your holiday was not what you expected. The pictures are always misleading x.'

Venga had described the Skerryn trip as a disappointing holiday, with friends, to Corfu, where the beach had been really narrow and coarse gravel rather than soft golden sand, as promised in the brochure.

'Might hit the town with my daughter tonight. Wish you could join us, winky face emoji, x.'

They'd exchanged a few pictures, but still not met after more than two months. It was unusual for Venga to take it steady, but it was a novelty and so far it was working. He replied.

'Would love to join you, blowing kiss emoji, but tied up for the foreseeable. I hear Chichester is a good night out x.'

'Some nice pubs and restaurants. Festival Theatre has some good stuff. You seen Moulin Rouge? x'

'Love the music x.'

'How about Southside? Sounds like it's all going on up there atm x.'

Distraction failed. He was back in the nightmare.

'Sorry. Gotta run xx.'

Chapter 18
2025, August 14, Thursday
Southside Crown Court, trial day 10

Defence barrister Petra Patel called Major Jensen from 22 Field Hospital, Royal Army Medical Corps, Aldershot.

'How well do you know Dr Flick Mendy?'

'I authorised his appointment. Top surgeon. Had the good fortune to work alongside him for almost ten years. Highly professional and a gifted physician.'

'And he worked with you after the team-building trip to Scotland?'

'His bail conditions only related to practising medicine. His role with us was, and remains, in the development of field equipment, some of which he carried with him to Skerryn and used, for the first time, with the successful transfusion to save the life of Venga Prost.'

'So your opinion of Dr Mendy has not been tarnished by the events of October 8, 2024?'

Major Jensen looked around the court with thinly-disguised contempt. 'Quite the opposite, Dr Mendy found himself in a highly compromised situation and, despite the extreme conditions he faced, went above and beyond to limit fatal casualties to just one man.'

Petra Patel noticed at least two jurors nodding their approval. She went on to call further character witnesses including Flick's boss from All Saints' Surgery, who confirmed what a popular and valued member of staff he was and how they were struggling to meet demand in his extended absence.

Lisa String as a friend of 25 years described him as a 'man of exceptional integrity'.

Petra's final character witness surprised everybody and sparked conversation in the jury box.

'That's Venga Prost's daughter.' Lesley Regan, juror six, whispered to Vicky Mather, juror five.

'Yes. Tasha Prost. And the murdered, oops, alleged murdered man's niece.'

'Wow. And she's helping the defence? What the…'

'Indeed. What a family.'

Petra Patel had faced the same problem with Tasha Prost as Botic van der Sar had faced with Jack String. Tasha would not discuss her answers before the trial. Prepared to appear, and prepared to answer most questions, but on the hoof. Raw. Honest. Take it or leave it basically and Petra had advised Flick, in the strongest possible terms, to leave it. He had been adamant that he wanted her to take the stand.

'But, Dr Mendy, my instinct tells me she could be the straw that breaks the camel's back and get you convicted.'

'So be it,' he had replied. 'I want her up there. She's part of the story.'

'It's your funeral Flick.'

He had not backed down and now Tasha Prost was sworn in and ready for Petra. She was equally ready for cross examination with Botic van der Sar, which could prove more of a test.

Petra tried to play safe.

'How do you know Dr Mendy?'

'He is my father's best friend.'

Everyone in the court room noticed the present tense and most observers assumed it was a slip of the tongue. A couple of jurors banked it as good information. A couple of others saw her as unreliable, given her obvious error.

'I've known him all my life.'

'Has he always been a reliable and constant friend of the whole Prost family?'

'I see him in many ways as part of the family and he's taken a lot of interest in my son Zac. He's been like a father to him.'

Venga, in the public gallery, tried to hide his discomfort. That was hard to hear.

Juror six Lesley Regan thought to herself, 'Surely you mean like a grandfather to him?'

'Looking around I see some surprised faces. You're probably thinking, surely you mean grandfather? He's the same age as your dad. But that's the thing about Flick, and his friendship with my father. He's such a solid and reliable man, that he's the first you call whenever there's a problem. That's what a father should be.' She stopped to glance at her own father, who was not enjoying his daughter's contribution.

'Yes. They're best friends, but when the chips are down, Venga goes to Flick, like most people would go to their father. It's a strangely paternal relationship.' She had the full attention of the room.

Petra said nothing, unsure if this was helping or not, but she was fascinated and left it.

'And at the end of this trial, when you've heard all the evidence, you'll probably be left thinking Flick or Venga? Who do I believe? Because that's all it is. But the way I see it, my father, whom I assure you all I love deeply, set the ball rolling on this trial in much the same way as a petulant child would rebel against a parent. Something very special was taken from him and he rebelled against the one person he has leant on all his life.'

Petra Patel was loving this, but fearing cross examination would bring it all crashing down. 'Miss Prost, could you give us an example, prior to the Skerryn trip, of how Venga Prost relied on Dr Mendy?'

She thought for a moment before settling on something suitable. 'I was involved in this tale, but only as a baby, about a year old, so I'm combining two versions of the event from my father and an almost identical version of events from Flick. I trust both versions, because it's a story that has happened over and over since then, as my father has tried and failed to commit long term to any partner.

'My mother Mira walked out. She was 19 when I was born, Dad 20, and she wanted to give me up for adoption. My father wanted to keep me.' She looked over at him now. 'Love you Dad.' Paused to collect herself. 'They tried to make it work, but she had big dreams. Me and Dad didn't fit. So. She left. Dad was devastated and had a meltdown. Went on his Playstation; *Call Of Duty, Grand Theft Auto* and *Simpsons Hit And Run*. Same games over and over. Didn't eat, didn't sleep, drank beer. In a trance. And it went on day after day. Flick, uncle Juan and aunt Megan took turns to look after me, apparently, but mostly Flick. He missed work to run everything. Dad just made himself ill and after 10 days on the Playstation, he went to bed. He was there for another week before Flick got him to eat, wash and think about going to work.'

'Miss Prost, you said it happened over and over?'

'Yes. Dad's partners come and go and the meltdown repeats. Flick picks him up.'

'Always Dr Mendy?'

'Yes. Mostly. And Juan, but mostly Flick.' Not quite true she remembered. 'Apart from the 10 years when Flick worked in Manchester. For those years it was me, some help from Juan and Megan, but just me really.'

'Just checking dates, you were a child for that period weren't you?'

'Yes. Seven to 17. And I scooped him off the floor every time. He got so bad one time, I drove him to the hospital.'

'Presumably when you were 16 or 17?'

Tasha laughed softly. 'I wish. Think I was 15. Thought he was gonna choke on his own vomit. Took the risk. But I so wish Flick had still been around to do it. Fortunately he came back and slipped straight back into the same role.'

By the time Petra handed the witness to Botic, she was very anxious. So far Tasha had been a marginal net gain, but that could easily be lost, or worse.

Botic stood, acutely aware that the trial was heading towards a contest between two big personalities and equally aware that Tasha Prost presented a big opportunity to improve Venga's stature with the jury. 27-year-old insurance clerk. Candy from a baby.

'Miss Prost. You've told us you love your father very deeply?'

'Yes.'

'He stood by you when your mother walked out?'

'Yes.' She wasn't going to be sucked in to volunteer anything.

'So you trust him?'

'Yes. Absolutely.'

'Venga Prost, under oath, has told this court that there was no consent given to Dr Mendy to perform the reckless blood transfusion, a procedure that cost your uncle his life. No doubt, when Flick takes the stand, we will hear a different story. Do you believe your father?' For the sake of clarity, he added, 'I'm looking for a simple yes or no here.'

She said nothing.

Botic waited.

Nothing.

'Would you like me to repeat the question?'

'No. I heard you.'

'Are you going to answer?'

'No.'

Botic turned to the judge, confused.

Judge Faith Haydn turned to Tasha with raised eyebrows. 'Miss Prost?'

She faced the judge calmly. 'Sorry Your Honour. He asked for a simple yes or no. There is no simple yes or no so I haven't got an answer for him.'

The judge looked across at Botic, said nothing, then back at Tasha. 'Please answer in your own words.'

'Thank-you Your Honour.' She turned back to Botic. 'It's complicated. He is convinced he is right. He believes what he is saying. But there's always grey areas. Whatever happened and whatever was said, if my father thinks no consent was given, I absolutely accept that is what he believes. I hope that makes sense. Probably not. But if Flick does come on later, and tells us something different, I would believe him too.'

Jon Frazer, juror eight, a Dire Straits fan, thought, 'Two men say they're Jesus. One of them must be wrong.'

Botic was losing this exchange and, what had seemed easy point scoring, was going against him. Gotta finish on a positive.

'Miss Prost, when Venga called to tell you what had happened in Scotland, did he express doubts about Flick's conduct?'

'No. Said he was a hero. Saved his life.'

Fuck. 'Thank-you Miss Prost. That's all.'

Tasha climbed down from the witness stand, slowly walked back to the public gallery and sat next to her father.

A hum of excitement rippled round the court room, and it grew stronger as Petra Patel called Dr Flick Mendy.

Petra Patel wanted strong clear answers to build Flick up with the jury. She had been unsure whether to put him on the stand at all, as he was brutally honest, even to his own detriment. She felt that could be harmful when Botic got his hands on him. Having worked through the basics of the Skerryn trip, she was ready to tackle the key points.

'Did you have consent from Juan to use him as the donor for the blood transfusion?'

'Yes.' Instant. Confident.

'Would you have done the procedure without consent?'

'No.'

Botic stood. 'Objection. Can we stick to what happened rather than speculating on what might have happened in different circumstances?'

'Sustained.'

'Did you believe that the emergency services would not arrive for 24 hours?'

'Yes. No doubt about it.'

'And your professional assessment was that both brothers would have died before help arrived.'

'Yes.'

'So you acted, with consent, in a manner that saved a life you knew would otherwise be lost?'

'Yes.'

'Did you hear Jack enter the building before you began the process?'

'Yes, he arrived as I was setting up.'

'So you could have aborted if you had heard his warning?'

'I could have done and, without doubt, would have done. Yes.'

'But you didn't hear him?'

'No.'

'Why not?'

If she hadn't warned him that she was going to ask that, he would have been irritated, but he had a prepared answer.

'The high winds were very noisy, Jack was 20 feet away in the open door, and I was concentrating, in the middle of a procedure that I had never tried before, with equipment that had never been used before, in horrendous conditions. I was focussed.'

'What did you hear Jack say?'

'Can't be certain, but I knew he'd been to check out the lifeboat wreck and I heard him say "lifeboat". Raised my arm to say I'd heard and he left.'

'You never at any point thought he was telling you help was on the way?'

'No.'

'Before you started the procedure, was there any mention of the money you owed him?'

'Yes. I raised the subject.'

'And?'

'I joked that it could look very bad for me, but assured him that he need not worry about that. He asked if I could give the money to Tasha for Zac. No problem I said and that was it.'

After a few more questions, Petra handed the witness to Botic. Again there was a hum of excitement around the court room.

Some simple questions to build rapport before Botic got to the meat in the sandwich.

'Dr Mendy. We have heard from the only other person present in the shack on that fateful day that you had no consent to carry out the transfusion.'

Botic waited.

Flick squirmed in his seat unsure what to say. 'What's the question?'

Botic had been expecting such a response and hoped it would make Flick look disrespectful.

'Venga Prost has told this court room that you had no consent. You have just told us you did. You can't both be right.'

Still no direct question, but for fear of looking antagonistic, Flick offered a view. 'I had consent. If I hadn't, both brothers would have died and I would have been compelled to let that happen.'

'Jack String has told this room, under oath, that he told you help was on the way before you started the reckless transfusion. "Blood is on the way." And you raised your hand in acknowledgement.'

Flick said nothing.

'You also claim to have reached a settlement with Juan on the owed money, but nobody else heard that.'

Nothing from Flick.

'I put it to you Dr Mendy, that there was no consent for your foolish operation. You heard Mr String's warning and ignored it when you realised there was an opportunity to kill a man you owed a large sum of money to. An opportunist striking for selfish reasons, exploiting the nation's trust in the medical profession. You saw your chance and murdered Juan Prost.'

A few gasps. Some jurors nodded.

Flick wasn't sure if he was allowed to respond but tried anyway.

'No Mr van der Sar. Not hearing Jack's warning is a mistake I will regret till the day I die, but I acted, under extreme pressure, with total integrity throughout.'

Chapter 19
2025, August 15, Friday
Southside Crown Court, trial day 11

Defence barrister Petra Patel called Dr Sarah Bruce to the witness stand.

'You were the first medical professional after Dr Mendy to get a close look at the Prost brothers following the accident on Skerryn island. Could you summarise what you faced on your arrival at the shack?'

'In the circumstances, challenging weather and modest accommodation, Dr Mendy had managed the situation with extreme professionalism. Both brothers had sustained injuries that would have killed them in minutes on the hilltop, without his intervention. And the transfusion had further contributed to giving Venga Prost a fighting chance.'

'Is it your professional opinion that Juan's life could have been saved if Dr Mendy had waited for help to arrive?'

'Too hard to be certain. But it is fair to say his chances of survival would have been much greater without the one-way transfusion to his brother Venga. But it's important to note that Venga Prost may have died without the blood taken from his brother.'

'So you can't say, unequivocally, that waiting for help would have guaranteed the survival of both brothers?'

'No.'

Botic van der Sar for the prosecution was more blunt.

'Can you confirm Dr Bruce, in your professional opinion, that the only chance for both brothers to have survived, would have been if Dr Mendy had waited for help?'

She thought about it briefly.

'Yes.'

'And any competent doctor would have known this?'

She looked over at Flick. 'Probably.'

'So we are, once again, back to the question of whether Dr Mendy heard Mr String's warning that help was on the way.' He checked his notes. 'Dr Bruce, what was Dr Mendy's reaction when you walked into the shack armed with vital medical supplies?'

'Horrified.'

'Horrified that his crime had been discovered?'

Dr Bruce looked thoughtful, but said nothing.

Freelance reporter Ginger Green was taking notes. This was all good bread and butter material, but she knew there was better stuff lurking in the shadows. Better stories waiting to be told. She had spent most of the morning in conversation with the chief reporter from the Southside Gazette, who sat alongside her. Messages had been passed back and forth, written in their notepads. She'd gained his confidence. Now it was time to go fishing. The Southside Gazette editor was one of the main witnesses. Surely there was some gossip from work. He must know a thing or two about Jack String.

She scribbled in her notebook. 'Must be awkward in the newsroom with the editor being a key witness?'

'Could be, but no. Jack's a pro. Taken a back seat on this. Just leaves us to it and trusts us.'

'Wow. Not pushing you at all? One way or the other?'

'Nothing. And he made it clear right at the start that he wouldn't.'

'But he must see what you do before it goes to print?'

'I expect so, but he's said nothing. Apart from the usual encouragement. Good job guys. That sort of thing.'

Ginger was struggling. Tried a new angle. 'He's still friends with Flick and Venga though?'

'Hard to say with Flick. Bail conditions. No contact, but probably sees Venga watching YMCA football. There's a game tomorrow. Jack always goes. Venga might. I'm covering the match. First league game of the season.'

'Mind if I join you? I'm a long way from home with nothing to do.'

'Sure. Away at St Day, 3pm kick off.'

Botic kept pushing.

'Was Dr Mendy's reaction to your arrival normal?'

She thought again. 'Hard to say *what* is normal in such strange circumstances. It was extreme. Consistent with bereavement I have seen in others.' She turned to the jury. 'He was devastated.'

This wasn't helping Botic. He moved on to her treatment of the surviving brother.

Venga, sat alongside Tasha, was hearing new information. He'd been unconscious and oblivious to the drama unfolding around him in the shack. He made a mental note to go to football the next day and talk more to Jack. In the nine months since the Skerryn trip, Venga had seen Jack many times, but they had always avoided talking about the fatal trip. Skerryn was their Lord Voldemort, *the trip which can not be named,* except for one very drunken day back in March, when Venga had endured one of his meltdowns. By coincidence, it followed the same football fixture as tomorrow's first game of the new season, Southside YMCA against St Day.

Saturday, March 15, had started badly for Venga. To be more accurate, his bad Saturday had started the previous day. He never went to bed after drinking a lot on the Friday evening. By midnight he was half drunk, enough to slow down his reflexes but not enough to knock him out. He sat down at his desk in the drawing room and turned on his Playstation, fired up *Simpsons Hit And Run*, then hit the mute button. He called up his Spotify account and played Leonard Cohen on repeat for the next 14 hours, sipping the odd beer until early afternoon.

He pulled on his coat and walked across town to the football club, grabbing a beer and selecting *Everybody Knows* by Leonard Cohen on the jukebox. As Cohen sang *everybody knows that it's me or you*, he walked out onto the clubhouse balcony, beer in hand, to see his club go 1-0 down, a 25-yard screamer from Dan Richards. Half a pint later, Nathan Taylor put the visitors two up. Venga returned to the bar and the jukebox. *Dance Me To The End Of Love.*

Three pints later the game ended two each, the other spectators, players and officials slowly filled the bar. Jack and the St Day manager Joff Malaber, joined Venga.

'Hey Ven, you got lucky there. We were all over you at the start.'

'Yeah. Saw two good goals.'

Joff's boy Eddie was pulling on his jacket.

'There's sausages. Can you get me some?'

'Grab 'em yourself. No-one will notice.' That was enough. He dived in. Got chips too.

Joff winced a little. 'What's this dreary music Ven? You trying to drive us away?'

Venga smiled. 'Sorry mate. I know. My fault. I put it on.'

'Pile of shit. No offence Ven, but… just saying.'

Venga nodded, the smile gone.

'We would have won today if we didn't have our best three players missing.' Joff always had an excuse. 'Stag night on a Friday. I told them not to. Three in hospital.'

Jack had half heard something. 'Go on. What happened?'

'Flaming arseholes.'

Venga nodded.

Jack was lost. 'What's that then?'

'A stupid dare game. Not something I'd ever do,' Joff quickly added. 'Something to do with toilet roll clenched between your buttocks. Two people do it. Someone puts a match to the paper and the winner is the one that holds out the longest. Stupid. Stupid players. The night before a big game.'

'Kids these days Joff. What can you do eh?' Venga responded slowly, taking care to pronounce each word clearly. 'Mate. You still decorating? I could do with some help. Couple of rooms and the garden wall?'

'Yeah. Sure. So busy though. How urgent is it? Probably be summer before I'm with you.'

'Summer's fine. Besides. You're good. Worth waiting for.' Venga forced a smile.

Two pints later, Venga sat back at a table with Jack after selecting another song. The away team had gone, a few players were still there and a few die hard supporters.

'Are you okay Ven?' Jack was worried.

'Yeah. Sure. All good. How about you?'

'I'm alright.'

'All good then. Let me get you another drink.' He didn't wait for an answer and headed for the bar.

Jack had noticed his speech was not as coherent as normal, even after a couple of post-match beers.

'Cheers Ven. Wanna get something to eat?'

Venga shook his head.

'You gotta eat.'

Venga shook his head again.

Jack had heard stories about Venga's meltdowns and was recognising the signs.

'When did you last eat?'

Venga rocked a little in his seat and shook his head again. Thought about it but couldn't remember. 'Dunno.'

'How about sleep?'

'Dunno.'

Then he twigged as Leonard Cohen sang *Last Year's Man* on the jukebox.

'Ven, you don't like this stuff.'

A slight shake of the head.

'He was *Juan's* favourite.' Jack remembered.

One short nod. 'Yup.'

Jack reached out a hand, squeezed Venga's shoulder.

Venga stared across the clubhouse at nothing and a single tear ran down his cheek. 'Today was his birthday. Would have been 52.'

Jack raised his glass. 'Happy birthday Juan. Always in our thoughts.'

Venga raised his glass in silence.

They sat through the rest of *Last Year's Man*, before Jack took advantage of the opportunity. If Venga had mentioned *the trip which can not be named,* it was on the table for further discussion.

'How is work Ven? Done much since Skerryn?'

'Nothing. Everything got cancelled. Nobody trusts me. Fair enough.'

'Shit Ven. That's terrible.'

Venga faced Jack, briefly a little brighter. 'Cleaned my car yesterday. First time since the trip.'

'Cool. That's a step forward.'

The brightness faded as fast as it had appeared. 'I had to clean it. Was so mucky, you could draw on the dirty paintwork. Somebody had done.' He paused. 'They'd drawn a large C on the TV Rush logo… just in front of the R.'

'That's just sick Ven.'

'Maybe. There's always haters. Fifteen minutes of hate follows 15 minutes of fame.'

'Sick though. Some people.'

'There's more. One of the jobs I need Joff for. Graffiti on the garden wall… *Juan and Venga went up the hill to fetch a pale of water*.'

'Arseholes.'

Jack and Venga were joined by a few supporters who remembered Juan from his playing days and they shared fond memories until the barman called time. Jack had an easy walk home. He called a taxi for Venga and helped him in.

Venga's meltdown was gathering pace and as they pulled out of the car park, he asked the driver to turn round and head for Milo Road. He paid and almost fell out of the car, the bracing cold March drizzle peppering his face. He walked carefully to the big front door and knocked. He heard footsteps. The outside light came on.

As Flick opened the door, Venga heard Leonard Cohen *Hallelujah* playing in the background. They looked at each other for about ten seconds before Flick broke the silence. 'Fifty two bud. I still feel like I have to listen to his shit music. Just opened a bottle for him. Whisky?' He stepped aside and Venga went in. They sat around the coffee table and Flick poured three glasses of Johnnie Walker.

Hallelujah ended and *Suzanne* played. They drank in silence for five songs before Venga topped up the glasses. 'I miss him mate.'

Flick nodded.

'No-one bickers like Juan. No-one irritates me as well as Juan, and no-one plays right back like Juan.'

'One in a million. I can picture him now, running down the wing swinging his arm like a windmill making car noises like he was changing gear as he got faster. Frightening. I'd get out of the way if I was a defender.'

'Such a piss-take. Class.'

'Always last to leave the bar after the game.'

'Yup. A lot of fun. Except for Megan.' They laughed. 'I was 16 when he first took me to the pub. After an away game, Wickstead I think. I'd been on the bench, played my first 20 minutes in shit weather, started snowing in the game and was sticking on the wings before the game finished.'

Flick nodded.

'Three hours in their clubhouse, then a 10 mile drive home through the back of beyond. Snow was thick on the ground by then. Untouched on some of those tiny roads. The weight of snow on the branches of one tree had snapped it off and it fell across the road. We had to stop and move it. Four of us got out. The snow had stopped. Everything lit up by the headlights was white. Middle of nowhere and it was weirdly quiet. After moving the branch, we stopped and listened to the silence. There was a crack in the distance, probably another branch falling under the weight of snow. Spooked Juan for some reason and he started barking like a dog. Funniest thing I've ever seen.'

They clinked glasses again.

'You got any food mate? I'm starving.'

Flick fed him and they shared more Juan stories and listened to more songs that neither of them liked.

'Did you ever meet that woman you connected with online?'

Venga was keen to tell Flick how well it was going. 'Still not met her, but still going really well. I now know why all my previous relationships have failed. Turns out it's best to avoid contact and sex. Stick to long-distance chat and I'm good.'

They laughed.

'Aren't you tempted to meet her?'

'S'pose. But it's a test now. Wanna see how long we can keep it going without physical intimacy. I think I'm genuinely falling for her and it's a completely new feeling, knowing that what we have is built on a meeting of minds instead of bodies.'

'Wow Venga. New man.'

Two drinks later, Venga fell asleep.

Difficult situation for Flick. His bail conditions forbade him from having any contact with key witnesses or their immediate family and friends. He couldn't drive Venga home. If he were seen there, he'd be locked up. He couldn't call a taxi. *Careless talk costs lives*. Or in this case, liberty.

Best option would be call Tasha. Get her to take him home. Similar to a taxi, but no chance of word getting out. Only danger being he wasn't allowed contact with her either. Gonna have to chance it. He selected her number and pressed call.

'Hi Flick. At the third stroke, the time will be six minutes past three…'

'Yeah, sorry. Bit of an emergency.'

'Does this have anything to do with uncle Juan's 52nd birthday?'

'You got it.' Flick could feel her rolling her eyes at Venga.

'Passed out I'm guessing. And you need him discretely removed before the police put two and two together?'

'I'd owe you a big favour.'

'Now Flick. That will never be true. I will cover up my number plates, pull on my red wig, false nose and glasses and be with you as soon as.'

Flick's heart raced. He hadn't seen Tasha for about five months, and despite breaching bail conditions, he felt it was a semi-acceptable but fleeting opportunity that would keep him motivated for the dark times ahead.

She helped him scoop Venga out of the armchair and belt him into her car before returning to the pool of light spilling onto the front doorstep of the house. After their forced time apart, restricted to Messenger conversations, much the same as lockdown, the embrace was firm and loving. They kissed. It was all the more sweet knowing it was a brief encounter.

'Stay strong Flick.'

'And you Tash.'

Venga roused momentarily from his stupor and glanced in the rear-view mirror. He cringed, but fought the urge to intervene.

The fan

Chapter 20

2025, August 16, Saturday

St Day Football Club, Vogue, near Southside

St Day Football Club manager Joff Malaber sat at the kitchen table deep in thought with a blank sheet of paper in front of him.

His wife Gemma handed him coffee in his favourite Number One Dad mug.

'Dunno why you're struggling. You do the same thing every week.'

'First game of the season though and its YMCA.'

She laughed. 'Makes no difference. You never change anything. You sit there trying to be tactical, then you pick your best players. I could do it.'

He pushed the blank sheet of paper across the table with a challenging smile.

'Okay. Big game. Need to be solid,' she said in a low voice. 'Scott Hopgood in goal. Gareth and Danny centrebacks, Wittsy left back, Hawkey right back.'

Joff raised his eyebrows. Okay so far.

'Perran Cooke and Tyler Oliver in the middle?' More of a question.

'Yeah. Still good.'

'Dan Richards up front.' Not so sure now. 'With Stuart.'

'Tough eh?'

She gave in.

He took back the team sheet. 'I'll go with that. Most important though. I need that promising young striker

Gemma Malaber in the kitchen doing the half-time teas and food.'

She groaned and walked away from the table.

'I need to pack for Canada next week and do some prep work.'

'But Gem. You're the best.'

'If I do it, you've got the kids all tomorrow so I can crack on.'

'No problem.' He hugged her. 'One more thing though. Venga Prost and Jack String will probably be at the game. And with Flick's trial still up in the air, best not mention... you know what.' He winked.

Gemma had nearly fallen off her seat with shock when Joff arrived home the night before after a week of decorating at Venga's house. He had been clearing his gear, when Venga took a call in the next room. With all the windows open on a blistering hot day, it had been easy to hear every word, at least on the receiving end.

'Gorgeous Mandy Mendy. How are you?' Warm greeting.

...

'Oh wow. Dive straight in. No *how about you Venga*?' Warmth fading.

...

'But I do think he's guilty.' Defensive now.

...

'How do you know? You weren't there.' Bordering on angry.

...

'Not enough? How can you say that?' Raised voice now.

The exchange got progressively more heated, Venga more animated until he snapped. Sort of *A Few Good Men* code red moment.

'Yes I did. And I'll tell you why. He fucked my 17-year-old daughter. He was 37. My "best" fucking friend and he's Zac's fucking father,' he shouted.

Joff could hear him smash the phone down on his desk.

Gemma assured Joff it would go no further.

'I did see Shika last night though in the shop. May have mentioned it, but told her to keep it to herself.'

'Shit Gem. She sells the raffle tickets.'

'Want me to have a word?'

Joff thought about it. 'Maybe not. If we make a big deal of it, could work against us.'

The first game of the season, on a hot sunny day, drew a crowd of around 200, with more Press than they normally got. Dave was there, chief reporter with the Southside Gazette. He normally covered their games about once every two months, and he was joined by a whole host of others, all acutely aware that Jack String and Venga Prost may be at the game. With Flick's trial almost at its climax, they were hoping for any related scraps.

Ginger Green leant on the railing that surrounded the pitch alongside Dave and quizzed him on the YMCA supporters, club officials and players.

'See that bloke next to the away dugout with black hair. White t-shirt. That's Mark Trigger. He used to play for YMCA. Same team as Jack String, probably had a few games with Venga as well.'

'Cool.'

'Over by the club house.' Dave pointed. 'Stocky bloke in the long red shorts.'

'Yeah?'

'That's Wazza.'

Ginger waited for more.

'Think he used to play on the same pub team as Venga.'

'Cheers Dave. Catch ya later.' She headed towards the dugout, introduced herself to Mark Trigger and they chatted.

Mark was full of praise for Jack. Great teammate, great club chairman, great friend.

'Used to play alongside me in the middle of midfield. Won the cup together.'

Ginger struggled to sound interested. Nodded encouragement.

'Can't believe what happened in Scotland. Juan was such a nice bloke.'

Now we're getting somewhere Ginger thought.

'And Jack took it so badly. Thinks he should have done more to make sure Flick heard his warning.'

'So he believes Flick didn't hear him?'

'Just a minute. You not gonna print this are you?' Mark retreated.

'Just background.'

'Well. Jack's a good man. He's here somewhere. You should talk to him.' Mark turned away to watch the game.

Ginger thanked him and headed over to Wazza, introduced herself and got the same story as Mark had told her. Great bloke. Gutted about Scotland. Blah, blah, blah.

'Thanks Waz. That's a great help. It's good to build up a clear picture of the people involved.' Then, out of desperation, she resorted to gutter tactics. 'To be honest Waz, I could do with something more spicy.'

He nodded.

'She flashed a fifty pound note. 'I'm happy to pay if you can tell me something about Venga that nobody else knows.'

Wazza's eyes lit up and he looked at the offered money.

Ginger was encouraged. He hadn't flinched at the offer. Promising.

'Okay.' He reached for the cash.

Ginger kept a firm grip on the note. 'Need the info first. Gotta be sure it's useful.'

Wazza wasn't happy but went along with it.

'Okay. About 25 years ago, when we played together for the Rose and Crown, Ven got sent off. He was so angry with the ref that he went into the changing rooms, while the game was still being played, found the referee's kitbag and pissed in his shoes.'

Not really what she was hoping for, but she felt obliged to hand over the cash.

Ginger was 500 miles from home, living in an Airbnb while she covered the trial, accumulating expenses and she was getting nowhere fast. As she walked back to find Dave from the Gazette, she saw a girl coming towards her selling raffle tickets. No thanks. She was bleeding money and didn't want to be accosted for a raffle. She headed right to give the girl a wide berth, but she had been spotted and the girl changed her route to intercept her.

'Hi. Raffle tickets? It's drawn in the clubhouse after the game. Lots of great prizes today including a plate of meat from the butcher's.'

'Ooh. A plate of meat.'

Shika missed the sarcasm. 'Over 20 prizes.'

Ginger tried to step past the girl but she moved to block and smiled.

Out of desperation, in the hope of ending the exchange and getting back to Dave, Ginger took a gamble. 'Okay miss. I'll buy £50 of raffle tickets if you can tell me something interesting about someone from today's away team.'

The girl's jaw dropped. £20 was her record sale.

'Didn't think so. Thanks.'

Ginger stepped past her and headed off.

'Okay,' Shika shouted after her.

Ginger stopped, hope rising, turned and walked back to the ticket girl. 'Go on then.'

'Do you know who Venga Prost is?'

'Yes I do.' Ginger tried to hide her excitement.

'How about Flick Mendy?'

'Yes.'

'Venga has a daughter.'

'Yes. Tasha.'

'She's got a son. Zac.'

'Yes.' Ginger knew this was big. Almost held her breath.

'Flick's the dad.'

Oh my God. Gold dust. Stay calm. Stay calm. Keep her talking.

'That's very interesting.' Understatement of the year. 'Where did you hear this?'

'Gemma.'

'And do you know where she heard it?'

'Joff.'

'Who are they?'

'St Day manager and his wife.'

Ginger nodded. 'And do you know where Joff heard it?'

'He's been doing some decorating at Venga's house. Overheard a conversation between Venga and Mandy someone.'

Bingo. Genuine. 'Mandy Mendy?'

'Yeah. That's it.'

Wow. This was the story behind the story. She could feel it when she first met Venga. There was something he had been keeping quiet. This would sell for a lot and the traffic on her blog would be through the roof.

She handed the raffle ticket girl a fifty pound note.

Shika started to write out tickets.

'Oh. No need. You have them.' She handed her a card. 'Call me if you hear anything more.'

Shika looked at it. Journalist. Shit. Big trouble. 'You not gonna print any of this are you? You can't. I heard it in confidence.'

'Don't worry. I won't say where it came from.' She looked around the crowd for Venga. On the clubhouse balcony with a beer in his hand. Jack by his side. She headed over.

'Hi Mr Prost. How are you today? Game going well?'

'Hi Ginger,' he looked at her briefly, then turned to watch the game as he answered. 'One each. Two good sides. Could go either way.'

'Do you mind if I ask a bit about the trial?'

He kept his eyes on the game. 'Sure. Fire away.'

'Are you happy with how it's going so far?'

'No complaints. Mostly in line with what I was told to expect.'

Jack gave Ginger a friendly warning. 'Obviously you are heavily restricted on what you can print from sources outside the courtroom.'

'Of course Mr String. Just working on background colour pieces for print after the trial has finished.'

'Fair enough.'

'So Mr Prost, closing statements on Monday, then it's over to the jury. Do you have faith in them?'

'Completely… oooh, did you see that Jack? Missed an easy through ball for a one-on-one.'

'Do you think you will win?'

Venga hesitated. Not altogether happy with that question, but he kept his eyes on the game. 'It's not about me. It's about Flick. Is he guilty or not guilty? And that's down to the jury. I'm sure they'll make the right decision.'

'But Mr Prost, it is about you. Dr Mendy is only on trial because you went to the police and accused him of murder.'

Venga didn't like that at all. Ginger Green had been very helpful in the past, but these questions were verging on hostile. He turned to face her.

'What's going on here Ginger?'

Finally she had his attention. 'Why did you accuse your best friend of murder Mr Prost?'

What the… where had this come from?

Ginger followed up with her next question before he had answered the last one.

'Is it because Dr Mendy got your 17-year-old daughter pregnant?'

Most of the supporters on the balcony had noticed the tension in the conversation and a lot of them heard Ginger's last question. Venga was a rabbit caught in headlights, surrounded by his football friends. He hated the cliché, but for that brief moment it was true. He wanted the ground to swallow him up. He needed to escape. This was his worst nightmare. The only thing worse than what Flick had done with his daughter was everybody knowing what Flick had done with his daughter. He was speechless. He found himself thinking about the 1980s film *Honey I Shrunk The Kids*. He felt like the raygun had been pointed at him and he was now only two inches tall. Little more than an insect that could be brushed aside.

Totally emasculated. Now that was fascinating. Why did he feel emasculated? For the first time it occurred to him that he was looking at it as something that had happened to him. Why? It was something that happened to his daughter. His shoulders sank and he walked through the clubhouse, out the front door, through the car park, opened the door and sat in his car with his head in his hands.

Jack ushered Ginger to a quiet corner of the clubhouse. Many eyes followed them, but it went quiet as the balcony door closed behind them.

'That's quite an accusation Miss Green.'

'I know.' She struggled to hide a smile. 'But his reaction confirmed it's true.'

'That's a long way from being sufficient proof to justify publication. You know that.'

'With respect. It's a different world from when you were a reporter Mr String.'

'Not entirely.'

'Fair, but different enough to work for me. Even now, I know *you* couldn't print what I've got. If he takes you to court for libel, you're in trouble and you've got a lot to lose. He could put you out of business and all your staff would lose their jobs. With this story, my blog will score more hits than you sell papers in a month and I'm on my own. No responsibility for other staff and Venga won't sue me. I've no money, so he's nothing to gain. And I'm happy to go with a defence of "it's true". You saw his face.'

'Miss Green, the judge could close you down. Contempt of court. We're in the closing stages of a trial.'

'Unlikely Mr String. I don't think you believe that. I stick to the family relationships, mention nothing about the detail of the trial and I'm safe.'

'But it will massively impact the trial. It'll taint the jurors' views of Venga and Flick.'

'I know that. That's why my hit counter will go mental. But the trial, officially, isn't supposed to be about the personalities.'

Jack knew he had lost. She was right. It would go viral before the jury retired to deliberate and he couldn't stop it, and if he were being honest with himself, he would have to accept that Ginger Green was spot on with her legal assessment of what she could do. Be nice if his reporters were that sharp.

Ginger was itching to get the story live, but had to stop by Tasha's first, try for a comment. Back into Southside.

She rang the doorbell.

Tasha opened the door, recognised the face, but couldn't place it. 'Hello.'

'Hi Miss Prost. My name is Ginger Green. I'm a freelance reporter working on the Juan Prost murder...'

Tasha started to close the door. 'How many times? No interviews.'

'This is about Zac.' Nothing to lose.

Tasha stopped just before the door clicked shut, waited a few seconds, then slowly opened again.

'I have some new information relating to Dr Mendy and Zac, which I believe may have prompted your father to trigger the murder trial.'

Tasha had a fair idea where this was going but absolutely no idea how Ginger Green could have found out. 'Go on.'

'Do you think your father went to the police because he found out Zac's father was his best friend Flick Mendy?'

Tasha struggled to keep her composure. 'Dr Mendy to you Miss Green. Doctor.' She felt exposed, like she was naked in the centre circle of Wembley in front of a 100,000 crowd. But her overriding emotion was relief. The burden of keeping the secret was gone, lifted from her shoulders. It was a good feeling, but it was mixed with fear. She had started to think Flick had half a chance of a not guilty verdict. But this would change everything. It could turn jurors against him. They would side with her father, who would probably be seen as a victim.

She closed the door and scrolled through her contacts to Flick's number.

'Just been asked by a reporter if you are Zac's dad.'

'Fuck.'

Chapter 21
2025, August 17, Sunday
Southside

Venga woke up in a good mood, but within seconds the trauma of the day before flooded back into his head and dragged him down. He made coffee, sat at his desk and called up Ginger Green's blog.

She wrote: 'The Juan Prost murder trial has taken an explosive new twist with the jury set to consider their verdict this week.

'My investigations have exposed a stunning revelation which sheds new light on Venga Prost's motivation for seeking the conviction of his former best friend Dr Flick Mendy for the murder of his brother Juan.

'It has come to light that the father of Venga's grandson Zac is Dr Mendy, the boy conceived when Tasha Prost was only 17. At the time, Dr Mendy was 37 years old.

'When I asked Venga Prost if the discovery of this information had prompted his request for a murder investigation, there was an awkward silence before he walked away. Click here to see his reaction.'

What the fuck? She'd filmed it. He clicked through to a video posted on YouTube, which showed the crowded balcony at St Day Football Club. He saw the humiliating interview come to life on his screen.

'Why did you accuse your best friend of murder Mr Prost?

'Is it because Dr Mendy got your 17-year-old daughter pregnant?'

He watched his reaction with horror. There were no words, but his face gave the clearest answer Ginger Green could have hoped for. His face said YES in the same size capital letters that famously spell out HOLLYWOOD. The hit counter on the video showed 11,866 views.

He closed down the blog and loaded *Simpsons Hit And Run* on his Playstation. He started the game, but pressed no buttons. His character died. He closed it down.

He wanted to escape, run away. His usual default wasn't enough. That would be hiding. No time for a meltdown. He had to find a positive way forward.

He logged on to Doting.com. Leanne had left three messages.

'Hope all is well. Thinking about you x.'

'Stupid thing to say. Sorry. I know it's not going well. The trial must be awful, reliving that terrible day on the island. Thinking about you xx.'

And finally. 'I think you need a hug xxx.'

He read them a few times, aware she would know her messages had been seen. Better reply.

'I think I do. Wanna pop round? x' They often joked about meeting up.

'Yeah. Be with you in about an hour xx.'

With Ginger Green's YouTube clip burned on his mind, he needed a big distraction. Maybe it was time to do it for real. Meet Leanne. He'd taken the bold step of telling her about the trial a couple of months ago and she had been very supportive. He expected her to disappear and was pleasantly surprised that it had brought them closer.

'Seriously. It would be great if you came round. I think it's time we took the next step x.'

He waited anxiously. Flashing green letters said she was typing, then disappeared. No message. Thirty seconds later the green letters reappeared. Gone again. Either her reply is long or she'd been spooked and … a reply came through.

'Venga honey. I'd love to. And yes, I could genuinely be there in about an hour. If you're sure? What's the address?'

He gave his address and assured her he was ready and couldn't wait to see her. 'What you fancy doing?'

She replied with a winky emoji and a kiss.

The banter bubbled along nicely until Venga let his trial anxiety intrude on their playful conversation. 'Can't wait to see the back of Ginger Green x.'

'Who's she? x'

'Reporter blogger hounding me with her poison.' Angry again. Forgot to add a kiss.

'Poor Venga. Way it is though honey. They're allowed in court xx.'

'I know, but she followed me to a football match yesterday. Posted a video on her blog.'

'I'll take a look xx.'

Venga waited for her reaction, looking for the green letters saying she was typing. Nothing after five minutes. That's long enough to have read it and seen the video. What's the hold-up? He waited another five minutes. Nothing.

'You okay Leanne? x'

Another five minutes. Nothing.

'You've got me worried now. Hopefully you're on your way. See you soon x.'

He could see she was no longer on line. Two hours later, there was no sign of her, but there was a knock at the door. He opened it. The day was getting worse.

'Hi Dad. Think we need to talk.'

He stepped back and she followed him in, took a seat in the lounge and waited while he made coffee. He placed hers on the table and sat opposite her.

They both felt like they had been called to the headmaster's office.

She made the first move. 'Interesting YouTube clip Dad.' Calm, but the words were loaded with sadness.

He looked her in the eye, but said nothing.

For the first time, she thought, hoped, she saw a hint of shame in his expression, but it was fleeting and soon disappeared.

'When did you find out?'

They looked at each other. He wasn't sure what to say, how honest to be, whether to be honest at all.

'No. Forget that Dad. I know exactly when you found out. Five minutes before you walked into Southside Police Station and accused Flick of murder.'

He looked away.

'Shocking Dad. And you sat next to me in court for two weeks knowing Flick is Zac's father. Saying nothing.'

He turned back and met her accusing gaze. 'That's right Natty. And you sat next to me for ten years knowing Flick was Zac's father. Saying nothing.' Surprisingly gentle, but full of pain.

It was quiet for a while, both unsure where they were going.

'I kept quiet to protect you Dad.'

He laughed softly. 'Protect me? A 37-year-old predator beds my teenage daughter and I'm the one who needs protecting? Are you serious?'

'Yes.' The fastest response of the conversation so far. 'You know I never loved Denzil. Or Dean. I wanted to be with Flick all the time, but we kept it quiet. I knew it would destroy you. You'd go into one of your meltdowns. And without me… or Flick… to rescue you from yourself, who knows…?'

Quiet again.

'Do you love Flick?'

'YES.'

Silence.

Tasha drank her coffee.

Venga watched his go cold.

'But why choose Flick? Uncle Flick...? And how could he pick out my 17-year-old daughter? He's a good looking bloke. He could have his pick.'

Tasha was ready for that one. 'I didn't. And he didn't. We met. We were instant soulmates, but we had absolutely no idea that we already knew each other. To me, he was some random hot man I met. Doctor M. And to him I was some random girl on a hen night called Tasha. As a kid, he knew me as Natty. Why would he recognise a seven year old he'd known ten years earlier?'

Venga raised his eyebrows. Not sure about that. 'Okay. Let's move past that. Why would a 37-year-old man hit on a teenager. That's wrong. I know we've been over this and we disagree, but that's a 20-year difference with a schoolgirl. Surely you can see that's wrong?'

'Okay, I'll concede some ground here. If I'd known that, I would have had second thoughts, but it wasn't like that. I was on a hen night with the netball girls from Vicar, all in their twenties and thirties. I'd done my work experience with them that week. I was one of the girls. Made up, I looked much older, especially in that company. And we approached him. Not the other way round. All six of us sat at his table, while he was quietly sat on his laptop preparing for his GP interview, drinking diet coke.'

Venga nodded.

'He thought I was mid twenties. He's told me since. I thought he was early thirties. He's aged better than you Dad.' She smiled. 'So we both believed the age gap was five years, maybe a little more, but certainly not 20 years. And neither of us had a clue that he was uncle Flick and I was little Natty.'

Venga screwed up his face a little. 'But you know now. That's what I can't get past. And you both know that when Zac was conceived, you were 17 and he was 37.'

'Right Dad… There's another issue we're missing here.'

Venga raised his eyebrows and sat back a little, inviting her to share her thoughts.

'Forget the law Dad, forget the age difference, forget morals and everyone's opinions… whatever age I was then, and whatever age I am now… it's *my* body. And I have an absolute right to decide what happens to my body.'

She paused. Her words hammering on Venga's defences.

'My body. My choice to sleep with Flick when I was 17. Not yours, or anybody else. So if I'm good with it, you should be able to accept my choice and give me your complete support. That's what would happen in my ideal world.'

Venga screwed his face up, scratched his neck and kept quiet, worried he may say the wrong thing.

'We were right to keep it from you. Flick's murder trial confirms that. But, and this is a big but, despite your catastrophic YouTube appearance, which will probably spark some Victorian views in the jury, I still love you and will be sat alongside you in the public gallery tomorrow with my fingers firmly crossed, hoping that the jury do the right thing.'

Later that evening on the other side of town, juror number 12 nurse Kate Ellis logged on to Ginger Green's blog and read about Flick Mendy and his son Zac, before watching the YouTube clip of Venga at the football club.

Always had my doubts about Flick Mendy. Had been edging towards not guilty, but this is wrong. I'm struggling to believe anything he's said now I know he's a paedophile. And wow. Look at the hit count. The clip now had 109,103 views.

She was about to close the website down when a fresh entry popped up. Ooh interesting, more on Venga. She clicked on it. This was the story that kept on giving. Who would have thought? Like London buses, you wait ages for one paedophile to show up and then two come along right next to each other.

Ginger Green wrote: '26-year-old Leanne Clamp from Chichester brands Venga Prost a hypocrite following her 12-month relationship with the 47-year-old owner of TV Rush.

'Earlier today on my blog, Venga Prost refused to deny that he had accused his best friend of murder after discovering Dr Flick Mendy had fathered a child with his then 17-year-old daughter.

'Within hours, Leanne Clamp, a year younger than Tasha Prost, contacted me to say she had been in an online relationship with Venga for the last 12 months.

'"He was completely at ease with me," she said. "We got on like a house on fire. It's only when I saw your blog this morning that I thought wtf, how can I trust this older man when he goes to the police screaming murder, when his best friend has only done what he is doing with me? Double standards or what?"'

'However, Miss Clamp did accept that she had lied about her age and Venga, for the whole year of their online relationship, had believed he was talking to Leanne's mother Olive.

'Challenged on what Venga had done wrong, Leanne added, "It's the sentiment that counts. Why is Venga so violently against a relationship between two people with a large age gap, without considering their compatibility? He looked at the gap between his daughter and Flick and threw his toys out of the pram condemning it as wrong. He didn't know I was younger than his daughter, but he let the bond grow without letting it influence his feelings for me. So, hypocrite."

'She makes a good point. How can we ever judge a couple based on stats alone? Love isn't a game of Top Trumps. To test the nation's views on this I've set up a poll called Twenty Is Plenty. Thumbs up if you support Tasha Prost and Dr Flick Mendy.'

Kate was incredulous. Now I don't believe either of them.

She clicked on thumbs down.

Chapter 22
2025, August 18, Monday
Southside Crown Court, trial day 12

Botic van der Sar had been on his feet for 40 minutes making his closing statement for the prosecution.

Tasha Prost listened carefully but her eyes were on the jury, subconsciously keeping a running score of nods and head shakes. Botic was scoring well. The blog effect seemed to have gone against Flick in favour of the man who had not only lost his brother, but also lost his daughter's innocence far too young. She would stay alongside her father throughout the trial but wondered, sadly, if distancing herself from him would reduce the sympathy for Venga. Perhaps she could sit at the far end of the public gallery wearing a T-shirt with the slogan Free Flick Mendy.

Botic was winding up.

'So, to summarise, this trial is about Dr Flick Mendy's abuse of the nation's trust in their health professionals. That trust is a fundamental building block of our society and Dr Mendy exploited that privilege for financial gain. His messy divorce was allowed to drag on for a decade with naive financial control forcing Dr Mendy into desperate measures.'

He paused for dramatic effect, nodding in approval of his own words.

'Our desperate doctor needed money badly, he heard Jack String's warning that help was imminent, acknowledged it with a wave of his hand and pressed on regardless. Not only did he ignore the potentially life-saving warning, but he proceeded without consent. Beyond Dr Mendy's perilous finances and the ignored warning of help, he still could not have gone ahead with his reckless, untested, and ultimately fatal transfusion, without the consent of the patients involved. None was given.

'So I put it to you that Dr Mendy coldly, and with total awareness of what he was doing, abused his position as a trusted doctor, ignored warnings of help, ignored the need for consent and murdered Juan Prost with no regard whatsoever for the horrific trauma he rained down on his closest friends.'

Tasha winced at the number of nods.

Petra Patel for the defence was equally thorough but took half the time in the hope that less is more, and her fewer words might have more impact. She could not mention what had been exposed in the media over the weekend, but she wanted to imply Venga had only gone to the police out of spite, a knee-jerk reaction to hearing Dr Mendy was the father of his grandchild.

'We will never know why Venga Prost left Skerryn hailing his best friend Dr Flick Mendy a hero, only to visit the police a week later convinced the same man was a murderer, but the facts speak for themselves, and Dr Mendy's actions were selfless and heroic in the most horrendous circumstances that any health professional could find themselves in.

'Medical experts have confirmed that both brothers would have died if they had to endure a 24-hour wait for help.

'The emergency services have confirmed that Dr Mendy was told the wait would be 24 hours and there was no chance of shortening that time.

‘We have also heard from the lifeboat station that their early arrival on the island was only made possible by a freakish string of good fortune and exceptional ability of the crew involved.

‘Dr Mendy did not hear Jack String’s words of warning, shouted, in a hurry from the open door twenty feet away at the height of Storm Vicky, the worst weather to hit Scotland for years, while he was focussed on a pioneering, life-saving operation with ground-breaking equipment in what must have been close to battlefield conditions.

‘He did not want to take such an enormous risk, but felt compelled to save at least one life when faced with the almost certain loss of two good friends.’

‘And Dr Mendy, who was unhurt in the hilltop accident, and fully alert, had consent from his patient to proceed… a patient who he carried a quarter of a mile to a shelter over his shoulder despite the barrage of a named storm.

‘This whole trial is a scandalous injustice against a gifted doctor painted into a corner by extreme circumstances beyond his control, who acted with absolute integrity and professionalism to do what any good doctor in our trusted health service would have done, and that is fight for the preservation of life. Dr Flick Mendy is a hero and you should find him not guilty.’

A hum of excitement filled the room as Petra sat down.

Tasha was pleased to see a few nods from the jury box, including one or two jurors who had reacted the same way to the prosecution’s closing statement. Were they changing their minds or were they undecided?

Flick looked over at Tasha. He could do that now, without fear of giving himself away. He had read Ginger Green's blog with mixed feelings. He had guarded their secret because that's what Tasha wanted. Without the shackles of their shared secret, he could probably have put up a better fight in the trial. But even though he faced possible conviction and a life in prison, he felt liberated. He looked at Venga. It was the best of times. It was the worst of times. It was the age of wisdom.

Judge Faith Haydn brought down her gavel to silence the boisterous crowd and sent the jury to consider its verdict with a final warning.

'There has been a lot of online chatter and media interest around this trial ever since the Scottish trip, especially over the weekend just gone. You must put it out of your mind and restrict your thoughts exclusively to what you have heard in this courtroom over the last two weeks. Ignore the noise.'

Jury foreman Steven Robinson, retired police superintendent, wanted to establish some ground rules. 'As the judge said, we must only consider what we have heard in court. Nothing else, however tempting, matters. It's just noise.'

Swimwear model Joe Wareham challenged him. 'From what I've been told about jury duty, nobody will ever know what we talk about. It's all confidential so we *could* talk about anything. Surely?'

'That's true, but I think we should do it properly and take the judge's advice.'

Nurse Kate Ellis enjoyed Ginger Green's blog over the weekend. 'How can we ignore the fact that 37-year-old Flick Mendy shagged his best mate's 17-year-old daughter?'

'Firstly it's not a fact, it's media speculation, it's not relevant to this murder trial and we're not here to reach a verdict on whether Dr Mendy should or should not have kept his trousers on ten years ago.' A hint of anger from Steve.

Sports therapist Imelda Morse offered her support. 'How do you know it's not relevant? Just because you are foreman doesn't mean you get to decide what is and what isn't relevant. Maybe…'

'He's a paedo.' Business owner Lesley Regan. 'I say that's relevant.'

They'd barely started and Steve was losing control. 'Just for clarity. The age of consent is 16. Tasha Prost was 17. He's not a paedophile and I'd appreciate you not throwing inflammatory words around. It's not helpful. We're a jury, not a lynch mob.'

'Paedo,' nurse Rebecca Pooley muttered under her breath.

They all started talking among themselves.

'Has anyone else noticed it's just the women here who think this is important?' Chef Alister Wilson almost shouted to be heard.

'Even more reason to ignore it.' Steve responded, but immediately thought his comment could be misinterpreted. 'Not because women think it. That's not the problem here. The problem is that something we should not be discussing divides us on gender lines. That's dangerous, whether it's women sharing a view… or men. And, as I've already said, it's not been discussed in court and is not relevant to the murder trial. Can we move on?'

They were quiet for a moment.

'I'm a woman.' Less forceful, but very assured, commercial solicitor Emily McGovern.

'Nobody will argue with that,' joked retired phone engineer Roger Temple.

No laughs.

'I don't necessarily think the age gap between Flick and Tasha is a problem. To be honest, I've no idea, I don't know them well enough and none of us knows how well they get on, but I do have to disagree with you Steve.' She waved a hand in his direction. 'We can't say automatically that it's not relevant.'

She had their attention.

'The problem we are facing is that everyone on this jury has read the news. I expect we have all seen Ginger Green's blog. The information is in our heads whether we believe it or not. And I expect it will influence some of us. So we have a choice. We can follow the judge's guidance and try to put it out of our minds or we can accept that it is in our minds already, it is highly likely to effect our thinking and it would be far better if we looked at it together in detail and gave it due consideration.'

They were quiet as they digested the suggestion.

Steve was determined. 'The judge was clear. Ignore the noise.'

Emily wasn't that sure how they should proceed, but felt it should be a group choice. 'We're stuck in this room until we all agree. Why don't we start with a vote to decide whether we include Ginger's blog in our discussion?'

A murmur of approval left Steve with no choice. He shook his head. 'Fair enough. Raise your hands if you think we should talk about "the noise".'

Eleven hands went up.

'Let's hope the first vote on a verdict is this easy.' Steve accepted the ruling. 'I'll kick it off then. Personally I thought the YouTube clip was very powerful. Venga's face said everything. Quite simply we're only here deliberating over a murder trial because one old man did his mate's teenage daughter.'

'That's quite a strong view from someone who wouldn't let me use the word paedophile.' Lesley smiled.

'He's not a paedophile. But his choices might be seen as immoral by some, but, again, that's not my point. I'm just saying Venga Prost appears to think like that, and I believe that's why he accused the doctor of murder.'

'So you don't think it's murder?' Lesley pushed.

'Dunno. Probably not. Hard to say, but I have my doubts about Venga's motivation.'

'I don't trust a man who slept with a teenager 20 years younger.' Kate wasn't moving. 'I accept it's not illegal, but I just don't trust him and if we are faced with a choice of believing the doctor or the father, I'd struggle to go with Flick. Sorry.'

Lift engineer Bradley Waters waded in. 'But you'd trust a man who had a relationship with a girl 21 years younger?'

Kate smiled. 'Venga never saw Leanne Clamp.'

'So a relationship between a blind man and a woman wouldn't count either? Because the man has never seen the woman?'

Kate laughed. 'Is that a serious question?'

'Yes.' Bradley's voice went higher. A little wound up. 'A relationship doesn't always need a visual connection or physical intimacy for validation. The fact remains, Venga is 47 and Leanne is 26. They got pretty close and she was gutted when she realised her age could be an issue with Venga.'

'My husband is 16 years older than me.' Teacher Vicky Mather. 'I trust him completely and for me, looking at Flick and Tasha, or Venga and Leanne, the age difference doesn't have any impact on how much I trust them. I'm probably leaning towards Venga at the moment. Possibly the consent is a bigger issue for me. A doctor can't do any operation without consent and Venga says there was none given.'

'Flick says there was.' Joe hit back.

Emily tried to summarise their collective mood. 'We all agree that consent is a straight fight between Flick and Venga. Who do we believe? At least one of them is not telling the truth. We all have issues to a greater or lesser extent over which of the two we can trust depending on how we view their partner choices. But beyond that, we should look at how likely they are to have accurate memories of the event. It was hugely traumatic for both of them. Trauma plays tricks with memories. Sometimes trauma can block difficult memories. But also we should take into account Venga's injuries, his loss of blood and his doubtless struggle to maintain any clear thought at a time when he was fighting for his life. We ought to give more weight to Flick's memory of events. He had a clear enough head to successfully carry out a ground-breaking medical procedure that kept his accuser alive.'

A few nods.

'Here's my thinking.' Bradley. 'I don't believe it's got anything to do with the consent or any questionable relationships. I think it's pure grief.'

That took everybody by surprise. 'I think Venga knows he has fucked up with the telegraph pole, his ego pushing him to take a photograph to prove what a bunch of tough guys they are, and he can't stomach the pain. He knows he killed his brother. It's too much and this whole thing is one massive deflection, passing the blame onto his best friend. We hurt the ones we love the most. His daughter said pretty much the same thing.'

Steve tried to keep order. 'I think we're going off on a tangent now. There's a lot still to discuss, but maybe it's time to take a preliminary vote and see where we are.'

That seemed a popular choice.

'Let's go round the table. Give your current verdict with a brief explanation. I'll kick it off with a not guilty. I don't think there's enough solid proof to convict beyond reasonable doubt.'

Mixed reaction.

All eyes fell on Lesley. 'Not convinced either way, but for now I'm going not guilty. Flick is more solid than Venga.'

Jon. 'Guilty. And I think we should bring back the death penalty.'

A few oohs of surprise.

'Why?' Steve pushed. 'And I don't mean the death penalty bit.'

'The money I suppose. And everybody trusts a doctor. Probably thought he'd get away with it.'

Steve nodded and waved a hand towards Roger. 'Guilty. I think he heard Jack's warning.'

Alister. 'Guilty. It's the money for me.'

Emily. 'Not guilty. Not enough evidence.'

Kate. 'Guilty. It's the paedophilia thing.'

Rebecca. 'Not guilty. I like Flick.'

Bradley. 'Not guilty. All seems very circumstantial and I'm sticking with the deflection theory.'

Imelda. 'Not guilty. I think it was all a terrible accident.'

Joe. 'Not guilty. Way too many grey areas.'

Vicky. 'Guilty. I also think he heard Jack's warning.'

Steve checked his notes. 'I make that 7-5 in favour of not guilty. We've got a long way to go. But, summarising, I think it's one man's word against another.'

'Or one paedo's word against another.' Lesley couldn't help adding.

Steve gave her a stern look.

'Sorry.'

Chapter 23
2024, October 8, Tuesday
Skerryn, ten months before the trial

The door of the shack closed and Jack was gone.

Flick was on his knees in the narrow gap between Juan's bed and Venga's bed.

'More morphine Flea?' Venga wheezed.

'You've had too much already. Any more would kill you.'

Venga and Juan laughed at that.

'More morphine Flea?' Venga was joking this time. 'Might be an easier end.'

'You wanna trade in some quality time with your brother for an easy end?' Sarcasm and an attempt at banter from Juan.

It went quiet and they all stared at the closed door, knowing Jack was their only hope, but at the same time knowing that it was not going to happen.

The wind was battering their crofting hut. At least they had shelter.

'*I am just going outside and may be some time*.' High-brow historic reference from Juan.

'Yeah. Nice try mate, but he's not selflessly walking to his own death to give us a fighting chance; he's walking out just before the final act of a Shakespearian tragedy. He just doesn't want to be here when we go.' Venga's glass was half empty.

'Wouldn't be the first time.' Juan remembered.

They all remembered.

Flick had scored a goal, but the three of them, playing a cup semi-final for YMCA were about to lose. With five minutes to go and losing 4-1, their manager at the time, Jack String, had walked out of the dugout, into the club house and bought himself a pint of beer.

'He missed my two goals.' Juan smiled. 'But he knew it was all over and he didn't want to be there at the end.'

'Same old same old,' Venga whispered. 'He knows it's all over and he doesn't want to see it happen. Fair enough.'

Juan mocked. 'I'll see if there's anything that can help us in the wrecked lifeboat. Yeah, right Jack. I'd rather he'd stayed. We could have grilled him on his appalling football management. Would have given us a final laugh.'

'We did have some fun though didn't we Juan?' Venga managed a smile.

'What about that game in the snow Ven? You must have been 16 and the beer went straight to your head. On the way home, you got out for a pee and started barking like a…'

'That was you mate.' Indignant loud whisper.

It was quiet for a moment.

'Actually you might be right,' Juan conceded. 'I do remember punching that bald defender about the same time. He'd gone in really hard on you. I waited for the ref to look the other way and got him back. Bastard.'

Venga tried to laugh.

'You both nearly got me arrested. Trying to pee discretely in a shop doorway after a night out. You both jumping up and down pointing at me with a police car parked up the road.'

Quiet again. All three lost in their thoughts. Enjoying their memories.

'How many times have we sat together asking dumb questions like what would you choose as your last meal on death row?' Juan dragged the mood down.

Venga quoted The Inbetweeners. 'Dunno, but it'd better be delicious.'

Flick had plenty of suggestions, but kept quiet. He didn't want to intrude on the brothers' final moments together.

'Hey.' Venga nodded in the direction of his phone. 'Let's have one last song each.'

Flicked called up a music App. 'Got anything downloaded?'

'Shitloads. Let me think.' Venga.

'I've got one.' Juan was ready. 'Doors *Unknown Soldier.*'

'Jesus Juan. How about something upbeat for once? At least it's not Leonard fucking Cohen.'

Flick played it.

They were all quiet as Jim Morrison sorrowfully sang it's all over for the unknown soldier.

After it finished, it's haunting chords stayed in the room, metaphorically blending with the howling winds of Storm Vicky outside.

'Okay, I've got mine.' Venga wanted something lively. 'Play Black Eyed Peas *I Gotta Feeling.*'

Flick played it.

'Uplifting mate. Thought mine was more appropriate tbh. Why'd you pick it?'

Venga was smiling again. 'To help me visualise the video. Fergie's lesbian scene. Hot. That's an image I'll be happy to take with me.'

Flick and Juan groaned.

Venga's train of thought had gone to a better place. A happy place.

'I had a girlfriend once...'

More groans.

'You never told us what happened to that girl at the gala dinner with the orange dress.'

'Wow Flick. That was a year ago, and you remember the colour of her dress?'

'Very striking. Hard to forget. We never saw her again. Was it... Maria?'

'Yup. Marija Brankovic.' Venga waited to get his breath back. 'That was the last time I saw her. She wasn't that into me. Think she chose me because she knew I would take her to the gala ball and she wanted to show off her dress… body.'

'Ha.' Juan laughed. 'A woman used you?'

'S'pose.'

'Nothing happened then?' Flick was surprised.

'I didn't say that. I just said I never saw her again after that night.'

'Ah right.'

'Got her home and it took about half an hour to get that dress off. Not because she was reluctant. It was just so complicated.'

'Did you have to undo all the safety pins?'

'Wasn't that bad. But even with the dress off, she looked,' he stopped to think. 'Unusual I suppose… covered with all those painted blue circles.'

'Bet she was relieved to get those discs off? What did she say to Jack? Nip clips?'

'Well there's the funny thing.' Venga smiled again. 'She said the clips had been turning her on, unclipped them, slipped them in her bag and pulled out some metal weights with bigger clips on the end.'

He paused.

'What the fuck?' Juan.

'Vibrating nipple clamps.'

Juan and Flick both shook their heads.

Quiet reflection again.

Venga was looking back at all his romances. There had been a lot. So many false starts. Tasha's mum Mira. She hadn't been his first choice when they got together, or even second, but once he'd committed to her, he gave it everything he'd got and was devastated when she left. They'd been so young. Was that the reason it didn't work though? Maybe. He'd always assumed it was, but after so many other failed efforts, the obvious conclusion was that he was doing something wrong. Perhaps he just wasn't capable of loving a partner. Juan was. Megan was wonderful and they had been so close. Venga had the same DNA. Why couldn't he do it?

'Juan.'

'Ven.'

'Looks like this is it.'

'Does mate.'

'Listen… I've lost count of how many hot women I've been with.'

'You're a machine.'

Venga rolled slightly. Ooh. Painful. So he could look his brother in the eye.

'I'd swap 'em all in a heartbeat to have what you had with Megan… the perfect soulmate. Love of your life. That's what I've always wanted really.'

They both reached across the gap and took each other's hand.

Juan held back a tear. His life had been so empty since she died. He was certain that a part of him had died with her, but it gave him an unexpected warm feeling to discover his Playboy brother did have some compassion after all.

'That's good to hear Ven. Hidden depths. After all these years, you surprise us all. Hidden depths.'

'Well Juan. There you have it. Your younger brother is genuinely jealous of you.'

'Megan would have loved to hear you say that… but we were both very jealous of you.'

'Why?' Venga was shocked.

'You have a beautiful daughter, stunning, bright, no idea where she gets that from, with a heart of gold. *And* Zac. What a great grandson. He's definitely got your charm and all the best of Tasha. Wish I could have seen him grow up.'

The past tense stopped the conversation. They were all lost in their thoughts. The wind seemed quieter as they immersed themselves in so many happy memories.

A fresh wave of rain hammered on the roof bringing them back to the present.

Venga had started to accept his fate and the feelings of guilt were growing as their final minutes ticked by. The Skerryn trip was his idea. The foolish photograph was his idea. Juan, as he always did, had offered his support. His big brother had helped him. He always did. And Juan didn't deserve to die. He didn't have to die. Flick had the tools to keep one of them alive and Juan was only in this horrendous position because of his reckless younger brother. The help would arrive too late. Jack String, Captain Oates, had left them to it. He didn't want to witness the final act. They had to talk about the unthinkable. Venga knew what he had to do.

'Doctor Flea.'

Flick got a bit closer.

'I want to talk about the transfusion.'

'I don't want to do it.'

'I know. Just tell me more. I want to know what our options are.'

Both brothers were struggling to stay conscious. Juan had slipped into a half sleep. He was talking but making no sense. He mentioned Megan a few times, Tasha and Venga now and then.

Flick explained again. It was possible. He had the equipment but it had never been tried and they were in the worst possible conditions to try it. And it would kill the donor with no guarantee that it would save the other brother.

'Mate. Me and Juan are both gonna die. You know that and there's no help coming. Am I missing anything?'

'Nothing. It's dangerous and it might not work.'

'Yeah. You said something else though. It's worrying me. Can't remember what it was.'

Flick thought back. 'Untried. Untested. Dunno. That's about it. I don't think we should do it.'

'Something about blood groups?'

'You're actually quite lucky. Works in either direction.'

'Anything else?'

'There is something else. One of you will die first if we do nothing. Could be either of you. Once they're dead though, I can't use their blood to save the other. I need a beating heart to complete the procedure.'

'Flick mate. What a fucking nightmare. He's gone quiet. Is he okay?'

'He's conscious. Sort of sleeping. Bordering on delirious.'

'Will he pass out completely?'

'Maybe… might come back. Hard to say. A bit of a kip could build his energy up.'

'Right Flick. Listen to me. This is what I want to do.'

'Go on.'

'This is my trip and I went for the stupid photograph. My life is a shit show and Juan *is*, no debate here by the way, Juan is a much better person than me. You have to do everything in your power to save him.'

Flick listened carefully. Not wanting to interrupt.

'I give you consent to use me as the donor. I'm not saying I deserve to die, but I am saying Juan deserves to live. So take my blood and save Juan.'

Flick felt obliged to make sure Venga had considered everything.

'You are the younger brother. He's already had five more years than you.'

'I know. Makes no difference to me.'

'You have a daughter and grandson who need you.'

'I know.' A loud whisper.

'Juan lost the love of his life. He's often told me a part of him died with her.'

'Listen Flick. I'm certain I've considered everything and if I wake up in a hospital bed tomorrow, you will have broken my trust.'

'I hear you.'

'Will you do it?'

'Miracles happen. Help may arrive. I'll leave it as long as I think possible.'

'That's not a yes. You're deflecting Flick. Don't do this to me. I absolutely do not give consent for you to use Juan as a donor. If that happens I will be… well I dunno. Just don't do it. For complete clarity, I don't consent to Juan being a donor.'

Flick waited for Venga to catch his breath.

'I accept you have consented to be the donor.'

'And Juan?'

'And as Juan's next of kin, I accept that you do not want Juan to be used as the donor.'

Venga knew there was a but.

Chapter 24
2025, August 19, Tuesday
Southside Crown Court, trial day 13

The jury had spent the whole of Monday getting no further than the 7-5 vote in favour of not guilty. Tuesday's deliberations had started with a similar entrenched feeling.

Steve had news that may push things along. 'I let the judge know how little progress we made and I've had a note back.'

They were quiet for a moment.

'She has allowed a majority verdict in the event that we can't all agree.'

Imelda asked. 'How would that work exactly?'

'She would accept 11-1 or 10-2. So we're three vote changes away from a verdict.'

'Or five.' Jon, bring-back-hanging, added. 'Depends which way you look at it.'

'Fair enough,' agreed Steve. 'But simple maths suggests we should first try and find three more not guilty votes.'

A few nods.

'So we're looking at Vicky, Jon, Roger, Alister and Kate. Are any of you borderline? And if so, what are the key details?'

All eyes were on the guilty voters.

Lesley stood. 'I need coffee. Anyone else want one while I'm up?'

Joe and Bradley joined her.

Foreman Steve held off. Allowed the guilty voters a little time to consider their position. First to offer anything was the chef Alister.

'I'm certainly not 100 per cent guilty, but the money tips it for me.'

'Okay, let's talk more about the money.' Steve encouraged him.

'It's a lot of money and he was, by the sounds of it, struggling. Doctors don't drive around in old bangers.'

Emily responded. 'Sounds to me like he was just careful. Not the sort of man that needs status symbols. And it's not like wiping the debt would have made any difference. He was already in the house and there was no paperwork. If he had stopped paying Juan interest on the loan, he was never going to be kicked out. No mortgage company. No contract. No repossession. Made almost no difference.'

Alister raised his eyebrows. Fair point he conceded.

'And, unlike some of you, I don't doubt his word just because he had a taste for a younger partner.'

Kate joined in. 'Morality. That's king here. If he breaks the moral code with teenage girls…'

'Just the one teenage girl actually.' Steve corrected.

'That we know about…'

'Wow. Kate, you shouldn't be judging him on a relationship he had ten years ago with a teenager, legal I remind you, and you absolutely shouldn't be judging him on questionable relationships you think he *might* have had.'

'Noted. I'll try not to.' Kate made sure she said the right thing, knowing she was at liberty to go on thinking whatever she wanted. 'Anyway, as I was saying. Morality is king. If any of us have doubts over the doctor's integrity as a result of his partner choices, it's bound to effect how much we believe everything he has said during the trial. Including the £100,000 loan from Juan Prost.'

Steve looked back at Alister. 'Okay Alister. Is your thinking on the money being effected by his choice of partner.'

'No.' He shook his head. 'I already said that.'

'Okay. So if we forget that, do you take on board what Emily said about his modest lifestyle and probable lack of desire for big ticket status symbols?'

Alister pursed his lip and looked into the distance, giving it due consideration.

Sports therapist Imelda could see Alister was wavering. 'I have two clients who play for the same football club. Professionals. Championship side, so, not the top level but close. Both very rich. One of them drives a flashy silver Porche, the other an old Ford Fiesta. I asked him why. He told me he did a test drive in the Porche with the other player, but it felt uncomfortable. He had lots of money, but it didn't feel right pushing it in people's faces. Besides, he inherited the Fiesta from his grandmother. Loved the old car. Reminded him of his gran. Simple needs. The doctor sounds similar. To me at least.'

Alister was nodding.

'Seems to me,' Joe said. 'That the loan was a harmless deal between two good friends and Venga Prost only mentioned it to get the police interested when he heard Flick was Zac's dad. A vindictive swipe to push the knife in further.'

'I did think the same.' Alister was close.

Steve nudged him. 'Okay Alister, the money was the deal breaker for you and it looks like you at least have doubts. Would you risk wrongly convicting a man when you can't even be sure about the one key issue that pushed you to a guilty verdict? The phrase that used to be the backbone of jury deliberations was *can you be certain of guilt beyond reasonable doubt?* And you look like you have reasonable doubt.'

Alister screwed up his mouth and rocked his head from side to side.

Steve kept the pressure on. 'Looks like you're edging towards a switch. Can we take that as a not guilty?'

Alister closed his eyes and faced the ceiling for a few seconds, before turning back to Steve. 'I don't want to get this wrong and I am unsure about the money. Yes. It was a deal breaker, but I thought the vote would be guilty. Given how many people said not guilty, I am questioning my own thinking and yes, perhaps I was wrong.'

They all looked at him waiting for more.

'So I'm gonna change to not guilty.'

Muted appreciation.

'Thank-you Alister. 8-4.' Steve turned towards his next target. 'Okay Vicky. Let's talk about your concerns.'

She looked around at them all, feeling a little nervous. Not enjoying being the centre of attention.

'Fine. Two things worry me. The first is consent. Venga Prost says there was none. The doctor says there was. It's one man's word against the other, at which point we get into the character assassinations we all witnessed over the weekend. Both as bad as each other. Or as some of you would have it, both as faultless as each other. Either way the issue is cancelled out for me and I move onto what is really troubling me.'

Steve nodded encouragement.

'I think Flick heard Jack say the lifeboat was on the way with help.'

They all waited for her to elaborate.

'Jack String knew how important it was to get the information to Dr Mendy as soon as possible to ensure the dangerous operation did not happen. He ran the whole length of the island, twice, to be certain of that. I can't believe he would have gone back to the beach unless he knew for sure that the message had been successfully delivered.'

Bradley reacted first. 'What about the time issue? If he didn't get back to the beach at exactly the right time to do the oil thing, the lifeboat could not have landed. And he only just made it.'

'Would one minute have been that critical?'

'Maybe. He's an old man. Seventy or something. It was quite a stretch for him to do it at all. Let alone with a time limit.'

'60 I think. Not 70.' Steve corrected.

'Still old.' Bradley held his ground.

'It was vitally important. One minute to walk 20 feet, tap the doctor on the shoulder and tell him again that help was on the way. Look him in the eyes and know for sure.'

Joe helped Bradley out. 'Easy to say, sat here in the comfortable sun-drenched court house. They were fighting for their lives with the storm battering them. And the doctor, like he said, was concentrating. As far as he knew, he had to lose one of his friends to save the other by doing a risky procedure that had never been done before. Only in this case, it was in a derelict, abandoned building with a hurricane raging outside.'

'Storm mate.' Jon added. 'A hurricane is much worse.'

Joe rolled his eyes.

'Well. I know, if it was me, I'd have made sure he heard me.'

Bradley again. 'Thing is Vicky, it wasn't. How old are you? 32?'

'36,' she smiled.

'Still young. 36. Half his age. Time was short and he saw a waved hand. Job done. And he was off.'

'Right. If I accept Jack String didn't need to try harder. Or couldn't because he was at his physical limit. I still think the doctor must have heard him. We know he raised his arm to acknowledge Jack. How can that mean anything other than *yes, I hear you*?'

Steve came in. 'Well, he says he heard something, but dismissed it as less important than what he was focussed on. So we're back to whether we believe him or not?'

Vicky rested her chin on her hand. 'I'm not totally sure I do.'

Nurse Kate had worked with a lot of doctors, and even though she was one of the guilty voters, she felt duty bound to contribute her experience. 'Doctors can be a bit blinkered to be honest.'

A few surprised faces.

'When you have someone dying in front of you and every second counts, you have to think fast. If you've got limited information and some of that conflicts, it's asking a lot and they get caught up in the moment. A three-legged giraffe could walk through the room unnoticed. And if it said something, the doctor might quite easily brush it aside as a distraction.

'Happens all the time.' Kate saw shock. 'Not the giraffe bit.'

Some nods around the table.

Rebecca was also a nurse. 'I do know something that is relevant here, but I didn't hear it in court.' She looked at Steve. 'Am I allowed to say it?'

That was a tough one for Steve. He had already reluctantly agreed to discuss Ginger Green's blog, but only because every juror had already heard it. This was new and only one juror knew about it. But he did feel enormous pressure from the other jurors to allow it, especially as it may help push them in the direction of a verdict. He followed precedent.

'Hands up if you think we should hear Rebecca's new information.'

Eleven hands went up again.

Steve waved an open hand in Rebecca's direction.

'Everyone at the hospital has been talking about the Scottish trip ever since the story hit the news last year. We had a new nurse start a couple of months ago from Manchester. Used to work at the same hospital as Dr Mendy. And, apparently, he got in serious trouble a few years ago and the hospital trust could have been forced into a massive payout because of an error.'

Rebecca had their attention.

'He was performing an operation and just before he closed the wound, one of his colleagues reminded him that some of the swabs had not been removed. He was so focussed, he missed it. He'd heard the warning, acknowledged it, but left them in. Sewed up the wound.'

'That's bad.'

'Yes. It's bad. And he had to remove all the stitches, open the patient up again and get the swabs out. Nasty scar when it was all finished.'

'That's terrible Rebecca.'

'Yes it is. But the point is this, even in a routine operation, Dr Flick Mendy gets so focussed that he misses the simplest of instructions. So the same doctor, faced with a much more intense life or death situation in extreme conditions, could easily do the same. Even if he waved his hand to acknowledge the warning, it is quite believable that he didn't take in the detail of what was said.'

Jon was not impressed. 'Maybe he should also be struck off for being an incompetent doctor.'

Steve was ready to seize the opportunity. 'Let's stick to the murder charge. Thanks for that Rebecca. Very relevant in my opinion. Makes me wonder why Petra Patel didn't bring it up in court. Missing the warning was a key issue and he's obviously got form.'

Emily came to Petra Patel's defence. 'We've seen how powerful Ginger Green's blog has been. It has massively tarnished the jurors' views of Venga and the doctor, fortunately both equally. My guess is that Petra felt the swab incident might lower jurors' opinion of the doctor and cast doubt in their minds over his integrity and believability.'

A few nods.

Steve returned to Vicky. 'Now you know the doctor has a history of missing vital information when under pressure, does it effect your view?'

She said nothing for a few seconds, then a single and very subtle nod. 'Probably. If I'm being honest, that does make a difference. Certainly pushes me into the category of not certain beyond reasonable doubt.'

'Can I take that as a switch to not guilty?'

Vicky looked around the table. The peer pressure was almost physical. She was ready to change her vote. 'Yes. Not guilty.'

More muted appreciation, along with some relief as the jury members started to feel momentum pushing them in the direction of a firm outcome.

Steve looked around the table for one more, and settled on Roger. 'Okay we're nearly there. 9-3. And if I remember rightly, you had the same doubts as Vicky. You've heard Rebecca's new information. What are your thoughts?'

Chapter 25
2024, October 8, Tuesday
Skerryn, ten months before the trial

Flick waited for Venga to catch his breath.

'I accept you have consented to be the donor.'

'And Juan?'

'And as Juan's next of kin, I accept that you do not want Juan to be used as the donor.'

The storm lashed the building. It didn't seem possible, but the wind got louder. The rain got heavier and Venga slipped into the same half sleep, semi-conscious state that had consumed his brother. Flick felt alone, watching two good friends' lives slipping away like the sun disappearing over the horizon at the end of the day. The sun was big and red. A spectacular Prost sunset was getting perilously close to its unstoppable conclusion.

He didn't want to risk the transfusion, but if he was going to do it, Venga would have to be the donor. He had given his consent and, as Juan's next of kin, he had made it very clear that there was no approval to take Juan's blood. That would not change unless Juan came round and overruled it. No chance of that. He was fading and the delirious chatter was slowing down.

At that moment, Juan tried to shout. It was quiet, but intense. 'Don't do it Joe. Mum said leave it.'

His closed eyelids were moving rapidly and his good arm was twitching.

Flick could see pain in his grimace. He was facing his fears as his mind started to shut down. Purging the demons.

'Help me Flick. Help me.' Trying to shout again.

That's encouraging. At least he's dreaming about something close and real.

Juan opened his eyes.

'Flick mate. How's Ven?' So quiet. So soft. A struggle to speak.

Out cold, but alive. 'All good. He's sleeping.' Flick sugar coated it.

'Any chance of a morphine boost? Arm's killing.'

Flick gave him a small shot. 'That's quite a dream. You were shouting.'

Juan smiled. 'What did I say?'

'Well, Megan came up a lot. Last thing was, "Don't do it Joe. Mum said leave it." And then you shouted for me to help you.'

It flooded back. 'Ah yes. We were gonna call our first son Joe. He was in his twenties in the dream. So mum was Megan.'

'You were shouting though. Didn't sound good. What did you need my help for?'

'We were in a boat. The four of us. Well… not really a boat. It was a huge bath tub out at sea. I was handcuffed to the hot tap, which, for some reason, was bigger than me and Joe was about to pull the plug out.'

'Weird.'

'Very. Megan didn't move or say anything. She called me on her mobile and asked me to tell him to leave the plug in.'

'Couldn't she just talk to you?'

'No.'

'Why not?'

'Hard to say.'

'Where was I?'

'You were the plug. Stuck in the plug hole reaching a hand out to Joe. He wanted to save you.'

'What happened?'

'Dunno. I woke up.'

'Strange dream. Wonder if it meant anything?'

'Think I know what it was.'

'Yeah?'

'Your life is supposed to flash before your eyes before you die. It's something like that, isn't it?'

'Maybe. Who knows?'

'I'm okay with it… dying I mean. I'm ready. I think the dream was Megan. She's waiting for me. Flick mate, we'll be together again.'

Flick put his hand on Juan's good arm. 'It could happen.'

'Joe was miscarried. So long ago. I'm finally gonna see him.'

Juan was smiling and crying at the same time.

They were quiet for a while.

'I hope you do Juan because there is nothing so precious as watching your own child laughing, playing and having fun. It's a beautiful gift.'

Juan could see Flick was sharing something real. This wasn't a story being passed on. Juan's body was failing, but his intuition was sharp as a pin.

'What can I see in your eyes doctor? Something.'

Flick was ready to share his secret.

'There's no flies on you Juan.'

Then it all fell into place for Juan. There had been so many signs and nobody had made the connection.

'It's Zac isn't it? He's your boy.'

Flick didn't need to reply. His proud smile said enough.

'My God. You spend so much time with him. And Tasha. You treat *him* like a son.' He thought a little more. 'You treat *her* like a wife in many ways.'

Flick could see Juan was happy for him.

Juan's smile faded a little as he put it all together and saw the obvious problems.

'Shit Flick, she was only 17. How did… what…when?..'

'I had no idea she was Natty. I came down for my GP interview, stayed at Hotel Petra and bumped into her. She was with a hen party. All much older.'

'Wow.'

'I thought she was at least mid twenties. She thought I was early thirties. She told me that later. It was instant. It just happened. But when I found out it was Natty and she found out I was uncle Flick, it could never be.'

Juan shook his head. 'Venga.'

Flick agreed. 'Venga.'

'The cause of, and solution to, all life's problems.'

'I know. Tash didn't want to risk it.'

'Fair enough. You never know what he's gonna do.'

Flick nodded.

'He's my brother and I love him, but he's an unexploded bomb.'

'Indeed. A one-man minefield.'

Juan winced and moved slightly hunting for a more comfortable position. 'The three amigos. One wanted a child, never had one, another had one but had to keep his distance and the third didn't want one, but got the best kid you could hope for. Life mate.'

'Them's the breaks Juan.'

They were quiet for a while.

'Funny thing.'

'Go on Juan.'

'I meant to tell Ven this, but didn't. Just never came up.'

'What?'

'I was on Facebook the other day, looking back. Tracking people down from years ago. You won't believe who I found. Almost by chance.'

Flick nodded.

'Mira.'

'What? Tasha's mum?'

'Yes. Mira Pellow. Obviously married now.'

'She look happy?'

'Very. And she had two kids. Not much younger than Tash, so being a young mum wasn't the issue she made it out to be.'

'Looks like Venga was the problem all the time then.'

'Maybe. We'll never know. Two daughters and the older one looked a bit like Tash. I was gonna tell Ven, but thought it might hurt. To see that she was happy with a family. Think I must have subconsciously decided to leave it. He was happy enough.'

'Fairs.'

They were quiet again. Juan considering what he should and shouldn't tell his brother. Why did it matter? He wasn't his father. He shouldn't control his brother in any way. He should pass on anything he knew and let his brother decide what to do with it. Venga should know Flick was Zac's father and learn to live with it, accept it and enjoy it.

'I think you should tell him.'

'About Mira? Or me and Tash?'

'You and Tash. I know it's wrong of me to stay quiet on Mira, but knowing about her would help nobody. But knowing about you and Tash should help all of you, especially Zac.'

Flick smiled. 'I would, but Tasha doesn't want to. Doesn't want to do it to him. Gotta respect her wishes… Besides, might not get the chance.'

Juan came back quick. 'I think you will.'

Flick had an idea what was coming.

'I want you to do the transfusion. I know you can't do it without my approval, so this is it. I consent to be the donor.'

Flick was torn again and found his thoughts followed the same lines as when Venga had volunteered. Was Juan certain he had considered everything?

'But Juan, this whole situation was caused by Venga. He came up with the idea, he set up the trip and his attempt to photograph the flag led to the accident.'

'I know, but he's younger than me, my life ended when Megan went, I'm so looking forward to seeing her again and Venga has family. He has a wonderful daughter, an awesome grandson, and he's got you Flick. I've always seen you as part of our family, and as it turns out, you are. I want you to have the chance to tell him, make it good and move forward. All together. The winning team.'

'It might be one team building exercise too far for Venga. I'm not so sure. I think we might be over reaching.'

'Flick. It's not in my nature, but I'm putting a three line whip under this one. It's non-negotiable. And Venga is out cold, so, as his brother and next of kin, I do not give consent for you to use his blood.'

'There is one other problem if I use you as the donor Juan.'

'Yeah?'

'I owe you money. Who do you want me to give it to?' Flick considered the money. 'Might even look bad. Some might think I saw an opportunity.' He screwed his face up. 'No. Forget that. Shouldn't make any difference. Forget I said anything.'

'Give it to Tash for Zac. But no hurry. Whenever. Doesn't matter.' Juan adjusted his position again and took a deep breath. 'But you have to promise me you won't use Venga as the donor. That is my final wish. Please Flick.'

Flick was conflicted. Both brothers had insisted they be the donor and both brothers had insisted that there would be no consent to take the other brother.

Juan pushed harder. 'Doctor Flick Mendy. Please acknowledge that you have heard me consent to be the donor. Please also confirm you have heard me give no consent to use my brother as the donor?'

Flick looked him in the eye knowing he had to give Juan the reassurance he was looking for.

'I accept you have consented to be the donor.'

'And my brother?'

'And as Venga's next of kin, I accept that you do not want him to be used as the donor.'

'One more thing Flick.'

'Go on.'

'Could you play me one last song?'

'Sure.'

'Leonard Cohen *You Want It Darker*.'

Flick raised his eyebrows. 'That's a sad one. You sure?'

'I'm ready my Lord.'

The conversation had exhausted Juan and he fell back into a half sleep as Leonard Cohen's deep bass-baritone blended with the merciless wind.

Flick was left alone with the painful dilemma of choosing which brother to save. With consent from both of them, the wishes of the next of kin were trumped. He had sufficient consent to take either brother and he didn't know what to do. He had vested interest for many reasons, but he removed that from the equation. It was irrelevant.

Venga was his best friend, but Juan wasn't far off. Venga was Zac's grandfather. That could push him either way. He could remove the one barrier between himself and Tasha, but he wouldn't be able to live with himself if he let that interfere with the decision. Besides, if Tasha ever thought it had been a consideration, the romance would come to an abrupt end anyway. Rightly so. Maybe he should favour Venga as he was a closer relative to Zac than Juan. But no. Made no difference.

He set up the equipment so he could do the procedure. He just had to make a choice.

'Blood on the way. Lifeboat coming.'

The choice was pure agony. His head was spinning with memories. Juan, Megan, Venga, Mira, Tasha, Zac, Denzil, the paedo from Vicar, the crazy bitch from the hospital, Lisa String and Jack… the Wise Old Man. Hold on. Was that Jack? He raised his hand. Heard the door shut and rested his head in his hands. He couldn't choose.

Venga was right though. Juan was a better person than him and the younger brother's life was, as he quite rightly said, a shit show. Then he considered their ages. Juan was five years older. That made Juan the right choice as donor, but no. He was a doctor. The whole ethos of health care was built on the belief that one life equals one life. Who lives and who dies can never be judged on age, colour, religion, sexuality, anything. One equals one. His choice could not be means tested in any way.

He checked both brothers' pulses. They were getting weaker. Time was against him and there was no help coming.

He was set up and ready to go. He just had to decide which brother to sacrifice.

Chapter 26
2025, August 19, Tuesday
Southside Crown Court, trial day 13

A buzz of excitement rippled through the blistering hot court room and across the packed square outside. Just after 3pm a rumour began, as the jury door opened and a note was handed to an usher. A verdict was imminent. The rumour travelled with the speed of a slow-burning cartoon fuse headed towards a stick of dynamite held in Wile E Coyote's hand.

When Ginger Green heard it in the cafe across the square, she left her half eaten sandwich and undrunk coffee and headed for the door. She was immediately accosted by a TV crew. She had become a character in the story and was happy to milk the opportunity for the publicity it gave her blog and the kudos it added to her growing reputation.

'Miss Green. What verdict are you expecting?'

'Given the revelations we've all read in my blog over the weekend, there's no surprise that it has become something of a popularity contest between Venga Prost and Flick Mendy.'

'Are you saying the two men's partner choices will decide this trial?'

'Strangely. Yes.'

'What is the current vote split on the Twenty Is Plenty poll?'

Odd question thought Ginger as it gave a running count online so they could see for themselves. No matter. All good publicity.

'With about 180,000 votes so far, thumbs down is winning with 81 per cent.'

'So only 19 per cent of your readers approve of Dr Flick Mendy and Tasha Prost's relationship?'

'Your maths is good.' Sarcasm from Ginger. 'Gotta run. See you in court.'

DCI Jon Jordan had been in the same cafe as Ginger Green when the rumour arrived. He stayed to finish his coffee before walking briskly back to court, passing a TV crew interviewing a reporter as he bit into his sandwich.

Shocking he thought, the Press are so hungry for something new that they are interviewing each other now. Pretty sure that was Ginger Green, the troublemaker who exposed the private lives of Flick and Venga over the weekend and started that appalling poll. A highly inappropriate vote to run alongside a murder trial. Although DCI Jordan had clicked thumbs down, quite certain that his wife Jo had not seen him do it.

He took his seat and ate his sandwich in a hurry as the jury retook their seats. He noticed juror number two and felt a tiny jolt of guilt… at the start of the trial he had admonished the young man for disrespectfully eating his breakfast in the court house.

With the judge not yet in her place, the jury chatted with the same excitement as the rest of the room.

Juror number one Rebecca still did not know where the name Flick had come from, but her surprise at Dr Flick Mendy's single status had been explained by Ginger Green's blog and she had warmed to him despite the potentially problematic age gap.

Juror number five Vicky was now certain who she wanted to survive with her following a nuclear holocaust. It had to be Flick. Her belief that he must have heard Jack String's warning had been put to bed. Rebecca's swab story showed he was prone to blinkered behaviour under pressure. He's only human after all, but his other qualities would be invaluable in a post apocalyptic world.

Juror eleven Emily was happy with how the deliberations had gone and comfortable with the verdict, but she still smiled every time she saw Tasha Prost in the public gallery. Spitting image of the naked roller-skating nun.

Juror six Lesley had been set against Flick in favour of family-man Venga, but now she knew Flick was also a family man, the same family as it turned out, she was more comfortable with their verdict. She had enjoyed a conversation in the jury room with Rebecca and Vicky, who had also had early doubts over Flick. They had all warmed to him as the trial progressed and considered Tasha's testimony as a character witness in a new light.

In the public gallery Zac Prost, now aged nine, sat between his granddad Venga and his mum Tasha. She had taken him out of school for what they had hoped would be the conclusion of the trial.

'Granddad.'

'Yes Zac.'

'I've missed uncle Flick.'

'We all have.'

'Are you sure Granddad? Because my friend Billy says he's only in trouble with the police because of you.'

If they weren't all packed so tightly on the benches in the public gallery, Venga would have fallen off his seat. 'Does he now? What else did Billy say?'

'His dad told him you threw your toys out of the pram because uncle Flick was such good friends with mum.'

Venga looked at Tasha. She had been listening, but gave him no easy way out.

Zac didn't let him off the hook. 'Is Billy's dad right granddad?'

Venga looked into his nine-year-old grandson's pleading eyes that demanded an honest answer. It was more powerful than any question Petra Patel or the judge might have asked him. He considered how best to word his answer. In the end he concluded there was only one very simple answer. The difficult bit was why.

'Yes Zac. I did.'

'Why?'

And there it was. The big one. The one he had been asking himself for the last ten months and coming up with a different answer every day. Usually when he had such a tough question to answer, he would take advice. Usually when he took advice he would go straight to Flick. Not possible this time. Failing that, he'd ask Juan. Failing that, he'd ask Tasha. Also not possible. The next alternative would be a two week bender drinking beer playing *Simpsons Hit And Run*. That never worked. He was on his own this time.

'That's a tough question young man.'

Zac waited patiently, wide eyed and expectant. Next to him, Tasha was equally intrigued to hear what her dad would come up with.

'To be honest Zac, I literally haven't got a clue.'

Venga was alarmed to see his grandson roll his eyes like Tasha.

'Although I have considered a few theories.'

The boy smiled again. Still waiting. So was Tasha.

'Uncle Flick is a good man.'

Zac nodded.

‘A better man than me.’

Tasha didn’t disagree.

‘I rely on him. He’s my rock. But when my brother, uncle Juan died, it hurt so much. I reacted badly. It *was* my fault he died. I couldn’t handle that and I looked for someone else to blame. Whenever I’m in a jam, uncle Flick is the answer. I blamed him.’

Zac thought about it for a moment. ‘That’s not very nice Granddad.’

‘You’re right. But, like I said, he’s a better man than me. Grief effects us all differently. Let’s hope the jury get it right and we can all go home together.’

Zac reached up and placed a hand on Venga’s shoulder.

Tasha noticed movement in front of the bench.

The usher stood. ‘All rise.’

It went quiet as Judge Faith Haydn entered the room and took her seat.

Looking around, she could feel the excitement in the room from the public gallery, the jury box, the Press box and the assembled court officials/counsel. Checking through her notes, she felt an enormous sense of relief. She had offered a majority verdict, but had been informed a unanimous verdict had been reached. The media interest had killed any chance of an impartial retrial, so a hung jury would have left her painted into a corner she didn’t want to contemplate.

It had, as she feared, turned into something similar to a US presidential election, a personality contest. It had become Flick versus Venga thanks partly to Ginger Green. Not something she enjoyed presiding over. She would lose all professional credibility if it ever got out that she had voted thumbs up. The hum of noise around the room came to an abrupt end as she bought down her gavel.

The usher asked the foreman of the jury Steven Robinson to stand.

Judge Haydn asked, 'Have you reached a verdict on the charge of murder against Dr Flick Mendy?'

'Yes Your Honour.'

There was silence in the room.

'Do you find the defendant guilty or not guilty?'

'Not guilty Your Honour.'

A collective gasp. The judge looked at Venga Prost and saw an unexpected look of relief. Next to him Tasha Prost was in tears. Between them a young boy, presumably Zac Prost, was celebrating like he had won The Lottery.

Venga's reaction had surprised her a little, but Flick's reaction surprised her more. He looked sad, deflated and lost. He looked… she couldn't put her finger on it… he looked… guilty. Almost as if he had been cheated out of his due punishment. He didn't move. His head slumped forward.

Judge Haydn noticed a fly land on her notes and in a flash she swatted it. If it hadn't been pummelled so thoroughly, she might have noticed it only had four legs.

She called over to the defendant. 'Dr Mendy. You are free to leave.'

He lifted his head, focussed on Venga at the back of the room on a seat near the aisle and took the steps down to the passage that led to the back of the courtroom. His brisk walk purposefully in Venga's direction was noticed. The court stopped emptying and went quiet as the gathered crowds anticipated a clash between the two main protagonists from the trial. It was like the parting of the Red

Sea as people stepped aside to facilitate the drama that was to come.

DCI Jordan considered standing between the two men, but was too fascinated to intervene.

'What the fuck?' Juror four said to juror five.

'Shit's going down,' she replied.

Judge Haydn was equally reluctant to interfere.

Flick was nearly there. Venga stepped out into the aisle. Everyone else backed away.

The whole room held its breath as Flick rushed up to Venga and threw his arms around his friend for the biggest bear hug any of them had seen.

'I'm so sorry Vee. If I'd heard Jack, it could have been so different. I deserve to be punished.'

'Mate. You saved my life and I put you through all this. I'm the one that should be sorry. You tried to save us both. Shit happens Flea.'

Venga pulled back a little and noticed Flick looking at Tasha. He let him go. 'We'll talk further on that one.'

Flick grabbed Tasha and lifted her off the ground. A bigger hug than Venga, but shorter, so he could reach down and lift up Zac. All three hugged.

Noise filled the room again. It was lost on nobody that Flick and Tasha kissed. Everyone in the room had voted on Ginger's poll, but even the thumbs down could see this was real. There were still a few tuts and rolled eyes though.

Flick ignored them all. He knew what he wanted and he was closer than ever to getting it. He felt a warmth in Tasha's arms that he had never felt before.

'I love you Tasha.'

'Same, Doctor M.'

Community chest

Chapter 27

2026, December 25, Friday
Flick and Tasha's house, 16 months after the trial

Tigger came through the cat flap in Milo Road. He walked over to his bed, clawed it a bit, twisting in circles, then settled. He preferred his new house, the garden was bigger and there was the occasional mouse near the bins at the end of the garden. No mice this morning unfortunately as his owner had put Christmas tinsel around his neck. Not ideal when he was trying to stalk prey, but the unexpected bowl of warm milk had been a treat.

His owner strolled into the kitchen and put on the kettle for a cup of tea, followed by her partner with a boy riding on his back.

'Merry Christmas Doctor M.'

They kissed with the boy still dangling from the man's shoulders.

'Merry Christmas Tash.'

'Had a message from Dad. They'll be here about eleven, so we've got two hours of harmony before the fun starts.'

Flick was ready for the fun. Zac loved winning, Flick's fault, and Christmas Day would not be the same without a family game of Monopoly.

Zac was sharp, but Venga was ruthless.

Venga took no prisoners and always hit back harder.

Flick had suffered through many of those battles with Venga. He now reflected, with a smile, on the most recent showdown.

Two weeks after Flick's trial ended, he called on Venga and was invited into his drawing room to 'share a few ideas'.

Venga sat behind his large desk, leant back in his office chair looking at Flick with a neutral, but quietly aggressive expression. Maybe not aggressive, but certainly challenging, confrontational.

Before Flick took the lower, and less comfortable, chair facing him, he walked around the end of the desk to the corner where Venga kept his shotgun. He pulled the double barrel towards his nose and sniffed the air.

'Fresh gun oil. You won't need to clean it during our chat.'

Venga smiled as he watched Flick return to his seat. He was about to lay the ground rules for the exchange, before Flick beat him to it.

'You are still my best friend… despite everything. There is a lot I want to say to you, but first you must know that I love Tasha… and Zac… and, if she agrees, we *will* be together.

'That will happen, with or without your approval.' Flick expected Venga to dive in at that point, but he didn't. 'But we would both prefer it to be *with* your approval.'

They were both quiet, taking in each other's initial reactions and considering the next move. Venga responded.

'I hear you Flea. But can you tell me why the whole idea gives me a bad feeling?'

Flick came straight back. 'I can take a guess.'

Venga's eyebrows went up and down to say this will be interesting.

'Firstly nobody will ever be good enough for your daughter in your eyes. Look how you treated Denzil and Dean.'

'The paedo from Vicar?'

'It's years since she ditched him and you still can't call him Dean.'

Venga nodded acknowledgement.

'Main thing though. You judge every man by your own standards.'

Venga pursed his lips. Not sure about that.

'You are 48 years old and your longest relationship is two years. I am different to you. I managed fifteen years in a loveless marriage before I conceded defeat. That's hard-core commitment. Foolish some may say, but you can't question my determination to make things work.'

'Fair.'

'And here's the big one.'

Flick took a deep breath.

'I'm also 48 and I've never fixed another man's wife to a workbench with 123 staples and nailed her legs open while that same man waited for me in the pub. And yes. I counted them. It took me two hours to undo your mess. And another ten years trying to repair the emotional damage.'

Below the belt and it hit home. Venga had already apologised, but it would never be enough.

'I'm not you Venga. And, sadly, you should see that as a good thing.'

Venga sighed and swivelled slowly in his chair. 'Okay. Maybe. I still have the feeling though.'

'Tasha told me she already had this conversation with you, so I'm gonna repeat what she said, but it won't do any harm to hear it from both of us.

'When we met at Hotel Petra 11 years ago, I did not know she was Natty, she had no clue I was uncle Flick, I had no idea she was 17 and she had no idea I was 37. I have youthful looks while Tash was made up, and out with an older group. We both thought the age gap was five years or so. Nothing that would raise any concern.

'As it turns out, the gap was 20 years. Yes. Wow. I thought the same. Jesus. I was horrified when I realised it was your Natty. Absolutely mortified.'

Venga nodded slowly.

'But it didn't stop me wanting to be with her. Same for her. It was legal. Two consenting adults. The only reason we stayed apart was you Venga… *you.*'

'Go on.'

'Tasha was so worried how you would react and she put you first.'

Venga's expression stayed neutral.

'For ten fucking years Venga.' Now there was anger in Flick's voice. 'Ten fucking years and then you found out and we all know what happened next.

'She was right. She expected volatility, something reckless and she got it… with interest. And I have to wonder why. I don't think you were reacting to what happened to your daughter. I think it's vanity. It's what happened to you. Somebody got your daughter pregnant at the age of 17 and *YOU* felt raped. Raped of your alpha, testosterone charged manliness.'

Venga looked shocked.

'Tasha has put you first all her life. She's been like a mother to you. I think you should start giving a bit back. You should respect her wishes, her choices and support her whatever they are. You have a paternal moral obligation to support your daughter, not a legal obligation to control her.'

Venga had a lot to digest and came back with nothing. He was shell-shocked and Flick's words were finding their target.

'I've always accepted Tasha's wish to keep you happy. Ignorance, for a long time, was bliss. And I also knew your reaction when you found out would be nuclear. It was that and more, but I think we would have got through it until the grief amplified everything. I understand that. I accept that and I absolutely make no complaint. I made a horrendous mistake and ten months of torment waiting for a murder trial is nothing compared to how much I deserve to be punished for my fuck-up. The mother of all fuck-ups.'

They both looked down, sobered by the reminder of their loss. Dispute suspended. Trivial by comparison. The quiet crept unseen around the room, like Juan was silently judging their exchange, willing them to move forward.

Venga broke the silence.

'Have you seen what happened to Ginger Green's Twenty Is Plenty poll since the trial ended?'

'No. Still going is it?'

'Yup. And it's changed direction.'

'Oh right.'

'Still 75 per cent says you're a paedo, but it was 81.'

Flick was encouraged. 'You realise that means votes since the trial have been running at about 50-50?'

'S'pose… yes.'

They were quiet again until Venga pulled out two glasses and a small bottle of whiskey. Half a bottle later, they were on lighter subjects and laughing together like old times.

'TV Rush is back in business and I've got more work than I can handle.'

'Wow. Thought that'd never come back. How'd you get it going again?'

Venga laughed. 'Slight change of direction swung it. The publicity was massive. I just used it to my advantage. Instead of team building weekends, I'm doing murder mystery trips and events.'

Flick laughed.

'Quite enjoying it to be honest.'

'Excellent. That's great news.'

They clinked glasses and it was quiet again.

Venga's neutral expression returned, but the edge had gone. It was more congenial with a rare hint of humility.

'Flick mate.'

'Vee?'

'You both have my blessing.'

That was sweet music to Flick. He wiped away a single tear and went around the desk to hug his best friend.

Half an hour later he shared a celebratory toast with Tasha, but the drama wasn't over for the day. That morning, he'd received an e-mail that concluded 11 months of research following Juan's revelation that Tasha's mum was on Facebook.

Flick's only clues were the surname Pellow, married with two kids. One that looked like Tasha. He'd eventually given up, but recently found a social media expert who had agreed to look into it for him. Today's email was a link from her to Mira Pellow's Facebook account.

'Tash.'

'Flick.'

'I have something to share with you.'

Tasha could see he was apprehensive and immediately worried what it might be.

'Okay.'

They got comfortable and close on the sofa.

'One of the last things Juan said to me was that he had stumbled across your mum.'

'What? Mira?'

Tasha was instantly on edge, almost angry. The woman had abandoned her. It was never a good feeling when her name came up.

'Yes. Mira… Mira Pellow. Married.'

'How come you never mentioned it?'

'I couldn't find her. Wasn't sure I'd heard right. And if I couldn't find her, why would I tell you? You'd be no better off and miserable, thinking an opportunity had been missed, or something. I've spent the last 11 months trying to track her down and I got confirmation today and I have a link, under the name Mr Pillow.'

Tasha was unsure how to think, what to do.

'She's married with two kids and one of them looks very much like you. Probably not much younger.'

Tasha nodded, knowing that told them a bit more about Mira. 'Looks like her big dreams faded fast and she settled down to a family.'

Flick pulled her close, kissed the top of her head.

'Nothing to do with being too young. Wanted a family after all, just not with me… or Dad.'

'I'm guessing you don't want to get in touch?'

She shook her head.

Flick watched a tear roll slowly down her cheek.

'Delete?'

'Yes please Flick. Delete. And I'd rather keep it from Dad too. It's the last thing he needs at the moment.'

They never told Venga and now they were together in Flick's house on Christmas Day, waiting for Venga and his girlfriend to join them for a gloves-off annual game of Monopoly.

There was a knock at the door.

Kisses and hugs as they made their way into the lounge, admired the tree and sat down for a drink.

'What can I get you Olive? Wine? Coffee?' Flick asked.

'Coffee would be lovely thanks.'

He poured it and handed her the glass. 'How's Leanne?'

'All good thanks. She said to say Merry Christmas. Would have joined us, but she's met someone new and it's their first Christmas together.'

'Ah right.' Tasha joined in. 'Meet him online?'

'Yes. Seems okay so far.'

'Doting.com?'

'Yes. Same site, but she insists on meeting them within 24 hours these days.'

They all smiled.

'Give her our love,' Tash concluded before they moved on to presents.

Zac was straight under the tree, pulling them out and handing them around.

The atmosphere was warm, no tension and Bing Crosby crooned softly in the background.

Tasha thanked Flick for her gifts, kissed his cheek and pulled him close, whispering in his ear. 'You know what I really want for Christmas? Maybe next year.'

'Anything.'

'A bigger family.' She kissed him again and laughed. It was banter, but they both liked the idea.

'Game on,' shouted Zac as he grabbed the Monopoly and started setting it up on the dining table.

After early exchanges and a few cut-throat deals, Zac established a lead and smugly headed to the kitchen for a can of coke.

With him gone for a moment, Flick added an extra card to the community chest pile, telling the others that it was a surprise for Zac.

The dice rolls were kind and Zac landed on community chest, reached for the card and looked confused as he read it.

'What does it say Zac?' Flick asked.

'Well, it's supposed to say you inherit £100, but someone has added three zeros.' He had his mum's sharp mind. 'This got anything to do with you Dad?'

Tasha reached for an envelope from the book shelves and handed it to Flick, who passed it on to Zac.

'One last Christmas present.'

'Nice. From you and mum?'

'No. This one's special. It's from uncle Juan.'

Tasha paused the music and put a small package on the sofa between herself and Flick so he could reach it when he was ready.

The atmosphere was immediately sombre, respectful. Zac recognised the gravity of the moment and opened the envelope carefully.

He read it out. 'You are precious. The son we always wanted. Megan and I loved you like our own. Walk tall, walk high and put your head up in the sky.'

Tasha and Flick had chosen the words, but felt they reflected what Juan and Megan would have said.

There was a document with a wax seal. Zac looked up at Flick, hoping he would explain.

Flick took the cue. 'It's a one sixth share in a house in Manchester to be held in Trust by Mum for you. The house is worth a little over £600,000. Mandy and I have had the deeds adjusted to include your share and, as she is still living in it, she will add £200 to the Trust every month by way of interest. And you have a veto, that says you can trigger a sale any time you want.'

'Really?'

'Yes. But she's confident that you'll take my advice to sit on it for now and watch it grow. She knows you're a great Monopoly player.'

Zac's head was spinning, but still thinking along Monopoly lines. 'Does that mean she pays you £400 for your remaining two sixths of the property?'

'You are sharp Zac.' Flicked rubbed his head.

'Does she?' Zac pushed for an answer.

'Well. She should I suppose, but I've never asked her for it. The value climbs so I'm not losing out.'

'You know you'll never beat me don't you?'

'I do Zac. You're the boss.'

Flick then raised his glass and toasted Juan and Megan. 'A love like no other. Juan and Megan.'

Venga raised his glass, but didn't say the words. He had a lump in his throat, swallowed hard and fought back a tear.

Flick reached for the package and handed it to Zac.

'Another present?'

'No. Just a key to the place. To make it official.'

He ripped it open and pulled out the key.

'Thanks Dad.' He looked closer at the double keyring; a coin and a disc. 'What's the coin?'

'Ah right. Yes. The coin.' Flick took a sip of his drink. 'It's a coin I got in my coffee machine change when I first saw you in hospital two days after you were born. And, coincidentally, it's from the year I was born.'

A ripple of appreciation from around the room.

What Flick didn't tell any of them, apart from Tash a few days after the Skerryn trip, was that he had used this very coin to decide which brother to use as the donor in the fatal transfusion.

Zac turned his attention to the disc and saw his name, NHS number and blood type B negative.

'What's this for?'

'It's like an army dog tag. All soldiers on active duty have one so if they get hurt, it is easier to treat them. You and I have a very rare blood type, only two per cent of people, so if you ever get hurt, playing in your tree house, or anything else, it could be a big help.'

'Ah, cool. Only two per cent. We're special.'

'Very special. You're my type on paper.'

Garry Kay is self published and could do well with your help. If you enjoyed this book, please tell a friend or give them a copy. Any reviews on Amazon would be hugely appreciated. Thank-you for reading

Thanks for your help: editors Ginny Kay and Vicky Lyne; technical and contemporary advice Hannah Kay, Sam Kay, Joe Allan, Lucy Regan, Brendan Gillies, Jon Jordan, Jo Jordan, Jackie Robinson, Kirsty Wilson, Emily Wilson and Trudi Temple; location research Frank Kay, Joan Kay, Jacky Lamb, Sandra Kay and Graham Kay; legal advice Emily McGovern and Steven Robinson; medical advice Kate Ellis and Jane Powell; writing location host Gabriel Pla from beautiful L'Estartit; jurors Rebecca Pooley, Bradley Waters, Imelda Morse, Joe Wareham, Vicky Mather, Lesley Regan, Steven Robinson, Jon Frazer, Roger Temple, Alister Wilson, Emily McGovern and Kate Ellis; St Day Football Club Joff Malaber, Gemma Malaber, Dan Richards, Nathan Taylor, Scott Hopgood, Brian Hawke, Matt Witts, Danny Watts, Gareth Jones, Tyler Oliver, Perran Cooke and Stuart Reynolds

Printed in Great Britain
by Amazon

53070177R00179